ChangelingPress.com

El Diablo/El Segador Duet

Marteeka Karland

El Diablo/El Segador Duet
Marteeka Karland

All rights reserved.
Copyright ©2022 Marteeka Karland

ISBN: 978-1-60521-848-9

Publisher:
Changeling Press LLC
315 N. Centre St.
Martinsburg, WV 25404
ChangelingPress.com

Printed in the U.S.A.

Editor: Katriena Knights
Cover Artist: Marteeka Karland

The individual stories in this anthology have been previously released in E-Book format.

No part of this publication may be reproduced or shared by any electronic or mechanical means, including but not limited to reprinting, photocopying, or digital reproduction, without prior written permission from Changeling Press LLC.

This book contains sexually explicit scenes and adult language which some may find offensive and which is not appropriate for a young audience. Changeling Press books are for sale to adults, only, as defined by the laws of the country in which you made your purchase.

Table of Contents

Diablo (Black Reign MC 5) 4
    Chapter One 5
    Chapter Two 21
    Chapter Three 39
    Chapter Four 50
    Chapter Five 67
    Chapter Six 82
    Chapter Seven 94
    Chapter Eight 113
    Chapter Nine 124
El Segador (Black Reign MC 8) 138
    Chapter One 139
    Chapter Two 156
    Chapter Three 168
    Chapter Four 183
    Chapter Five 195
    Chapter Six 212
    Chapter Seven 222
    Chapter Eight 233
    Chapter Nine 246
Marteeka Karland 255
Changeling Press E-Books 256

Diablo (Black Reign MC 5)
Marteeka Karland

Jezebel -- Life in a gilded cage isn't all it's cracked up to be -- especially if the whole purpose of the cage is to keep me a virgin till I'm ready to be sacrificed to the man of my father's choosing. I want out, and don't think I haven't tried. It's not that easy with Daddy's Brotherhood guards all over the place. But that doesn't mean I want to trade one cage for another. And, let's face it, I have no idea how to live on my own. I've never had the chance. Now I'm not sure I want to learn, because my new jailer -- err, rescuer -- is the sexiest man I've ever known. El Diablo's not the monster everyone's made him out to be. But can I tame the beast of a man without losing my heart? All I want for Christmas is a chance to find out...

El Diablo -- I went hunting for a victim. Instead, I found a Christmas Angel. She's the daughter of my enemy, used as a pawn in a deadly game of chess. All I really wanted was the Brotherhood out of Palm Beach. Instead I found an innocent who brings out a side of me I'd thought long buried and gone. But Jezebel's younger than my own daughter, and just as much trouble. And I'm El Diablo -- a title I earned heart and soul. I'm so not what she needs. And now she's under my protection in the Black Reign compound. She should be completely off-limits. I won't let the Brotherhood take her back and force her to give up her dreams. But who's going to protect her from me?

Chapter One
El Diablo

Sitting off in the distance next to a densely wooded area, the house looked like something out of a horror movie. Sure, the grounds were immaculate and the structure itself a beautiful, Gothic architecture, but with the trees bare of leaves and the full moon hovering above it with a halo of fog around it, not to mention the tall, imposing fencing with razor wire surrounding it... Yeah. The place could have been an asylum in a slasher film.

From what I'd found out from Drago and Pretty Boy, the girl I had been searching for was being held in this house. Had been in this house her entire life. Not just living there. By all accounts, she'd never once left it.

"No change, Liam," El Segador -- the Reaper -- said to me on our personal line. He was one of a very few people who knew my real name. Mainly because we'd grown up together, and he'd willingly followed me for close to thirty years. "She's still on the upper floor. West wing. Giovanni swears he got it right, and that there's a tracker on her person."

"Very well. Is there any way to get in and contain her before we breach the house from below?"

"Negative. Security equipment's too sensitive. You can go up the side of the house and breach from the roof, but Giovanni says the only viable entrance opens up two rooms away from her. You'll still have to navigate the hallway, which is probably full of Malcolm's men."

"That's my entry. You come up from below and eliminate as many as you can... quietly. If I need a distraction, you call in the boys, and you're it."

"Copy that."

I switched to the team channel. "It's a go. El Segador and I will enter first. Other than that, follow the plan."

"Not comfortable with that, boss," Archangel keyed in. "Everyone agreed I should take point. Besides, Samson will kill my ass if you come back with so much as a scratch. I know, 'cause he told me so."

"I'll endeavor to appease Samson's delicate sensibilities," I replied dryly. While I trusted my club with my life, I wasn't willing to take the chance the girl was out and about in the house. Or that she could sneak out of her room. Drago had spoken highly of her intelligence and skill. While he'd been able to speak, that is. The fewer of us in the house until she was in my custody, the less likely it was there would be accidents.

"Going on the record I'm objecting strenuously to this. Something happens and El Diablo gets hurt, you motherfuckers better back me up," Archangel replied crossly.

On any other occasion I'd have taken pity on him and let him lead the mission. Or El Segador. But this was too important. I let my club do many things in the guise of safeguarding me. Only because it pleased them, and I was willing to give a little and look weak if it made them happy. Every single one of them was more than capable, so, as long as the risk was acceptable, I indulged them. They always did what I asked of them to the best of their abilities. It was the least I could do when none of them asked for anything. Typically, I had to force on them their heart's desires. This, however, was different. Malcolm was a fierce opponent, one I knew almost as well as I knew El Segador. I didn't want to risk my brothers on someone so unpredictable without knowing exactly where the bastard was and how much he was expecting from me.

"I got your six," Hardcase spoke up. I could detect the faintest amount of humor in his voice. "For all the good it will do you." There were chuckles over the radio as throat mics were activated with the sound.

"If you are all finished, El Segador and I would appreciate it if you kept an eye out. Let us know if any surprises are coming our way. Particularly if it's in the form of a small woman. Aye?"

"Eyes open, mouths closed," Archangel said. Immediately the chatter stopped and the operation began.

"Suppressors or bows only," El Segador reminded. "Do not shoot unless you have a clear shot at what you're firing at and won't miss. No mistakes or you'll answer to me." No one replied. No one needed to.

We used a spray acid to make a hole in the chain link fence on the defensive weak side. There were fewer guards and more obstacles. We'd been expecting more, but it was possible they suspected we were going to make a try for the girl and had pulled some men back to the house for extra guards there. I was sure I'd gotten the truth out of Drago before I allowed him to die, but I was also convinced they'd told him exactly what they knew I'd want to know. Pretty Boy had confirmed nearly everything Drago had said, but I wasn't sure how much that man had really known to begin with. No matter what he'd wanted to believe, Pretty Boy wasn't a big player. He was a means to an end. He killed people. But he was messy. Anyone could do that job.

El Segador and I separated as planned, each going to a different corner on opposite sides of the house. While I was gaining the room and entering that way, El Segador found an opening in a basement window. Security was good, but Ripper, from Salvation's Bane, and Shotgun had hacked the security system and had a real-time feed of everything going on, plus a loop feed they were prepared to use if there was a danger of their men being spotted.

They needn't have worried. El Segador had been doing this a long time before any of these men had ever been brought together. This was our life's work. A skill we could perform like no other. We killed in the shadows. No camera had ever caught us. No one had ever found a trace of us, no matter how high-level the kill. Tonight would be no different. Not only were we here to rescue an innocent who'd been a captive her entire life, we were here to make a point. To send a message.

The Brotherhood prided itself on being a permanent institution. Once you joined -- or were drafted -- you never left. While El Segador had never been an official member of the Brotherhood, I had. In fact, as far as I'd been able to tell, no one had ever made El Segador while I'd still been active within their ranks. He was still a ghost. He was a patched member of Black Reign, but, other than the name and ethnic similarities, no one could link him to me. Even though we were closer than brothers.

The Brotherhood thought they'd had a hold on me all these years, that I hadn't really left. That no one could ever really leave. The fact was, I was biding my time. I knew Malcolm was trying to buy an alliance with his largest rival, I just wasn't sure who that rival was, or where he was keeping his currency, his only child. At least, I hadn't until recently.

"I have eyes on you." Samson's voice was calm

over the radio. He was watching the whole thing taking place from the safety of the Black Reign compound. "Whatever the tech is Giovanni gave you, it's fuckin' brilliant so far. Not only can I spot both of you through any obstacles, but I can see everything around you, including people and animals."

"Good," I replied softly. "Reaper. You good on your end?"

"I'm ready."

"Girl is still hanging out in the West wing. You're almost directly above her, El Diablo. Are you sure there's no immediate entrance?"

"Everything's boarded or electrified. The real tech is much more subtle, but still noticeable if you know what to look for. Giovanni's assessment of the place seems to be spot on so far."

"Go slowly," Samson warned. "I want time to be able to get you out if things go to shit."

No way that was happening. El Segador and I worked a certain way. We knew how the other worked. This was a scenario that had played out a thousand times. We knew what we were about. My club knew what they were doing as well, but they tended to be overprotective. Samson would be fine. So would Reaper and I.

"Just let me know at the first sign of anything not going right."

"Boss... "

"Enough. El Segador, *rasgue-o*."

"*Sim, senhor.*" Ripper's voice was like a carnivorous caress, the start to this extraction and execution we both needed. I could almost see his evil smile. It likely mirrored my own.

"Let's get these fuckers," I purred.

The entry we'd scouted for me opened into a

narrow stairway, just right for a kill box. If I failed to disengage any alarms, there was literally no way for me to escape as the stairway was straight. It didn't diverge into sections, but ran the length of the building until it reached the ground. Thankfully, the prep work done for this extraction was spot on -- as always.

When I reached the bottom, I waited until Samson murmured, "All clear up top. Two bogies around the corner to the left, three suites down from the target suite."

I walked calmly down the hallway and turned the corner. Not missing a beat, I took the first guy out with a quick twist of his neck. The other one took a knife to his throat before I yanked out the blade and broke his neck as well.

"Two down," I informed.

"Three on my end," Reaper shot back. I couldn't help but grin.

"You always have to make it a competition, don't you?" I tried to sound annoyed, but I knew my long-time friend would see straight through me.

"Just keeping you on your toes. Otherwise, you might be tempted to leave someone alive, you're so soft-hearted and shit."

"Just clear the way for us to go outside. I made one kill with a knife in the hall. I'd appreciate it if you'd cover it with the other body in case the girl is squeamish."

"You can always drug her," Samson added. "You have the means. Might be less traumatic."

"Only if she wishes," I said. "I'll not have her equate us with the bastards holding her now." There was always the possibility she was too scared to leave. Especially if she'd never been outside before as Drago had suggested.

"Give me fifteen minutes," Reaper said. "I'll be there to escort the two of you down."

I continued on. The place wasn't heavily guarded, but I did take out five more guards before I reached the suite I was looking for.

"Anyone in there with her?"

"Only one occupant," Samson said. "Likely female by the body mass index. Jesus, this equipment Giovanni gave us is fuckin' detailed!" He paused a moment. "She's moving around one section of the room. Seems to be around a table or something. Unsure."

"Any sound? I can't hear a thing out here."

"Nothing, and this equipment would pick it up. My thought is the room is soundproof, because I can hear sounds from most other areas of the house. This one and the suite at the opposite end are the only ones silent."

"Understood," I said, looking at the door. I quickly disabled the sensors I found, and there were three. I pulled out the phone Giovanni had given me and brought up the app that went with the equipment he'd sent. "Shotgun, you and Samson look at this and look hard." Shotgun was back at the compound, but he had a real-time view of what was going on. "I disabled three sensors here." I waved the phone camera around the door and surrounding wood. "Make sure I didn't miss anything." They had me repeat the motion several times, then again around the doorknob and the locking mechanism, which was a deadbolt, and the knob lock on the outside of the door instead of the inside.

"I see nothing else," Samson confirmed. "Shotgun?"

"There are no wires around the knob to suggest it was hot in any way. Far as I can tell, you're clear."

Without further hesitation, I unlocked the deadbolt, then the knob lock. The second I opened the door, I was nearly knocked off my feet by the noise and the smell.

* * *

Jezebel

"Get up, come on, get down with the sickness!" I screamed out the song from Disturbed as the video played on the huge TV covering one wall. I had ground beef browning with onion and had just put in peppers, garlic, mushrooms, and tomatoes. It wouldn't be long before it was time for the cheese and noodles. I rubbed my hands together. This was gonna be *so good*!

I stirred the egg noodles, testing their tenderness. Yeah. It was close. I cut up the Velveeta cheese into small blocks, then poured in the tomatoes. After mixing it, I dropped in the cheese a few blocks at a time and stirred until melted, all the while belting out song after song. Disturbed. Five Finger Death Punch. Alice Cooper. AC/DC. Rammstein. Yeah, I liked it hard and loud.

I'd just stirred in the noodles when a movement near the door caught my eye. A man. Correction, a *huge* man was shutting the door behind him, his eyes on me, but wincing as if the sound was a bit too much for him. Which, likely, it was. I hadn't met this guy before, but I was used to Malcolm sending in men to intimidate or scare me. Sometimes he sent them to get to know me, to try to cajole me into toeing the line. Especially when I was being particularly difficult. I hadn't been, though. Not for a couple of months. I'd had my fill of the outside the last time I'd snuck out. I suspect Malcolm knew I was capable of bypassing his security and sneaking out and had simply set up a bad situation for me to fall into.

Instead of muting the TV, I smirked at the big bastard and turned it up even louder. He merely shook his head, then motioned at the remote. Obviously either wanting it or wanting me to mute it. Instead of complying, I shoved it down the garbage disposal and flipped a switch on the wall, turning it on.

The big guy ground his teeth, pulled a gun from his back, and shot the TV.

"Well," he said, shaking his head slightly as if to clear it. "I guess I won that round." He gave me a shark-like smile. "My name's El Diablo. I'd say I was a friend of your father's but that would be… oversimplifying things, shall we say." His rich voice was accented lightly in some kind of English derivative, but his features were Hispanic. Short, dark hair with a smattering of silver, dark eyes, and lightly tanned skin gave him a rakish if sophisticated look. Though he was dressed in some kind of black military-grade clothing, he looked like he'd be just as comfortable in an expensive tailored suit.

I tried to hold in my reaction. "My father doesn't have friends," I said. "He has people who either owe him or whom he's blackmailing."

El Diablo looked like he was contemplating that assessment before nodding. "I think that is a very accurate description of Malcolm. You're a very perceptive girl." He held out his free hand to me. "Now. If you'll come with me, please. We're on somewhat of a tight schedule."

I shook my head. "I'm not going anywhere with you willingly. How'd you get in here, anyway? There are always guards outside the door."

Again, he gave me that smile. It wasn't exactly evil, but it gave me a shiver. It was a smile that said not to fuck with him if I wanted to live long. "Let's just say the guards won't be a problem anymore."

Had he killed the guards? My heart started to pound. I knew the name El Diablo. He was spoken of in hushed tones -- the Devil he was named.

"Look. I don't know what you want, but if you think I know anything about what my father is up to, you're wrong. I might be biologically related to him, but I'm not in any way an associate or partner. I'm nothing but another tool for him to use." As I said that, I tried not to wince. I hadn't had a normal childhood, but I'd watched TV. I'd see what the world looked like, at least a small part of it. The life I lived and the life I wanted were polar opposites. And neither was something this man would be able to understand.

"I'm not here to get all your secrets. That will come later," he said with a smirk. "I'm merely here to take you out of here."

"And go where?" As we spoke, another man opened the door and stepped inside. There were several other men lined up outside as well. All of them large and lethal looking, carrying either knives or guns with suppressors attached to them. I backed up a step.

El Diablo took a step toward me, his brows knitting together in both confusion and maybe a little bit of anger. "Away from here. I hear you're a prisoner here, no matter how well kept. That you've been here your whole life."

I nodded, narrowing my eyes. "Yeah? What of it?"

"Consider yourself free," he said. But he didn't back away. In fact, he was inching closer.

"Fine," I said brightly. "I'm free. Thanks so much for your help. I'll just pack my shit and be on my way." When none of them moved. I made a shooing motion with my hand. "You can go now. Thanks again."

The guys around El Diablo -- and there seemed to be more and more coming by the minute -- looked uncomfortably at him. The man just stared at me for long, long moments. I could hear my concoction on the stove bubbling lightly in the silence.

"Let me rephrase," he said, his voice hard. "You're coming with me. I'll show you more freedom than that fuck Malcolm did. But you will need to stay within the club compound."

One of the men, the first one to arrive, stepped close to El Diablo and put a hand on his shoulder. "Easy, Liam. What the fuck? And who broke the damned TV?"

El Diablo, or rather Liam, actually blushed slightly, his back straightening defensively. "Well, it was already a few decibels above a rock concert, and she turned it up when I entered the room. The polite thing would have been to turn it down." He glared at me. "Or off."

"So you threw something through the thing?"

"No," Liam grinned, his gaze still firmly fixed on me. "I shot it. But only after she dropped the remote into the garbage disposal."

"Jesus," the other man growled, turning to me. "Don't mind him. He's obviously having a bad day. We've been looking for you for several months. Ever since we had word you existed. It was really a frustrating race against time. Just please understand, we have your best interests at heart."

I snorted. "So you fuckers believe in the prophecy too, huh?" I shook my head as I moved to the stove and turned off the burner. I was not letting my noodles go to waste, no matter what these fuckers decided to do. I was gonna eat my fill and get sick. Just like I'd planned.

"No," Liam said. "Hell, I doubt even Malcolm believes. But he knows *They* believe. He'll keep you here until he finds the group he needs an alliance with the most, then he'll sell you to the leader."

"If by *They*, you mean the Brotherhood, yeah. I got that. Malcolm's hip deep with them. Trying to buy his way out, but it doesn't seem to be working. I figure that was where I came in. But he's not come for me yet. At least, not yet."

"What do you know about the Brotherhood?" Liam snapped. He took a step forward, looking every inch the Devil he was named.

"OK," the other guy said. "Time to go. You." He pointed at me. "Pack anything you want to take so we can leave. We've got time, but I'd rather not stay here."

I crossed my arms over my chest and leaned lazily against the counter. "I'm not going anywhere with any of you."

"You'd rather be a prisoner here?" Liam asked incredulously. As he grew angrier, his accent slipped from a distinguished English to something like a cross between Arabic and Hispanic. It was an exotic combination I found oddly sexy. Just like the rest of him. Didn't mean I was giving in. He was still on the same level as Malcolm, which meant, whether he admitted it or not, he was still my enemy.

"Why not? I have a whole floor to myself, I can get anything I want delivered, and I know the place. I know what to expect. If you think I'm just gonna leave with you because you say it's a good idea, you're not as smart as you think you are. Or as Malcolm thinks you are."

"I'm sure you didn't know, but El Diablo isn't exactly on his game. He's normally a charmer of ladies of all ages." The man gave Liam the side eye. "In fact, I've never seen him behave this way."

"So, shooting my TV wouldn't normally have been his first choice?"

"Uh, no. And I'm El Segador," he said, reaching out a hand to me. Yeah. Not falling for that one.

"The Reaper. Really?"

"You know that one, eh?"

"I've lived here my entire life. Played political games of the highest stakes, even though I'm a prisoner. I know who El Diablo and El Segador are. More than just the Spanish translations. He's the one who got away. You're the one who never was."

El Segador raised his eyebrows. "The one who never was?" He nodded. "Think I like that."

"We don't have time for this," Liam snapped. He stalked toward me. I took a few steps back. "We're leaving."

"Like hell," I said, snagging a butcher knife from beside the stove. My kitchen was the one concession I hadn't had to fight Malcolm on. In fact, he and his men sometimes joined me for supper. Apparently, even by the standards of the Brotherhood, I was a pretty good cook.

"You realize I could take that from you and gut you before you even realized I had the knife, right?" His voice was deadly, and El Segador snagged his arm.

"Brother... "

Before either of them could react, I lunged with the knife against my forearm and cut a gash across Liam's cheek. It wasn't particularly deep -- just a scratch -- but I'd made my point.

Liam bared his teeth at me and swiped a piece of my Le Creuset cookware off the counter to the floor. I hit my limit. "You fucking bastard!" I launched myself at him, out for more blood. Wrapping myself around his body, I turned my blade so I could stab the bastard. He somehow avoided it and was able to disarm me, but trying to fend off my knife left him open to another attack. Snapping my head forward, I connected my forehead with his nose. Hard. Blood sprayed and his body stiffened.

He didn't let go of my knife hand, nor did he let go of me. Instead, he pressed his thumb into the pressure point in my wrist, causing me to drop the knife. Then he somehow maneuvered me to the counter where he zip-tied my wrists behind my back.

"Liam!" El Segador barked. The other man had left the room, but I got the feeling they were probably not far away. "What the fuck are you doing?"

"Taking a wayward child in hand." He sneered. "If you can't behave, you get punished."

"All right, that's enough," another voice snapped from the doorway. "Reaper, take El Diablo out. I'll deal with the girl."

"My name is Jezebel," I bit out. "Not girl, or honey, or sweetie, or anything else. Jezebel!"

The big guy nodded. His head was shaved, and he had tattoos creeping up his neck behind his ears. With his looks, combined with his height and muscular frame, he had to be the scariest son of a bitch I'd ever seen. "I hear you, Jezebel. I'm Samson." His tone was quiet and level. I got the feeling nothing much shook the bastard. Then again, I'd first had that impression of El Diablo. Turned out the chink in that one's armor was in the form of a five-foot-nothing, smart-mouthed female captive. Made me wonder how he normally liked his women if he was known as a charmer. 'Cause, yeah. He wasn't charming in the least.

"Well, Samson, please inform Liam over there

that the cookware he just swept to the floor is extremely expensive and something very dear to me. I will not tolerate abuse of it, nor will I be intimidated by some ham-handed lout intent on revenge against a rival or whatever other reason he has for kidnapping me."

Samson held out his hands in a non-threatening gesture. "Not here to kidnap you, Jezebel. We only want to get you out of here and safe. If Malcolm sells you to his biggest rival in the Brotherhood, your life could very well be in jeopardy."

I tilted my head, unsure if I was hearing him right. "You know who Malcolm's selling me to?"

"We have a good idea. Ever hear of a guy called Cipher?"

Cipher!

"He wouldn't," I whispered as my throat closed off. I couldn't get in enough air. Abruptly, I sat down on the floor, hanging on to the kitchen island.

"We're pretty sure he's deep in negotiation." Samson crouched down in front of me. He didn't touch me or even look sympathetic. He just gazed at me, letting me make up my mind. "Besides, if you know Malcolm at all, you know he most definitely would."

He was right. If it furthered his position, he wouldn't care about what he'd done to me to secure himself.

I looked up. Samson was directly in front of me, his huge frame blocking most everything behind him. But then Liam stood beside Samson. He seemed better under control now. Strangely, I found my gaze drifting to Liam. El Diablo.

The Devil.

"What are you planning on doing with me?"

"We're just going to take you to our compound.

Once there, we'll get you settled in your own place," Liam said. "It can even be as nice as this if you like. Your own space."

I looked away, sighing. "No matter where I go, it seems I'll always be a prisoner."

"Not always," Liam said, crouching beside Samson. The other man gave him the side eye but stood and backed off. "Once we get rid of both Malcolm and Cipher, you'll be free to do whatever you please. You can stay with us, in our big family, or go your own way. The choice is up to you." That smooth accent was back. I now knew it was fake. I wondered what else about the man was false. Certainly not his reported ability to do violence. I could see it, barely controlled as it was. 'Cause the man definitely wanted to throttle me.

"Doesn't look like I really have a choice."

"Not at present, no," Liam agreed. "But it won't always be like this." I had to give it to the guy. When he was on his game, he was one smooth son of a bitch.

"You know, if you'd approached me like this, I wouldn't have been so difficult."

He snorted. "I have the feeling you'd have given me hell no matter what. Now. The cookware is obviously important to you. Anything else you need to take with you immediately? My men will collect everything else in here once the place is cleaned."

"Just some clothes. Oh. And supper." When he opened his mouth to argue, I interrupted. "I have leak-proof containers, and I've been looking forward to this all day. If you're nice, I'll even share."

He chuckled but nodded. "Don't think you'll always get your way, Jezebel. You won't."

We'd see about that.

Chapter Two
Jezebel

After the initial SNAFU, Liam was actually a really nice, charming guy. Just like El Segador said. Which meant I didn't trust him as far as I could throw him. It was an act. All of it. *Fake.* Why was anyone's guess, and I didn't really care.

I wasn't sure if I trusted what Samson had said, but the mere mention of Cipher's name would give me nightmares for several nights. It always did. He was the man Malcolm had told me about since my childhood. The boogeyman. Cipher wasn't the leader of the Brotherhood. On the contrary, he was just on the verge of being as dangerous to them as El Diablo. If Malcolm was trying to make a strong ally against the Brotherhood, giving me to Cipher would make sense. At least, that was the opinion I'd formed after eavesdropping on Malcolm several times. I wasn't sure if I should tell these men or not. So, for now, I'd keep it close. There would be plenty of time to give them information if they truly were helping me.

The ride to their clubhouse was a winding, forty-five-minute drive through Palm Beach and into Lake Worth. As we approached the front gates, I had to admit, I was fucking impressed. At first, I thought it was just one big mansion or something, but, unlike Malcolm's setup, this place was a fenced compound. Multiple buildings. Still more in the distance, some large buildings with multiple floors that resembled hotels, and others that were elegant, but more intimate. Like individual homes. Whoever these people were, they had money. But then, didn't they all? Malcolm did. The Brotherhood certainly did.

We were in a convoy as we drove through the

gates. Had been since we left Malcolm's stronghold. I was in a state-of-the art Hummer with Liam and a man he called Mechanic. I got the feeling the Hummer was the real thing, not the street version. Military grade. All around the large vehicle were motorcycles with big men on them. Malcolm employed men as large, but none of them seemed as dangerous as these guys. It was a heavy confidence, but more. They just knew they would win. And all of them looked to Liam. El Diablo. The only time any of them had been uncomfortable with the situation was when Liam had lost his calm.

It also hadn't escaped my notice that no one had mentioned that Malcolm was dead. It would surprise me greatly if they'd caught him. He had a sixth sense about impending danger. He'd have been long gone before this group of men -- Black Reign -- was anywhere on the property.

The convoy drove past the front building and to a large garage attached to the main building. We all rolled in, and the vehicles were turned off and parked. Liam got out of the Hummer's front passenger side and opened my door for me.

"Here we are, little Jezebel," he said, his facade firmly back in place. His smile was warm and inviting. "I'll apologize in advance. The party in the main room will be raucous, but there's really no avoiding it."

"We could go in the back," I said, raising my eyebrows at him. The bastard was looking forward to whatever waited in that room. Or, rather, he was looking forward to seeing my reaction to whatever was in that room.

"Hmm... I suppose we could, but this is the most direct route." His smile looked a little like anticipation. Maybe, he just wanted to embarrass me.

"What the hell have I done to piss you off?" I

asked, getting quite pissed myself.

He gave me a mock-surprised look, as if he thought I knew very well what I'd done. "Why, little Jezebel. Why would you think I was upset with you?"

I shoved him out of the way, hopped down from the vehicle and grabbed my noodle dish and marched off. No one stopped me or directed me which way to go. They just fell in behind and in front of me. Liam moved in beside me before four other men flanked us, effectively closing the two of us in a ring of protection as we approached the door to the massive structure. It looked to be about six stories tall with balconies wrapping around the structure at every level. It was impressive, and I wasn't too proud to admit I wanted to see the rest of it.

Too bad I was tossed into the lion's den.

The second the door was opened, a blast of noise hit me. I wasn't opposed to the music -- sounded like Rammstein, unless I missed my guess. It was that the room didn't leak sound at all. Soundproof. Just like my room. I glanced at Liam. He smirked. Seemed all he wanted was a little payback. Fucker. Then I stepped inside, and the rest of it hit me.

If there was a man or woman not completely naked, I didn't see them immediately. Granted, it was hard to actually see anything other than the orgy. It was two in the morning, and I knew the wildest parties were now in full swing. But I'd never seen anything to compare with this.

"You've been to parties?" Liam had his mouth next to my ear to be heard over the music without yelling. Had I spoken out loud?

"Yeah," I said absently, too mesmerized by all the hedonism going on all around the room. "I figured out how to bypass security, and I occasionally sneak out. I've never seen anything like this, though. Ohmigod!"

"Snuck. Out."

"Yeah. Out of that fucking house." I spotted one girl kneeling between two men, sucking the cock of one while she stroked the other. Another woman stood from where she'd been sucking off a guy only to be pulled onto his lap. She straddled his hips and reached behind her to grasp his cock and guide it into her pussy. Once she sank down on him, she started moving, the guy grasping the cheeks of her ass and kneading as she fucked him. Two other girls were going at it on the pool table, grinding their pussies together in a display that had more than one man watching and stroking his dick.

"Wow," I breathed in awe. I felt my face split with a grin. "This. Is. The. Tits!" I whirled around, looking for the bar. If I was gonna try to find a place in this lovely orgy, I wanted two shots of Fireball first. There was a fine line between a pleasant buzz and drunk off my ass, and I knew exactly what it took to get there without falling over. I wanted my inhibitions stunted. I did not want to be sloppy drunk.

When I spotted the bar, I made a beeline for it, shoving my escorts out of the way and making my demand. "Two shots of Fireball!" I yelled over the music. "Quickly!" The guy glanced away from me, probably at Liam. I didn't care, I was too busy watching the beautiful mayhem taking place.

"Which ones are couples?" I asked, not wanting to embarrass myself. "Who's just havin' fun with a convenient partner?"

Surprisingly, it was the bartender who answered. "The couples are the ones with the guy growling at anyone looking at his woman."

"Vague, but I'll take it."

"Look," he said. "None of the threesomes or more have a permanent partner. None of the chicks fuckin' each other are couples. No man here who has a woman would ever approach you, but, if you're in doubt, I'd be glad to show you a good time." He winked at me as he handed me the first shot of Fireball.

I giggled as I took the glass and downed it in one gulp, wincing only slightly. "Thanks, but you might be a little much for my first time."

"I'll be as little or as much as you need, babe."

I turned back to the guy. He had an infectious grin I couldn't help return. I was feeling the burn from the first drink when I downed the second, never taking my gaze from his eyes.

"You don't have anything that could satisfy her," Liam growled. I glanced at him but decided to ignore the grouch. Why spend effort arguing with him when there was so much to see and do?

I caught the gaze of a girl who'd just entered the room. She was fully clothed, but before my avid gaze, she stripped off her clothing before stretching out on a couch with her face in the lap of a muscled, naked man. He immediately buried a hand in her hair as she engulfed his cock in her mouth.

"There!" I pointed at the couple. "Are they together? She went right to him."

"Eden?" The bartender asked. "Na. She's just a friendly, fun-loving girl. Iron's one of her favorite fucks in the cam shows, but they ain't a couple."

"Can I do that?" I asked no one in particular. "Because I *really* want to do that!" As if reading my mind, Eden winked at me, never stopping her ministrations to Iron's cock. She crooked her finger at me in a beckoning gesture. "Oh, I'm *so* there!"

Without another thought, I stripped off my clothing as I hurried to join the pair. How far was I willing to go? I wasn't sure. I just knew I wanted to be a part of the celebration of life and sex going on all around me. There would never be a better time than right now.

* * *

El Diablo

In all my life, I'd never witnessed anything like what I was seeing in that moment. I was completely mesmerized by Jezebel as she moved toward Eden and Iron where they were playing on one of the plush couches in the great room. Her hips swayed seductively and muscles played across her back, arms, and thighs as she moved away from me. I managed to hold in my growl of displeasure. Just.

I wasn't displeased about her naked body. On the contrary, her form pleased me greatly. Gently rounded hips and ass, narrow waist, and small but perky breasts teased me. Normally, I'd have sent her on her way with my blessing, instructing Iron to look out for her and make sure she had a private place to sleep. Instead, I found myself ready to pull her back, to force her to her knees and tell her that, if she wanted something to suck on, I'd be providing the cock.

Still another part of me wanted to see what she'd do. How far she'd go. I thought she'd been captive in that house her entire life. Knowing she'd managed to sneak out made me wonder what mischief she'd gotten into. And if this was her first sexual encounter or if she'd found a man to fulfill those desires for her. It was another dual moment for me, torn between being glad she'd learned how to slip her leash from time to time, but wanting to kill any other man who'd known her body.

When she reached Iron and Eden, she dropped gracefully to her knees between Iron's legs. I fully expected her to reach for him, to take his cock in her mouth and suck with a look of bliss on her face. Instead, she sat back on her heels and watched avidly as Eden stroked Iron's cock in her small, pale hand.

"He's so beautiful." I heard Jezebel's soft voice even over the commotion in the room around us. "Will you fuck him?"

Eden shrugged one delicate shoulder. "If he makes me want him enough." There was a growl from Iron followed by a giggle from Eden. Then Jezebel's face brightened with a breathtaking smile and my world... shifted.

I knew I wanted Jezebel with a fierceness I'd never wanted with another woman, but now I felt like I'd die if I couldn't have her. Immediately. Instead of acting like a Neanderthal, like most of the boys would, I resolved to watch things play out. If she needed more than I was comfortable with, I'd deal with it then. I wanted to see what she'd do. See what I was getting myself into with this girl. Motioning to Mechanic, who was now tending the bar, I snapped, "Beer." Mechanic raised an eyebrow but didn't say anything. Just handed me my preferred Heineken.

Iron reached out a hand to her. "Come sit with me, sweetheart. You don't have to sit on the floor."

I fully expected her to crawl up onto the couch beside Iron, but she didn't. Instead, she did the strangest thing. She took his hand and brought it to her cheek so that Iron's big palm cradled the side of her face. Jezebel closed her eyes like she was in heaven. That simple touch meant something to her. Iron noticed it, too. Immediately, his focus was on Jezebel.

"Honey, are you good?"

"I'm wonderful," she said, opening her eyes. Her smile was genuine. "I just love being touched. I've not had that a lot in my life."

She was killing me. How the hell was I not supposed to take this sweet girl back to my home and worship her body all fucking night?

"We're more than willing to touch you to your heart's content, honey." Again, Iron made a move like he might lift her onto the couch beside him, but she shook her head.

"I just want to watch for now. But thank you for the offer. I might take you up on it if you're really good to her," she said, nodding to Eden. "What are your names?"

"I'm Eden," she said, reaching out a small hand to Jezebel, "and this is Iron."

"Do you both live here? I mean, does everyone here live here or do you all go your separate ways when the parties are over?"

Eden gave her infectious, melodious laugh. It was a sound everyone in the place always appreciated. Iron's answering grin said he appreciated it as well. "Some of us live here. Iron and I both do. Not everyone, though. Only those belonging to Black Reign get to live here. The rest are just here for fun. Some to transact business, but that's all club stuff." She waved off her comment like it was nothing, but I often used parties to help ease the way for business.

Jezebel nodded. "I understand. Malcolm always said blackmail got him the deals he wanted. I imagine that some people would do anything to not have their involvement in this kind of party get out."

Immediately, Eden sat up. "Oh, no, honey. Not like that. The better a mood someone is in, the easier they are to make transactions favorable to the guys. We girls... well." She grinned. "Sometimes we get to see to it the other party is in a *very* good mood."

It took her a moment, but Jezebel finally returned Eden's smile. "You enjoy your role."

"Absolutely," Eden said, turning her attention back to Iron's cock. She engulfed the head and sucked hard enough to hollow her cheeks before letting it pop free. "I enjoy sex in all forms." She looked up at Iron. "Don't I." It wasn't a question. I glanced around and found Samson conspicuously absent. He was highly uncomfortable with what his baby sister did for the club, but refused to deny her since, as he put it, at least she was in a controlled environment acting out her fantasies. He knew she was safe with his brothers.

"You certainly do, babe. And I, for one, love that you enjoy all kinds of sex." Iron grinned as he gently pulled Eden back to his cock, tunneling his fingers in her hair as she took him into her mouth.

She winked at Jezebel before taking Iron deep once. When she pulled out, Eden fisted Iron's cock, stroking lazily. "What's your name? Who are you with?"

"Jezebel," she said. "Some guy called Liam brought me. There were a bunch of them, actually," she said, furrowing her brow. "Do you think they all meant for me to have sex with them? Because they didn't say that."

"Liam?" Iron looked confused, then he found my gaze as I watched them intently. His eyes widened. Yeah. Liam wasn't how my brothers knew me. When I nodded, Iron's eyes got wide. "Liam have a hold on you? Are you his?"

"No," she said, her eyes fixed on Iron's cock. "He took me away from Malcolm. I think I'm a trophy or something."

"Honey, we don't bring trophies here. Maybe you better go back to Liam."

"You don't want me here?" Jezebel looked up at Iron, then to Eden. "But I thought it was OK."

"It is," Eden said quickly, reaching out to Jezebel with her free hand. "Come. Watch. Join us if you want." Jezebel couldn't resist Eden's ready smile. No one could. I even found myself smiling, though the thought of her joining the horny couple nearly made me crazy.

"I just want to watch you suck him," she said. "Do you mind?"

"Not at all." Eden grinned before turning back to Iron's cock and engulfing him as far as she could.

"Wow," Jezebel gasped. "That's so hot!"

"You like watching?" Iron asked, his jaw tight. Apparently, little Eden was very good at sucking his cock.

"I love it," Jezebel gasped. "This is so much better than Porn Hub."

Iron barked out a laugh. Eden took Iron deeper, gagging slightly when she did. Jezebel gasped and leaned closer.

"You like taking him deep?"

Eden moaned, then pulled away long enough to reply, "Yeah. I do." Then she went back to sucking Iron. The big man moaned, tightening his grip in her hair and moving her the way he wanted, taking control.

"You guys look so hot," Jezebel whimpered, cupping one small breast in her palm. Instantly, I was hard as a rock. My cock jerked every time she rolled her nipple between her fingers. She even licked her lips, like she'd like to be the one sucking Iron. It was a huge turn-on. Also made me angry as hell. The combination was wreaking havoc on me. And making me horny as fuck.

"Do it again," Jezebel said softly. "Take him as deep as you can." Eden did, humming slightly, her eyes closing. "How does it feel when she takes you deep?" Jezebel looked up at Iron. Thankfully she was sitting at an angle where I could see her face, because no way was I missing her expressions. As she spoke, there was genuine excitement in her voice.

"Fuckin' awesome."

"Eden, do you like it when he pulls your hair like that? It looks so hot, but doesn't it make you afraid he won't let you up if you can't breathe?"

Eden's eyes shot open. She took one last, deep, long suck, then pulled away. "I trust Iron with my life, Jezebel. Same as I do any man here. He may push my boundaries from time to time, but he'd never really hurt me. Especially not like that."

Jezebel looked from Eden to Iron, a hesitant look on her face. She swallowed, then looked at Iron. "I didn't mean to offend."

The man, God damn his soul, just smiled at her. "You didn't at all. It's good you've got a streak of self-preservation. Though, I promise you, here in this clubhouse, you can explore anything you want to without having to worry about getting hurt. We're a drunk and rowdy bunch sometimes, but there is always someone watching over us. Especially the women." He pulled Eden up by her hair for a lusty kiss before guiding her back to his cock. "No one's gonna hurt Eden -- or you. Least of all me."

Jezebel looked back and forth between Iron and Eden several times before a slow smile spread across her face. "I believe you." Reaching for the pillow beside Iron, she asked, "Do you mind?" Iron handed it to her, and Jezebel stretched out on the floor at the couple's feet. "Did I kill the mood, or do you feel like continuing?"

"Honey," Eden said with a giggle. "There is no way you could possibly kill the mood. You're sexy as fuck and so Goddamned innocent you make me feel like everything is new again. Thank you." Iron opened his mouth -- probably to respond as well -- but Eden engulfed his cock, taking him deep. The only thing that came from Iron was a loud groan.

His head fell back on the couch, and his hips bucked. Eden hummed around his cock and started bobbing her head, letting him fuck her mouth as deeply as he would fuck her pussy.

"Wow," Jezebel said, one arm behind her head as she watched, the other lazily rolling her nipple between her fingers. "You're really taking him deep. I could never take a guy that deep." I ground my teeth even as my cock twitched, anger and jealousy at war with lust and need.

"You know," Iron said as if contemplating what he was about to say. "If Eden doesn't mind, you could always practice on me. She could help you."

Eden let go of his cock and giggled. "'Cause that would be such a hardship for *you*." She kissed the head of his dick. "But, yeah. You can join us in any way you want."

"Maybe," Jezebel said, but made no move to go to them. "But right now, I think I just want to watch."

"Feel free to join in any time you want," Iron said, stroking Eden's dark hair away from her face so Jezebel could better see her sucking down his cock.

She nodded, but just continued to pluck at her nipples. First one, then the other, then the first. Over and over. The faster Eden worked Iron's cock, the harder Jezebel worked her nipples. Her breath came in little gasps. Sometimes, Jezebel would moan with Iron. It was as surreal as it was erotic.

After a while she got braver. "I want to see you lick Eden's pussy," Jezebel said softly, almost to herself. "She's playing with her own clit. I'm sure she would love you to help her."

Iron grunted, pulling Eden off him and tossing her to her back. Eden giggled and reached for him, threading her fingers through his hair and pulling her to him with a sigh. Eden's sighs soon turned to whimpers and moans as Iron worked her sex. I admit, as scenes went, it was hot as hell. Their scene paled in comparison with the solo scene going on below them.

Jezebel now had one hand playing with her nipples and one lazily stroking her clit. I could see her glistening sex as she dipped one finger between her lips and stroked up and down, pausing occasionally to circle her clit. Her breaths came in little pants, her lips parted slightly.

"You look like it feels good," she said to Eden. "Is he licking your little clit the way you like?" God, what was this girl doing? This was fucking hot and uncomfortable at the same time. I got the feeling she wanted to participate with them but was either too shy or just wasn't comfortable enough to take Iron up on his offer.

"It feels amazing," Eden gasped. "I need... Oh, God, Iron, I need you to fuck me."

Iron lifts his head and looks back at Jezebel. "What do you think, little Bell. Does she deserve to be fucked?"

Jezebel gasped, her body breaking out in a sheen of sweat. "Oh, God," she echoed. "Oh, God!"

"Hm," Iron said, sitting back on his heels. "I'm not sure she's quite ready." Then he brought the flat of his fingers down on Eden's pussy with a sharp slap. Eden and Jezebel both cried out, Eden in ecstasy, Jezebel in surprise. Jezebel sat up fully, getting to her knees and moving toward Eden. She laid her hand on Iron's where it rested on Eden's pussy.

"Did he hurt you?"

"No, baby," Eden said, shaking her head and smiling through her pleasure. "He made me feel good. Sometimes, a little bite of pain can make the pleasure more intense."

As if testing the waters, Jezebel dipped her fingers back to her own sex and circled her clit a few times before slapping her own fingers down on her pussy. She gasped, then did it harder. Gasped again before circling her clit once more. Then she slapped herself harder. And harder still.

"Holy fuck." Iron shot me a glance, and I realized I'd said that out loud.

Jezebel whimpered. Pulling her hand up, she stared down at her fingers in a kind of wonder. "I'm all wet," she said, looking to Eden as if for reassurance. Eden, bless her heart, reached for Jezebel's fingers and pulled them to her mouth, licking and sucking each finger and humming in delight as she did. Jezebel cried out but didn't pull away.

"Do it again," Eden said. "This time, fuck your pussy with your fingers. Then let me taste."

Jezebel nodded eagerly before doing exactly what Eden asked. Her fingers came back wetter than before, and I noticed a thick drop of moisture sliding down Jezebel's inner thigh. It took all my willpower not to drop down beside her and scoop that drop up with my finger and taste for myself, but I wasn't about to break the mood.

"What do you want to see next?" Eden asked, her eyes bright with lust. "Tell me."

"I... I want to watch Iron fuck you. Would you mind letting me watch?"

Instead of answering, Iron crawled his way up Eden's body. Stretching over her to the end table, he snagged one of the many condoms in the bowl sitting there. During parties, condoms were on nearly every flat surface. Usually with a beer or three next to them.

He tore open the package and sheathed himself before guiding his cock to Eden's entrance and sliding home. Eden sighed as Iron growled. Jezebel reached for Eden's hand and held on. I could tell the experience meant something to her. She watched everything avidly. I was surprised -- and grateful -- she didn't ask to participate.

"Tell me what it feels like," she begged, bringing Eden's hand to her cheek and rubbing it much like a cat might. "I need to know what it feels like to be filled like that."

"It stretches me. Iron always does," she said, her words coming in little staccato pants as Iron thrust into her over and over. "He hits my clit at just the right angle... Oh, God! That's so fucking good, Iron!"

Iron just grunted, dipping his head to suck on one of Eden's tits, never stopping his thrusts.

"Is she tight around your cock?"

"As a vise." His voice was husky. Raw. The man was obviously enjoying himself. "She's soft as velvet. Hot as hell."

"Are you going to come?" When Jezebel asked that question, I almost came myself. She sounded so Goddamned innocent, yet dirty at the same fucking time! It left me with more questions than I could wrap my mind around. Especially when I needed to wrap my fist around my dick and stroke off to Jezebel masturbating while she clung to Eden's hand.

"I might," Iron said. He raised himself up so he gripped Eden's thighs with his hands and pulled her to him with every surge forward of his body. "I might if you'd lean down and lick her nipple for her."

Jezebel whimpered, and Eden gasped. "Oh, God! Oh, shit! Bell! Will you please lick my nipple?" She cupped her small tit and offered it to Jezebel, turning pleading eyes her way.

For the first time, Jezebel looked at me. There was a question in her eyes, and she didn't move until I nodded at her, indicating she should. "But, my lovely little Jezebel, only if you want to. This is your choice." It was the first time I'd spoken to her in a sexual situation. She seemed to need my permission. Not Eden's. Not Iron's. Mine. I wasn't sure why, or why I cared, but my chest swelled with pride. The girl was mine, even if she didn't know it yet.

Hesitantly, Jezebel leaned down and licked her tongue slowly over Eden's nipple. When Eden cried out and arched to her, Jezebel closed her lips around the ripe peak and sucked gently. The effect on Eden was instantaneous. She screamed her orgasm, her body shuddering and writhing beneath Iron's. Jezebel stayed latched on until Eden stilled, then she let go with a soft pop and licked the peak over and over as if soothing it.

Iron threw back his head and roared his own release, pumping the condom full of cum. When he'd finished, he sat back, slipping out of Eden and putting his hand over the cum-filled condom so it didn't fall, but making no move to dispose of it. Instead, he heaved in breath after breath, wiping his free hand over his brow.

"Fuck," he gasped out. "Just… *fuck*!"

Eden sat up and pulled Jezebel into a tight embrace. "Thank you, Bell. Thank you so much!"

"I didn't really do anything," she said with a dazed smile. "That was so beautiful."

"It was, wasn't it?" Eden smiled and kissed Jezebel's cheek. "Maybe next time you'll feel comfortable enough to join us. Iron can make you feel good. It's part of his job so he has to be good at it." She giggled while Iron just groaned.

"His job? He makes women feel good by fucking them?"

"Pretty much," Eden said. "When the cam girls are putting on their shows, sometimes they need someone to get them in the mood. To help them orgasm on camera. That's part of what Iron does. He sometimes fucks them on camera, too." She shrugged. "If they want."

"Wow," Jezebel said, smiling once again and making me lose just a little bit more of my heart. "I think I'm gonna like it here. Can I be a cam girl?"

"Why not just get used to being here first?" I interrupted, not able to help myself. It was time she brought her focus back to me. "You can look around, watch some shows. See what you like. After that, you can decide what you want to do. If anything. Besides, you may find something else you like."

Like hell she was going to be a cam girl. No fucking way. I held my hand out to her. "Come. I'll show you to your room and get you settled." Which was code for, *"I'll take her to my room and get her settled."*

She didn't know it, but I was pretty sure Iron got the message. The other man nodded, giving me a lopsided smile.

Yeah, this wasn't going away any time soon. It

wouldn't be long before the whole of Black Reign knew there was something up with their fearless leader and a certain little brown-haired vixen.

Chapter Three
Jezebel

When I took Liam's hand, I fully expected him to help me to my feet, then lead me away. Instead, he helped me stand, then scooped me up in his arms, naked as the day I was born. Strangely, I had no inhibitions in this place. Zero. Since I'd found my first porn site on a computer I'd stolen from Malcolm, I'd wanted to watch something like it in real life. The previous scene with Eden and Iron had been absolutely perfect. I'd stolen the computer because I'd wanted it to be able to look up recipes, but had quickly found other uses for it. Until he'd found out I'd taken it, that is. It had opened up a whole new world I'd wanted desperately to explore. Tonight, I'd gotten to experience just a small slice of it, and I was eager for more.

Liam took me to an elevator and pressed a button. The car shot up, and the motion made me squeal a little, wrapping my arms around him a little tighter.

"Easy, my beautiful Jezebel," he said with a chuckle. "I won't let anything happen to you while you're in my care."

God, he smelled good! I used my small fright as an excuse to bury my face in his neck and inhale. Unfortunately, I made the mistake of sighing. When he gave me another warm chuckle, I gave up pretending and just smelled him at my leisure. I even stroked his hair, marveling at the silky texture of the rich salt-and-pepper strands. He was well-groomed. Clean-shaven and an expensive cut. Under his shirt, however, I could see a peek of a tattoo creeping along his shoulder and chest. There was also a smattering of chest hair I was dying to run my palms over.

The door opened, and he carried me into an opulent suite bigger than my own at Malcolm's mansion prison. It was clean and neat, but obviously lived in.

"Where are we?" I asked, getting the feeling that I wasn't going to like the answer.

"My suite," he said, carrying me through the room to a bedroom that was very Spartan. Obviously not a room used very often. "This is your private room. If you want an office, I'll get furniture for the other bedroom, and you can have whatever you want. Just say the word."

I squirmed, wanting him to let me down. Surprisingly, he did. Suddenly, I was very aware of my nakedness, hating that I was this vulnerable to him. There was no way to stop the hurt in my voice or, likely, in my expression. "Am I a prisoner here?"

Liam winced, and my heart sank. "You're not," he said, scrubbing his hand over the back of his neck. I got the feeling he didn't show indecision or regret -- or whatever he was feeling now -- often. It gave me the tiniest bit of hope he'd throw me a bone and not keep me sequestered any longer. I wanted to live a little. "I just thought you might need a period of adjustment and someplace safe you could retire to if it all gets to be too much." He waved his hand to the bed. "I'll get you whatever you want to cover the bed. Your clothes are already in the closets and drawers, most of them new because we didn't want to take a chance on Malcolm tracking you."

"So he wasn't in the house when you took me?" I wasn't surprised. The man always had a sixth sense about trouble.

"No."

Hearing the confirmation hurt. I was his daughter, yet he left me knowing there was danger. "He's my biological father, but he has no love for me, you know. Taking me from him will gain you nothing."

"I didn't do it to gain leverage, beautiful Jezebel," he said, taking back the two steps I'd put between us to brush a strand of hair off my forehead and tuck it behind my ear. "I came for you to free you. We'd heard you'd been a prisoner there your entire life. I know now that you were able to gain some freedom. But tell me, when you escaped, went out into the world, why did you come back?"

"How far have your people dug into my past?"

His brow furrowed. "Not far. I understand there's not even a picture of you to be found anywhere."

"Right. I'm sure I photobombed photos at parties and such, but no one would know who I am. I slip in, experience the event, then leave." I shrugged. "Pretending to know people isn't hard. You just have to fully commit. Anyway, yeah. There's nothing on me. Nothing. I have no birth certificate, no social security number, no bank accounts… nothing. As far as anyone knows, I don't exist. There's no way I could survive out in the world on my own."

"So, what exactly did you do when you got free?"

I shrugged. "I went to bars. Clubs. Anywhere I could get in. I found that, if I got close to the right people, I could usually get in with little trouble. After that, I'd go wherever the next party was. When I was done, I'd go home. Sometimes I was gone for a couple of days, others I'd be home before daylight. Malcolm always knew I'd been gone and was waiting for me when I got home. After a while, I just started coming in the front door." I shivered. "Until the last time."

"What was different about the last time?"

I sighed, trying not to shiver or cringe away. If I let Liam see how it had affected me, I might find myself locked in this room forever. He was a lot of things I'd yet to figure out, and very much the asshole, but he was also protective. I believed him when he said he'd keep me safe. "The last time I snuck out was two months ago. Malcolm could never figure out how I bypassed his security, but he was tired of it. I think it was because it was close to being time for him to sell me or whatever. Anyway, he was prepared for it. The second his guards spotted me, they were told to go after me and hold me for a couple of days. While they were apparently under strict orders not to take my virginity and not to bruise my face, those were the only limits they were given."

Liam's face turned hard, and I took a step back before I found my backbone. He wasn't going to hurt me, and I got the feeling it would insult him for me to think otherwise. "How bad did they hurt you?"

I met his gaze steadily. "Bad enough I had no intentions of sneaking out of the house ever again."

He turned, swearing softly. "This was a bad idea," he said, scrubbing both hands through his hair before turning to me. "You know, you don't have to participate in the sex at parties. I know you liked when you spanked yourself, but, even if you do decide to find a partner or two for the night, that doesn't give them the right to strike you in any way unless you tell them to."

OK. That wouldn't do. "I can already tell this place is nothing like where I've been. Besides, I knew Malcolm was on to me. I was just arrogant and stupid.

Getting caught was my own fault." I started moving toward him, crossing the distance he'd put between us. "And you should also know, I never do anything I don't want to do. Not willingly."

I kept moving, highly aware of my naked body. When I reached him, I put my hands on his chest, sliding my palms up his shirt to circle his neck, pressing my body close to his. Those wonderfully big, rough palms of his settled on my hips. He didn't push me away or bring me closer. Just gripped my hips as I pressed myself ever closer until, finally, I pulled him low enough I could stretch up on my tiptoes and press my lips to his.

His mouth was firm against mine, parting slightly to let me dart my tongue inside. My naked body shivered against his, and I swore I could feel every single muscle in his arms and chest. His arms came around me, holding me firmly to him as he let me kiss him. And, God, I loved his taste! His tongue slid against mine sensually but not persistently. I was craving for him to take control like I knew he would need to. He wasn't a man to let others lead. Not in life and certainly not in sex. Instead, he let me continue to explore for a time before gently ending the kiss and pulling back.

I looked up at him, trying to get an idea of what he was thinking, but my brain was too lust-stupid from the previous experience with Eden and Iron. To say nothing of experiencing my first kiss with such a sensual, perfect man. He just looked at me with those dark, intense eyes until I finally relaxed.

For long moments we stood like that. Me naked in his arms. Liam staring into my eyes. My body was on fire! I knew my sex dripped for him. It certainly ached to be filled by him. I might be a virgin, but I knew what those urges were. How they felt. I'd been turned on before and been tempted to take my own virginity. I hadn't because I'd known there'd be hell to pay if Malcolm traded me for a hard-negotiated alliance and I went to my new home not a virgin. But with no experience, I had no hope of understanding the things going on behind Liam's lovely dark eyes.

Finally, I couldn't take it any longer. "What? Did I do something wrong?" I didn't think I had. Unless he didn't like women sexually. Embarrassing, to be sure, but not disastrous.

"No, beautiful Jezebel. You did nothing wrong." He smiled gently at me. "But sex is not in the cards for us, my dear."

Had he physically punched me, I'm not sure I could have hurt worse. "I-I don't understand."

"You're a guest in my home, my club. Not only would it be bad form for me to take advantage of you in that way, I just can't be what you need. Explore sex with any of the men here who don't have women of their own. Explore it with women who don't have men of their own. It just can't be me."

"But, why?" I crossed my arms over my breasts before realizing what I'd done and dropped my arms to my sides again, lifting my chin and putting my shoulders back. I was a pretty woman. I might not be experienced like Liam was used to, but I was willing to learn. All he had to do was teach me where he wanted me to go.

"We're just too different. I'm probably more than twice your age, and the women I choose know the score. I'm dominant in bed and very demanding."

"I'm willing to learn," I said in a rush. "I can be whatever you want me to be."

"That's just it, little one. You need a man who is

happy with you as you are. One who has the same needs you do so he doesn't push you out of your comfort zone. You've had a whole life of men pushing you around. You don't need another. My needs and demands will be way too dark for you." He smiled slightly. "Your kisses are as sweet as your lush little body, but I'm not for you, beautiful Jezebel." He reached out and stroked my cheek, giving me a slight smile. "I'll help you find a man more suited to you if you wish. Until then, I'll protect you ruthlessly. You need not worry on that account. And Malcolm will be gone from this world, never to bother you again."

I just stood there, watching his departing form. All my life I'd been taught I had value for only one thing. My body. My untouched sex. I'd been treated like a piece of meat, but for the first time in my life, I felt decidedly unworthy.

* * *

El Diablo

I hated leaving Jezebel like this. The hurt on her face cut me to the bone, but I had to be strong. She was mine. I knew that as well as I knew my own name. But I couldn't claim her. I was too old and too twisted for her to try to take me on. Hell, she was probably younger than my daughter, Magenta. I meant what I said about finding her a man to take care of her. I would find the most ruthless bastard I could find so she'd always be protected. It just couldn't be me. Finding a man would be hard, but protecting her? Yeah. I could do that. Starting with her bastard of a father.

Malcolm. I was going to hunt down that son of a bitch and flay him alive. At one time, Malcolm had been first in line to take over the Brotherhood. From what I was getting from Azriel Ivanovich, second-in-command with the Shadow Demons out of Rockwell, Illinois, Malcolm had fallen out of favor for unknown reasons. My own brothers here had come up with much the same, but Azriel was a former Brotherhood member -- just like me. I trusted his information on this better than just about anyone else's. So when my cell chirped two days later, I was more than ready to act on his discoveries.

I called the officers to Church, needing to let them know where my interests were. Many things I'd set into motion had led to the start of all this, but finding Jezebel had sped up my timeline. I wanted those fuckers, the Brotherhood, out of my fucking city.

"You've all met Jezebel," I started. I was usually quiet and let Samson or Rycks lead the meeting, but I needed them to know how serious I was about this, and that this was a rapid culmination of everything I'd been working for the past few years. "She's the daughter of a man named Malcolm. Malcolm was the number two in the Brotherhood."

"Was," Samson barked. Not a question.

"Was," I confirmed. "There has been a falling out of some sort. A power play he lost. The man at the top is still shrouded in secrecy, but that's the way it's always been."

"But you know how to find him, right?" Archangel always knew how to get to the heart of the matter. He already knew the answer to his question. He was just keeping me honest.

"Not at all. As deep as I was, as important as I was to the organization, no one but the number two knew who the number one was. That was how they kept their leader safe. Malcolm's job was not only decoy, but ultimate bodyguard. Going head-to-head, he would be the most capable fighter and assassin in the group, other than someone in my former position. For all intents and purposes, Malcolm was the leader. Only he wasn't."

"So, with this falling out, with Malcolm being ousted from his second seat, is it possible he's moved up?" Archangel continued. "Succeeded his boss, so to speak?"

"Very possible. In fact, likely, given what was getting ready to transpire." I sat back and crossed my arms over my chest. "Malcolm was getting ready to trade his daughter to a man known as Cypher."

"Wait," Rycks sat up, leaning forward. "Is this the same Cypher who made a play for Malcolm years ago in Texas?"

"The very same. Only this time, I think he's out for blood."

"Any idea why now?" Samson asked.

"Azriel Ivanovich believes Malcolm tried to take over a lucrative international high-end escort service Cypher's organization runs. Cypher shut down the takeover, but now he's after the Brotherhood and Malcolm in particular. His intention is to shut them down in this area of the country." I looked around the room. Every man at the table was focused entirely on me. "My goal and Cypher's align. For now. It will free up all our contacts in the DA's office, though we will still need them in place. Their main jobs will now be to keep the corruption at a minimum with law enforcement and trial officers. Kiss of Death may not be completely out of the picture, but, after Fury cleaned house last month, they have more pressing problems than harassing my city."

"We're set to finish them off at your word," Samson commented. "There's really not much left. I think a strong warning will move them back to Nashville for good. Or dissolve them."

"I want them gone for good," I said. "They leave Palm Beach alive, I want it understood that, if they ever show their faces here again, even for a fucking vacation, their lives are forfeit."

"Consider it done," Samson said. "What's the plan with Cypher?"

"When he gets inside our territory, he'll contact either us or Salvation's Bane. Rycks, I want a dialogue set up with Thorn. If Cypher contacts him, I want to know about it."

"On it, boss."

"As to Malcolm." I pinned Shotgun with a stare. "Work with Giovanni and Azriel. I want to know the second he's located. He'll be coming for Jezebel. The only question is if he'll come with diplomacy or an army."

"We'll find him," Shotgun said. "And your girl will be safe until then."

That brought me up short. "She's not my girl," I said automatically. Immediately, I wanted to retract the statement, but bit my tongue. I never showed indecision. Couldn't afford to.

"Uh, boss?" Samson said, leaning forward. There was a smirk on his always emotionless face. "She's in your suite. You carried her up there naked. Even if she was just a convenient lay, you never take women to your personal space."

"Fine," I said, flippantly, calling up my usual swagger. "She's mine. No one touches her. Make sure everyone is aware so there are no mishaps." My hope was to throw them off the scent. Even my admission would be questioned as my brand of humor. And some of them might be fooled, thinking I was being sarcastic.

I even rolled my eyes. But not the ones who knew me best. That included Samson, Rycks, and El Segador.

The Reaper looked me in the eyes. He was my backup. The one man who knew how I'd fought and sacrificed my soul to protect not only my daughter, but the nest of women and girls the Brotherhood had tried to sell to their super-wealthy clientele. Some might have ended up in safe homes, but most would have been used and likely killed when their owners tired of them or got caught by their wives. It was the end of my tenure as their assassin, and the only reason I was still alive. The nest was large enough that, if I'd exposed it instead of merely liberating the girls, I would have brought the Brotherhood into the light for the first time since its conception before the Dark Ages.

Every crime organization has someone to answer to. The mafia in Chicago. A drug lord in Central America. Even the leader of a world superpower. All of those people who seemed like they were at the very top of the food chain answered to someone. That someone was the Brotherhood. I might not be able to take down the whole network, but I intended to force them out of Palm Beach and maybe Southern Florida altogether. And that fucker, Malcolm, was going to die.

Chapter Four
Jezebel

"I've had enough of this," Lyric said, hands on her hips. I entered the great room, where most of the parties were held, to find the women I'd been introduced to as being ol' ladies of some of the club members. Lyric, Celeste, and Esther were doing their best to turn the party room into a Christmas wonderland. Why? Because Celeste's and Lyric's daughters, Holly and Bella respectively, said it should be that way. Obviously someone disagreed because, for the past several days, no matter how much they decorated, the next day everything was gone. After feeling sorry for myself for a couple of days, trying to get to understand the layout of the place and how the hierarchy worked, I'd fallen in with this group of wonderful ladies and their bratty little girls. They were absolutely amazing.

"Who's taking our decorations, Mommy?" Bella asked. She looked up at her mother, Lyric, with the earnestness of a child who knew her mother would make everything better. "Doesn't Daddy know?"

"Of course not, sweetie. Do you think Rycks would let anyone take down decorations he knew you loved?"

"It's got to be one of the guys, but who?" Celeste said, looking around in dismay. Just last night, they'd finished stringing lights around the bar and the column at either side. They followed the lights with garland and a big Christmas tree in the center. The girls had danced around the thing, so excited I had to smile. Now, Bella looked sad and anxious while Holly, Celeste's daughter, looked angry.

"I bet it was that asshole, Jax," she muttered. The

child was all of seven or eight, but her nickname was Maddog. I was beginning to see why. I liked the kid.

"Holly," Celeste chastised. "With language like that, Santa will be rethinking putting you on the nice list."

Holly waved her hand dismissively. "I ain't worried 'bout that. Jax better be worried."

"I'm sure Santa will see him on the naughty list if he did this, sweetheart," Celeste assured.

"What? Who cares about Santa? Daddy Wrath will make him pay big-time!"

I raised my eyebrow, glancing at Celeste. "Bit bloodthirsty, isn't she?"

"You have no idea," Celeste said wryly. "Especially if it's Jax. Can't say the boy doesn't have it coming. Whether or not he did this."

"So what do we do now?" Lyric asked, looking from Celeste to me.

I straightened, squaring my shoulders. "We decorate again. And we keep decorating until this place is covered in tinsel and lights." It was the only solution.

"Yeah!" Bella jumped up and down, clapping.

I knew the men would never let us out of the compound as long as Malcolm was still out there, but it didn't matter anyway. I was queen of getting shit delivered. In a couple of hours, I had so many Christmas decorations for the girls to fuss with, Celeste and Lyric just shook their heads at me.

"You might be more than a little crazy, girl." Lyric giggled. "But I love your brand of crazy."

"We can do this," I said. "First decorate. Then we find who stole the other decorations, and we write a letter to Santa. If we can't find out quick, we'll call him."

Bella's eyes got wide and round. "You know Santa's phone number?"

I picked at the hem of my shirt, realizing I was caught. "No." When Bella and Holly both sagged in disappointment I added, "But Google is a wonderful tool. I bet if we get Shotgun or someone to help us, we could find it."

"Not Shotgun." Holly scrunched her nose. "He's a *guy*. He's probably in on it with Jax."

"Now, Holly," Celeste chided. "You don't know Jax had anything to do with it."

"Coulda been one of the club girls trying to get back at me," Lyric muttered.

"I bet it was Jax," Holly insisted. "He said this place didn't need no lights 'cause it was a clubhouse for men. Not women and kids." If the look on Holly's face was any indication, the more she thought about that encounter, the angrier she got. "I'm gonna get that asshole."

"All right, young lady. That's enough," Celeste said firmly. "Get to decorating so we can go bake cookies. You know how Wrath loves your cookies."

"Oh, boy! Can we make the cookie ornaments? We could pretend they're real cookies and let Daddy Wrath take a bite. I bet he'd growl all mean and stuff." Holly giggled.

Bella bounced. "We could do Rycks, too! That would be the best prank ever!"

"Bella!" Lyric tried to look stern, but her lips twitched. The girls were really a handful, but I loved them already. "You'd give Rycks a salt dough cookie instead of a sugar cookie? He'd be horribly disappointed."

"Ah, Mom. It ain't like we wouldn't have real cookies. I just like to give him a fake cookie first." She and Holly continued to giggle. "I bet their faces will look funny."

"Yeah," Celeste agreed. "They would. We can make ornaments, but we're not pretending they're cookies."

For the rest of the day, we put up decorations all over the common room and even down the hall leading to it. We got a few disgruntled looks from the guys, but the club girls, for the most part, gave us smiles and thumbs up. I smiled back, loving this banter. Besides, this was going to be the first real Christmas I'd ever had. I was probably just as excited as the children and couldn't be happier.

The next morning, I woke to the sound of banging on the door. I heard Liam's smooth, English accent even through the walls. Holly was excited, as was Bella. I heard another deep, male voice, then one I thought might be Lyric.

I sat up in bed just as the door eased open. "Sorry to wake you, Jezebel." It was Lyric.

"It's time I get up anyway. What's going on?"

The girls burst into my room, crying out in dismay.

"They're gone!"

"All gone!"

"Those assholes!"

"They need to be on the naughty list!"

They both talked over each other, but I was pretty sure the asshole comment came from Holly.

"What's gone?"

"The decorations!" Bella whined. "Every little bit."

"Not even an icicle!"

"What?" I looked up at Lyric for confirmation.

"I'm afraid so," she said. "It's like the tree was

never there."

"You've got to be fu -- ah, freaking kidding me." I winced, mouthing "sorry" to Lyric at nearly swearing in front of the girls. She grinned and brushed it off.

"Nope. Not at all."

"It's the Christmas Bandit," Bella said in a conspiratorial voice. "He's stealing all the decorations, trying to take away Christmas. Like the Grinch!" Neither girl would admit it, I was sure, but they looked and sounded more excited than angry or hurt.

"Surly not," I gasped, playing along. I glanced at Lyric, and she nodded, smothering a grin. Guess I was right to play along.

"It has to be!" Holly agreed. "But I still bet that asshole, Jax, is helping."

"That's enough calling people names," Lyric said, giving Holly a gently stern look. Holly just shrugged, not contrite in the least.

"What're we gonna do about it?" Bella asked, her eyes wide.

I thought about it a moment. What *were* we gonna do about it? Then I shook my head. "Only one thing we can do." When both girls looked at me questioningly I grinned. "Put up more decorations than the Christmas Bandit can possibly handle."

Both girls whooped and danced around, jumping into my bed to wrap their skinny arms around me like a well-loved aunt. God! It felt good!

As a rule, I didn't touch anyone. Liam was the first man I'd touched willingly for any reason. Even when I'd played with Eden and Iron, I hadn't touched him much. Or Eden. But I'd clung to Liam, practically begged him to have sex with me. His arms around me had felt incredible. This was different, but just as good. Better, even. Because these girls wanted to hug me.

They barely knew me, but something in me had called to something in them, and they genuinely liked me. Lyric and Celeste, too. They always included me in anything they did together.

When they let me go, they started bouncing around on the big king-sized bed I slept in. On a whim, I got up and jumped with them, joy in my heart. When was the last time I'd had fun? Real fun? Not just enjoying myself with my cooking or watching a good movie. Fun.

We were all laughing, Lyric and Celeste kicking off their shoes and climbing up on the bed with us, when there was a decidedly masculine voice in our all-feminine environment.

"What's all this?" His deep, rich voice was full of warmth. His eyes danced with mirth. "I have a small talk with Rycks outside, then you have a party and no one invites me?"

"Uncle El!" Both girls squealed his name and bounded over to him for hugs. He scooped up both children in his arms and kissed their cheeks while they giggled and wrapped their arms around his neck. Same as they had me.

"Uncle El?" I asked, looking at Lyric.

She shrugged. "Short for El Diablo."

"Uncle The?"

She giggled. "It's phonetic. I'd rather them call him that than Uncle Devil, anyway."

"Auntie Jezebel said we could decorate again!"

"This time, we're gonna do so much that mean ole Christmas Bandit can't get it all down!"

"Oh, you are, are you?"

"Yeah!" They both squealed, wiggling to get down. Liam set them down gently and patted their heads.

"Well, if you're to spend all day decorating, you should eat a good breakfast," he said, smiling at both. "Off you go. All of you."

I was still in my pajamas while the other women were dressed. "I'll meet you in a few minutes. Just let me get dressed."

"Take your time," Celeste said, glancing at Liam. "We need to get some more decorations, anyway."

"We can make some more while waiting on the delivery. I'll get that set up before I join you."

Then they were all gone, and it was just me and Liam. *El Diablo*. He looked at me with amusement, but his eyes heated just a little as his gaze roamed over my scantily clad form. I'd worn a small tank and bikini panties to bed. When the girls were with me, playing and having a good time, I hadn't thought about my attire. I'd never had to worry about it before. Even if someone had entered my suite unannounced, they'd have never dared to touch me, but I never had a reason to be naked either. It just never came up.

"You are... exquisite," Liam said in a low voice, almost absently. I froze where I stood by the bed, half turned where I'd intended to get clothes out of my dresser. "How could any man resist you?" He crossed the room to me in slow, deliberate steps. Reaching out, he stroked my cheek gently.

"I thought you said you didn't want me?"

"No," he said quickly, his full attention back in the moment. "I didn't say I didn't want you. I said you and I wouldn't have sex."

I shrugged. "Same difference."

"Not at all, beautiful little Jezebel. I want you very much. But you're too young, and you deserve a man who can commit to you." He dropped his hand from my face and shrugged. "I'm just not that man."

"Like women too much to commit to one, eh?" I tried to smile at him, like it didn't matter to me. It *shouldn't* matter to me. I didn't know him and didn't want a commitment anyway. But, I also knew men like him took women they wanted, regardless of what the best course of action might be. If he didn't have sex with me, it was because he didn't want me. Pure and simple. I was just trying to give him something to say to take the sting out, even knowing there was no way he'd say what I needed to hear.

He didn't respond but didn't back off either. I felt like I was trapped in a sensual web, the heat of his body seeming to radiate to me. Why I did it, I have no idea, but I reached out and laid my palm on his chest, feeling the muscles beneath his immaculate black shirt. When I looked up at him, his expression was so intense it took my breath away.

"Never make the mistake of thinking I don't want you, beautiful Jezebel." He cupped my cheek with his big hand. Though his palm was rough and callused, his nails were clean and neatly trimmed. Just more evidence he wasn't what he seemed. For several moments he rubbed my face lightly, then his thumb slid under my chin for him to hold me still. His other hand slid into my hair. The next thing I knew, Liam's lips were pressed firmly to mine. Unlike last time, this kiss was all Liam.

He coaxed me to open my mouth before sweeping in with his tongue. I thought he'd let me go then and wrap his arms around me, but he didn't. He just kissed me over and over, licking the insides of my mouth and making me whimper with need. Hand tightening in my hair, Liam moved over my lips, taking complete control. The longer he kissed me, the more I trembled. I was completely out of my depth with Liam. We both knew it. Maybe that was why he'd kept his distance since bringing me here. Likely, there was no way I could ever keep his interest, and he was just being nice.

One thing I knew absolutely was that Liam was protective of his family. By bringing me here, it seemed like some of the others considered me family. Maybe Liam did, too. Maybe he was as protective of me as he was the rest of them. All I knew for sure was that I loved his kisses. Could get lost in them easily. In him. Liam. *El Diablo*...

It took me a moment to realize he'd ended the kiss, his forehead pressed to mine. He was breathing just as hard as I was. A deep, rumbling growl came from his chest, low and soft, but there. Like he was expressing his displeasure with... something. Me? Was I a horrible kisser?

"If you're going to help my girls with the decorations today, you need to get dressed and eat."

"I'll need to get more stuff. We used all we had," I said, soaking up his touch. His arms now held me close. One hand was still bunched in my hair, but the other was securely around my back. I was pressed against his warm body tightly with no real desire to move.

"I'll take care of that. You just get yourself ready and make sure to eat breakfast. I'll know if you don't."

I couldn't resist my next question. "If I skip breakfast, will you punish me?"

He stiffened around me, actually jerking as if someone had hit him. "Don't even joke about that, Jezebel," he rasped. "I have quite a bit of control, but it seems to be tested where you're concerned."

Knowing all the lust and need I was feeling would be obvious on my face, I looked up at him.

"Maybe you should just let it go? Give in to what you want?" I didn't mean to sound unsure of myself, but I was. How could I not be? All I knew was Liam was my choice. Not Cypher or whomever else Malcolm wanted to choose for me. I wanted Liam.

He sighed, then dropped his hands, putting distance between us. "I'm afraid that can't happen. I'm not what you need, and you'd end up hating me."

"What is it you think I need, Liam?" I asked the question, truly wanting to know the answer. What kind of man did he think I needed? What kind of lover? Did he think I couldn't handle a one-time thing? Because, with him, I could.

"More than I could give you, beautiful Jezebel," he said a bit wistfully.

"If you think I can't handle a temporary hookup, Liam, you're wrong." I spoke as he turned away from me. Needing to not be looking into his eyes when I said it. I meant every word, but I was beginning to wonder if temporary with him would satisfy me. I thought it would, but there was doubt.

He turned slightly, not facing me. "No."

"But you don't understand," I said, hoping he'd let me get the words out I needed to say. "You're my choice. For my first time. I've lived my whole life knowing Malcolm would sell me to someone for something of value to him. My wants were never a factor in his decisions. Now, for however long this lasts, I get to make the choices for my life. And I choose you." I gave a little helpless shrug. "Can't you just give me this one thing? I'd be one woman in a string of many to you. And I promise, when you say it's over, I won't hang on."

"Why is it women assume that, just because a man may have had sex with multiple partners that he doesn't want something more as well?" He sighed. "Sure, beautiful. I could give you what you say you want. I could make it good for you, show you more pleasure than you've ever imagined." He turned and reached for me once again, laying his palm on my cheek like he had earlier. "But one night with you would never be enough for me, beautiful Jezebel. And if you think you'd ever have your freedom again --" He pinned me with his dark gaze. "-- You'd be wrong. I'd be the man who ruled you from the first time I fucked you until the day I died."

"But... all the other women --"

"Meant nothing to me, Jezebel. You do."

I thought for a moment, trying to figure out what he meant. Then it dawned on me, and a stab of pain went through my gut. "You want me for the power it will get you. Just like Cypher and all the others Malcolm brought around."

"No," he said immediately, pulling me to him closer, wrapping a hand around the back of my neck. "I want you because there's something about you that calls to something deep inside of me. I've never had a woman of my own, Jezebel," he said, squeezing my neck harder. "Not because I didn't want one, because I never found someone to make me not want anyone else. I'm many things, but to my family, I'm as honest as I can be. I take a woman as mine, I absolutely will not cheat. So no matter how much I like a woman, I've never made that commitment to anyone."

"I'm still not seeing the problem, Liam. I'm not asking for a commitment. Besides, why not just break up or get a divorce if you decide a woman's not right for you? Isn't that what married people do when they don't want to be together anymore? Even committed couples break up sometimes."

"No, you're not asking for a commitment, but I'd force one on you. No other men for you. No other women for me. As to a breakup or a divorce? I don't believe in them. I take a woman as mine, that means I trust her enough to bring her into my world. She knows what I know, because I won't keep secrets from her unless she asks me to. I won't put either of us through that."

"So, a partner?"

"Any woman of mine would be the person I went to when I could go to no one else. My confidante. My moral compass. She might not hold the rank of president -- or even be a patched member -- within the club, but she'd get to voice her opinion to me in private before anything went to a vote."

"Meaning you'd have to trust her to not try to take something that wasn't hers. You're the president. Not her."

"Precisely. There aren't many men or women out there I'd trust with that. Not to mention the role she'd have to take within the club. Taking care of the women and children, being an advocate for them. Even the club girls. I do it all now. My woman needs to be willing to handle all that. And believe me, it's a lot."

"So, why are you mentioning it to me now?"

He shrugged. "You wanted to know why I wouldn't fuck you."

Again, I thought about everything he'd said. "Why would you hold me against my will, Liam? If you don't want me, why not just take what I'm offering, then move on?"

He chuckled, but it had no humor in it. "Because, you're the one woman who'd forever haunt me, the siren luring me back over and over. Once I'd had you, I'd never be able to let you go. Hell, I wouldn't even try."

* * *

Jezebel

It was three weeks until Christmas, and we had yet to get a single decoration to hang around past the day they put them up. The children were angry, or pretended to be, and the women frustrated, but I was having the time of my life. Every day, I had Liam bring in new decorations. I expected him to set his foot down at some point and refuse to spend any more money on Christmas stuff, but he just chuckled and ordered more the next day than he had the previous. If we ever found this Christmas Bandit, he'd have enough decorations to decorate the entire compound in lights, garland, and tinsel. To say nothing of the Christmas trees. There might not be enough for every single room in the compound -- the place was like a resort -- but there would be enough for anyone who wanted one, with several left over.

"Delivery!" I shouted, bringing a slew of children. And dogs. Seemed like the number of Saint Bernard dogs and puppies had multiplied since I'd come here. Since we were in a race to get as many Christmas decorations up as we could before bedtime, I'd enlisted help. Some of the club girls had nieces and nephews or children of their own, and I'd insisted they bring them to the clubhouse to help us decorate.

We'd taken a huge room, used as a dining room when Liam had "fancy guests," as Lyric had explained, as our workroom. Not only was El Diablo a notorious motorcycle club president, but he was a prominent fundraiser for the community of Palm Beach as well. He also had political fundraisers and some for various charities of his choosing. I didn't pretend to know how all that worked, but it wasn't my problem.

There were tables set up as various stations for making salt dough ornaments, painting and glittering those ornaments, stringing popcorn garland, making wreaths, and all kinds of things. Some of the older girls sat in a corner together cross-stitching ornaments while they giggled at the boys who were putting together wooden toys and ornaments for the younger kids to paint. The kids were having a ball, and I was in heaven. I don't think I'd ever smiled so much in my life.

"Someone seems to be having a good time." Liam came up behind me where I was setting boxes on the tables lined up at the front of the room. The kids were digging through them, putting paint and glitter and string and whatever at the appropriate stations. The women in the room tried to keep it orderly, but this was Christmas. If the kids wanted to make a mess, as long as no one got glitter in their eyes, I said let 'em have at it. I was surprised to see things were for the most part orderly. Most had special projects they wanted to make, while others were just having fun. Wasn't that the whole point of decorating for Christmas? Having fun?

I grinned at him over my shoulder. He'd wrapped his arms around my middle and kissed the side of my neck. I shivered but knew better than to get my hopes up. "Hard not to when this is all so exciting," I said. "I decorated my room during the holidays and made my own Thanksgiving and Christmas dinners, but I've never celebrated it with other people. I never got to be this excited with so many people because it was always just me and nannies or tutors. I only knew about Christmas through them and the TV."

Liam stiffened briefly, but relaxed and pulled me

tighter against him. "Well, looks like you've gotten more than you can handle. But as long as you're enjoying yourself, I don't suppose it matters."

"Oh, I'm fine. Great in fact! Only... "I trailed off, unsure how to put my small worry to Liam.

"Only what, beautiful Jezebel?"

"Well, I just hope these decorations don't turn up missing like the last five days' worth have."

"I wouldn't worry. I've got my best people on this. I'm sure we'll find the culprit or culprits, as well as the missing decorations."

"You do? Doesn't a man so important in the community have better things he could use his resources on than finding a Christmas decoration thief?"

"Sweetheart, nothing is more important than you and the children."

"Holly and Bella are treating it like it's a big mystery. I think they've been the ones responsible for getting the other kids involved."

"I heard you insisted the club girls help out. I'm not sure there's an MC out there where the ol' ladies let the club girls mingle with them, especially during family events."

I stiffened. "Did I do wrong, then? I just saw some of them watching like they wanted to help, so I invited them."

"No, my beautiful Jezebel. You didn't do anything wrong. You included them and their families. That's never a bad thing, especially for the children." He kissed my cheek and, stupid me, I basked in his praise. "Besides, there are a couple of the girls I worry about. They came from bad backgrounds and find it hard to trust people. I think they came to Black Reign thinking we were like every other club around and that they could punish themselves in some way." He shook his head. "I never want any of them to feel that way. I won't let Black Reign be that kind of club."

"You're not. I see the way everyone here treats the women. Club girl or ol' lady, the men are nice. I mean, there are a few men who are gruff and rough around the edges, but they aren't needlessly cruel. There is a distinct line between wives and club girls, and there are rivals, but no true animosity."

"I also see you've managed to find some of those rivals and separate them."

I shrugged. "Makes the day run smoother."

With a kiss to my head, Liam released me. "Have fun. Order anything you need to. I want this whole place ready for Christmas as soon as possible." He gave the order like he was a king. I giggled.

"Yes, Your Majesty," I said over my shoulder before turning back to my work. I heard his warm chuckle as he left the room and, not for the first time, I wished I had the courage to go after him. The more I was around him, the more I wanted him. We spent our evenings together in his suite's sitting room either watching TV or just sitting in front of the fire talking. It was so domestic I wanted to gag. I seemed to have acquired a man in every form but the sex.

I also never saw him with another woman. And believe me, I watched and looked hard. Sure, women approached him all the time. Even clung to him. I mean, the guy was seriously hot. What woman wouldn't want to be with him? Every single one of them he sent on their way. He wasn't mean about it or overly obviously with his brush-offs. But he never let a woman linger for more than a few seconds before asking her to move on. While that wasn't anything in and of itself, it gave me hope when I had no right to expect it. Liam made it clear to me he wasn't having sex with me and that he wasn't the settling-down type.

I was brought out of my musings when I was approached by Eden and Winter and Serilda. The latter two were sisters and only a year or two older than me. I didn't know their stories other than they'd had it rough. But I knew getting them here, participating in anything with a large group, was a huge thing. I tried to give them my best inviting smile.

"Hey guys! I'm so glad you came to help!"

"We've got an idea," Eden said. "Or, rather, Winter does." She nudged the other woman, who squared her shoulders.

"We need to set up guards," Winter said.

Serilda added, "At night. Someone who can sound an alarm if they see something strange."

"That's a great idea," I said. "I have no idea why we didn't do that from the beginning. Talk about a duh moment."

"I can get the girls together," Eden offered. "We can do it in shifts, maybe."

"That way no one has to worry about staying up all night. We can just do it a couple of hours at a time." Winter actually looked excited. Serilda looked to her sister to guide her responses, and I could tell she wasn't sure how she should feel.

"Get everyone together," I said. "See who wants what shift. Set it up like you said. Two- or three-hour intervals. We can start tonight."

"Great!" Eden said, clapping her hands. "Come on," she said, pulling Serilda with her. "Let's get started. We need at least two or three lined up for tonight if we start at ten or eleven."

"Let me know if you need me to take a shift," I said, waving as they went about setting up their plan.

Chapter Five
El Diablo

Black Reign MC wasn't the typical motorcycle club. In fact, there wasn't much, other than the parties, that resembled any other club I'd ever had dealings with. But having Jezebel here now made it more like the family I'd always envisioned it being.

The boys were dicking with the girls and the Christmas decorations. So far, they'd been careful not to get caught. It was definitely an all-hands effort, though. I was a little concerned at first. But, after watching for a while, I found Rycks and Wrath were in on the scheme too and knew it would all work out. Those two would never let Bella and Holly down for Christmas, to say nothing of Lyric and Celeste. As to the women, while aggravated and annoyed, they were all banding together on this project. Club girls included. Oh, there were a few who sulked and stayed out of the game, but I had no doubt they'd soon either move on from the club or give in and join the fun. Black Reign was slowly but surely becoming a very large, very tight family. Just like I'd wanted. Jezebel was becoming the center of that family.

Currently, the women were huddled together. I was on the dais above them, watching the whole thing from afar. It gave me more pleasure than I could describe to see everyone so absorbed in this simple task. Given all we'd gone through the past several months with Kiss of Death and Southern Discomfort, not to mention the fucking Brotherhood, I was glad they had more things to do besides work and worrying about the men. We might try to shelter our women -- whether ol' ladies or club girls -- from the violence in our lives, but they worried about every single man in the club. It warmed my heart. Given how cold my heart had become, it was a nice feeling.

"When're you gonna put a stop to this nonsense?" I glanced to my left to find Hardcase with Tank slightly behind him. Both men were frowning down at the scene below.

"I'm not," I answered with a wave of my hand.

"Why the fuck not?"

"Because they're enjoying it."

"Yeah, well, the cam shows are nil the last few weeks. Even Celeste and Wrath have stopped coming. Wrath says Celeste is refusing in protest."

That got my attention. "Protest? Of what?"

Hardcase looked around, as if to make sure no one was listening before he leaned in and spoke softly to me. "Look. It started out as a prank. And we have every intention of putting it all back. Like all at once. It's fun seeing them add more and more stuff and getting all huffy and put out when they're really having a good time."

"By 'they,' we mean all the women," Tank added. "Ol' ladies and club girls included. Hell, the club girls even brought kids and nieces and nephews to help. We were thinking about seeing if the kids from some of the homeless shelters and group homes wanted to help, but it's getting a little out of hand."

I raised an eyebrow. Because I could totally make all that work as a community event. A community Christmas party on Christmas Eve sounded pretty great to me. "How so? What's the problem?"

"The girls all went on strike," Hardcase said in a rush. "They're refusing to do any more cam shows with men present. Some of the women have started doing shows on their own. The ones who still let us record them refuse to let us participate."

"No one said they had to let you touch them to be a cam girl," I said immediately, all business now. "We don't operate that way."

"No one's saying we do, boss," Tank said. "But it's not really that." He glanced at Hardcase who just clenched his jaw. Finally Tank stuck his chin up and just blurted it out. "They've cut us off," he said. "All of us."

I contemplated that, not understanding. "Cut you off."

"Yeah."

When nothing else was forthcoming, I asked, "Cut you off from what?"

"Everything," they both said. Tank was as agitated as I'd ever seen the man while Hardcase just clenched and unclenched his jaw.

"I'm sorry, but you're going to have to be more specific," I said.

"Sex!" Tank threw his hands up in the air in exasperation. "They've cut us all off from sex! I think even Rycks, Wrath, and Shotgun are having a hard time! What the fuck, boss?"

"They've... cut everyone off. From sex," I said slowly, trying very hard to suppress my glee. This was rich.

"Yeah," Hardcase said. "And we hear it's because your woman put them up to it."

"I see. So, you've come to me for... what? To make them let you back into their beds? Put them back in front of the cams where you get to play with them when you decide they need a little fluff to get them ready for the action?"

The boys looked at each other, clearly uncomfortable with my description of their request. Finally, Tank answered for them both. "Yeah, maybe.

It's unnatural! Club girls are here to put out for us. They knew the score when they came to live here!"

I just looked at both of them. I knew they didn't really believe what they were saying, though it was that way in most clubs. Most of the time, the girls would let the men indulge in their bodies. It wasn't a requirement, nor was it expected. They did what they wanted to do, when they wanted to do it. Everyone knew that.

"Come on, boss," Hardcase pleaded. "Get your woman to back off. We're all dying here."

"Blue balls never killed anyone," I said, waving him off. "In any case, if you want back in their beds but still insist on taking down their decorations, I suggest you get creative." I sat back, crossing one ankle on top of the other knee. "I hear they're getting ready to set up guards," I said seriously. "They're taking a shift each night." I shrugged. "Be a shame if the guard got… distracted… "

At first Tank and Hardcase just stood there. Then their eyes got wide, and they nodded. "Yeah, boss," Hardcase said. "Be a damned shame."

I grinned, then raised a finger for them to wait. "But I expect every single decoration taken down to be put back up in time for the Christmas Eve party. I want the place looking like a tacky Christmas parade float inside and out."

They winced but nodded in agreement. "We'll pass on the message, boss."

"See that you do."

* * *

Jezebel

"You've *got* to be fucking kidding me." I'd woken up early for my shift, pulling my weight with my sisters in determination. "Eden? Where are you? Are you OK?" If someone had hurt Eden...

"I'm here! I'm coming... Oh..." I heard Eden running down the hallway leading to the great room we'd been guarding. Her eyes widened when she entered the room again to find every single decoration gone. Had she gone for a bathroom break? It was only three hours, but maybe she forgot to go before her shift started. Or maybe she'd just drunk too much coffee.

"Where were you? Is everything OK?"

"Yeah. Except for everything's gone. *Again!*"

The more I thought about it, the more things didn't make sense. If she'd gone to the bathroom, it wouldn't be nearly enough time for the guys to take everything out of the great room. It took five minutes tops to go down the hall to the bathroom, piss, and return. Probably less. So... did she get locked in the bathroom? "What happened?"

She looked up at me, sheepishly. "Iron happened," she said. "Bastard."

"Did he lock you in the bathroom or something?"

Eden sighed. "You know how I told you before me and the girls decided we weren't fucking the guys until all this stopped?"

"Yeah."

"Well, I think it backfired on us."

I froze. "They're not forcing you guys to --"

"NO! No. Nothing like that, I swear, Jez!" She gave me a sheepish smile. "But it might be as hard on us as it is on them. We like sex just as much as they do."

"So, what happened? The whole place is cleaned out."

"Yeah, I saw." She sighed. "I might have gotten a little distracted by Iron on my way to relieve Vanya.

The next thing I knew, we were doing the hunka chunka out by the pool. Then in the pool. Then --"

"I get the picture," I said, trying hard to suppress a giggle.

"You're not mad, are you?"

"Mad? Oh, honey, not at all! They just don't play fair. Though I have to admit, I expected something like that when you guys cut them off." I did giggle then. "Brilliant move. Both times, actually."

Eden scowled. "This means war," she muttered. "I'm getting the girls together. We're going to the toy shop and buying a bunch of stuff to keep us outta their bedrooms!"

"Did you even make it to the bedroom, Eden?"

She sighed. "Not even close. But I'm sure he'll try to get me there."

"You gonna resist?"

"Oh, absolutely! I resisted this time!"

"Just didn't do much good?"

"Jez, the man has a body that won't stop. And a big swinging dick that he knows how to use. I'm gonna be so sad to see him get a woman."

We both laughed.

"Look. Get the girls together again. And the kids. How many more days until Christmas?"

"Too many," Eden said. "Twelve days."

"God, when those decorations show up, where the hell are we going to put them all? And will the kids be decorated out before then? It just keeps getting bigger and bigger!"

"Na. The kids love it. Especially those at the homeless shelters. The shelters try to do some things, but all their stuff is old and falling apart. Better things to spend the city budget on than decorations."

I put my hands on my hips. "Then we'll just have

to make up for the shortcoming. Get the girls ready. I'll go talk to Liam and see if he can commandeer a few city busses to bring in kids to help decorate. Again."

"Liam?" Eden looked confused, then her eyes got wide. "Oh! You mean El Diablo. You think he'd help with this?"

"Won't know until I ask. Either way, we've still got shit to do. Get the women together. Go get some fucking toys. By then, I hope to have the place brimming with children from every homeless shelter and group home in the city. Last time was a small group. This time... yeah. We're gonna rock this place with Christmas! And we're gonna do it every day until Christmas Eve if we have to."

Right. I'd just go ask El Diablo to help me. No sweat. I left the girls to do their thing and wondered how I was going to get my courage up to go to Liam with this.

I didn't see him until that evening in our suite. I made dinner. Nothing fancy, just tacos from a recipe I'd found on the Internet. It was my favorite, and I was hoping it would be a new experience for him. Something homemade. I made a pineapple upside-down cake to go with it and couldn't wait for him to try it. The man had a serious sweet tooth he tried desperately to hide. But I knew where all my cookies went because I'd caught him red-handed more than once since I'd moved here.

"Something smells delicious," he said as he shut the door when he entered the suite. "I smell cumin... basil... garlic?"

"And a few other things," I said, wiping my hands on my apron. "Homemade tacos. Care to eat with me?"

He dropped his jacket on the floor -- he'd missed

the peg it always hung on -- and hurried into the kitchen area. He sniffed several times, his eyes darting around looking for something not on the stove. "I smell something else, too." He kept looking until he spotted a raised cake plate with a clear glass cover. The inside had condensation on the glass, but it was clear there was something in there. He lifted the lid and, I swear, the man's eyes rolled back in his head and he heaved a great sigh. "Is that... pineapple upside-down cake?"

I raised an eyebrow. "Might be. Why do you want to know?"

He snagged a knife from the block and started to take off the lid.

"Oh no," I said, staying him. "You don't get a piece of that cake until after dinner."

"But this is a perfectly acceptable dinner." Liam actually looked like a forlorn kid.

"Not in my home."

He raised an eyebrow. "So, you think this is your home now?"

"You made it so. You wouldn't give me my own space, so here I am. I've been here forever without you making a move to get my own place, so?" I spread my hands wide. "Home. Now, sit. I'll bring the food to the table, and we can dig in and have a discussion." If he raised his eyebrows about the "discussion," I didn't see it. What he did do was snag the cake plate and set it on the table as well. It was all I could do not to laugh.

Once the table was set and the food ready, we dug in. Liam ate his tacos in the shell while I made mine into a salad. 'Cause I'm a crazy-messy eater. The man didn't stop until the last of the meat was gone. Then he looked around like he expected more. He looked up at *me* like he expected more, but I just laughed.

"Cut the damned cake."

His eyes lit up, and a smile split his face. He cut two pieces. One square around a pineapple around the edge, the second around the pineapple in the center. I didn't get the center piece.

"You do know that's not how you cut a cake. Right?" I laughed.

"It is if you want the center. Now. Tell me, beautiful Jezebel. What did you wish to discuss?"

It was now or never. He was in as good a mood as I could get him. "I want you to see if you can bus in kids from all the homeless shelters and all the group homes in the Palm Beach area to help decorate for Christmas."

He paused, his fork halfway to his mouth, then scowled at me. Instead of answering, he slowly brought the fork to his mouth. The second his lips closed over the cake, his eyes closed in bliss, and he let out a loud moan. He chewed slowly, making sounds like I imagined he might during a slow round of lazy sex. Then he did it again. This went on until the whole piece was gone. I can honestly say, I've never seen a man enjoy his food as much as Liam enjoyed that fucking cake.

"My dear, if you make me another one of these, I'll get you however many children and however many decorations you want." His eyes popped open, and his gaze zeroed in on the cake again. He cut himself another slice and dove in. Faster this time. Then he paused. "Wait. I thought you and the girls had a bunch of local children help you yesterday?"

I sighed. "We did. But Eden got distracted on her guard duty -- pretty sure Vanya did, too -- and the decorations are gone again. We've got to start over."

Liam chuckled. Then threw back his head and laughed until tears rolled from his eyes. "The Christmas Bandit strikes again," he managed to get out between guffaws.

"It's not very Goddamned funny."

"Try to see it from my perspective, my dear. The guys pretend to hate the decorations. The girls are determined to have them. The children think it's the greatest caper of all time and are determined to catch the bandit. Then here you are, enlisting my help by feeding into my weakness for sweets and home-cooked meals for something I'd gladly give you just to continue to enjoy the holidays." He gave me a warm smile. "You bring joy and liveliness to my home, Jezebel. I never want that to end."

That caught me off guard. "Thank you. I wasn't sure how you felt about it all, especially with the only end in sight being Christmas Eve itself. Seems to me like your home is in chaos."

"I can only hope this is something that will continue every year." He chuckled. "Maybe with fewer decorations, but it is what it is. And it's something I'd gladly fund every single year as long as everyone is having so much fun."

"You're a remarkable man, Liam. Thank you for bringing me here."

He waved that away. "I should be the one thanking you. You've brought joy into this house, and the locals in the community are abuzz with how much fun the children had yesterday."

"I need to do the dishes." I was suddenly nervous and had no idea why.

"I've already arranged for someone to come clean. Now. Is there anything else you need from me? If so, tell me, and it's yours."

When he extended his hand to me, I took it. Liam pulled me to my feet and took me to the living area, his big palm on my back to guide me as we walked. He caressed my hand, bringing it to his lips and kissing the palm lightly. While I was still hoping for sex, I was afraid that ship had already sailed. Sure, he touched me every time he saw me, even if it was just to put his arm around my shoulders or touch my back as we walked. Like earlier, he often kissed my cheek or the side of my neck with his arms wrapped around me from behind. It was torture and heaven at the same time.

My breath quickened and I bit my lip. "I-I need..." Again, he kissed my hand, looking into my eyes.

"Why are you doing this, Liam?"

"Doing what, beautiful Jezebel?"

I jerked my hand away and paced to the other side of the room, refusing to turn back to face him. "Playing with me! Are you wanting me to tell you I need you so you can deny me again? Because I've been sheltered all my life from the real world, but even I know how pathetic I'd look if I kept throwing myself at you."

I felt his hand on my shoulder and stiffened, trying to shrug him off, but he held on. "Stop," he said sharply. It was a soft command, but a command nonetheless. I wanted to keep trying to get rid of him, but my body responded to his demand. "You're right, sweetheart." He kneaded my shoulders before pulling me back against him and wrapping his arms around me. "I'm being a bastard, but I find myself drawn to you more than I've ever been to anyone in my life."

"You said we couldn't have sex. That you wouldn't."

"So I did. I can't." He gently turned me to face

him. Cupping my cheek gently, he stroked my bottom lip with his thumb. "But I need another taste of you, beautiful Jezebel," he said, closing the distance between our mouths. "Just one more taste..." Then he kissed me.

The second our lips touched, Liam took control. I was beginning to learn what he needed when he kissed me. In a way, it almost felt like he was testing me. Seeing how far I'd let him go before I pushed back. What he hadn't figured out yet was that I had no desire to push back. I wanted his dominance. His control. Even now, both of his hands had slipped to my face, and he controlled my movements so he could deepen the kiss to his liking.

He teased me, lapping at the insides of my mouth, but not for long. When he adjusted his grip on my face, holding my chin in one hand and sliding his other arm around my back to hold me to him. I felt the warmth of him seep through my clothing, making me hot and achy, needing more when I had no idea if he was going to give it to me. I promised myself in that moment, no matter what, I was not begging him. Not again.

"Open for me, Jezebel," he rasped against my lips. As before, I obeyed, unable to suppress my moan of pleasure. The rough rasp of his beard over my skin was like a separate caress. He held me tightly to him, wrapping me securely in his big, strong arms. I could feel the muscles flex against my body with every movement, and it only excited me more. What would he look like naked? Would he like the way I looked? Did he want to see me naked? I sure as hell wanted to see him naked.

I clung to him, whimpering as he continued to kiss me. My breasts ached where they were mashed against his muscular chest. When one of his hands slid down to grip my ass, my knees gave way. Liam took full advantage, lifting me into his arms and marching through the suite. I had no idea where we were going but wasn't at all surprised when he placed me on a big bed in another room. Were we in his bedroom? His bed?

I was sitting and, before I realized what he was doing, Liam whipped off my shirt. Gasping, I looked up at him, shocked but so fucking turned on I was unable to process this was actually happening. Liam followed me down after that, stretching himself out over my body so that I was pressed into the mattress. Somehow, he managed to get my bra off and fling it over the side of the bed. Again, he kissed me, sweeping me away on a sea of pleasure.

Liam raised himself off me briefly to pull his shirt apart and shrug out of it. Buttons flung in all directions, and I distinctly heard him growl as he stared down at my naked breasts. I had a nearly uncontrollable urge to cover myself, but the hungry look in his eyes stopped me. Instead, I stretched my arms over my head and arched my back in offering.

I wasn't disappointed. Liam lowered himself on top of me once again, this time latching on to one nipple with his mouth. His arms slid around me, holding my chest to his mouth as he sucked and nipped. I couldn't hold back my little whimpers and cries, the sensations overwhelming me. I'd never been touched like this by anyone, and Liam was an expert. I didn't have a prayer of resisting. All I could do was hang on until Liam decided the ride was over.

"Fucking perfect," he muttered around one nipple. "Absolutely fucking perfect." He kissed up my neck back to my mouth, rubbing his naked chest over mine. "Is this what you needed, my beautiful Jezebel? Did you need my body over yours? Working yours?" He kissed me again, then breathed softly in my ear. "Do you need me to make you come?"

I had to make a conscious effort to keep my mouth closed, to not answer him. It felt too much like begging him. Instead, I pulled him back to me for more of those drugging kisses.

Gradually, Liam made his way back to my breasts, sucking and nipping until I was writhing mindlessly. I tangled my fingers in his hair, trying to hold him to me. He just continued to play with me as he wished, sucking first one nipple, then the other.

Swearing viciously, Liam sat back on his heels, raising my legs and peeling my shorts down my legs along with my panties. He held my gaze as he tossed my shorts over the side of the bed but brought my panties to his nose and inhaled. His eyes closed, and a loud groan escaped his throat.

"Ah, my beautiful Jezebel. These will be a source of many nights of pleasure for me."

Wow. The guy was shamelessly admitting he was keeping my panties and was going to masturbate with them. For some reason, his admission was the hottest thing I'd ever experienced. Even the outrageous things I'd read in books and seen online couldn't compare to the real thing. Liam was an experienced guy. He didn't want a relationship, but he admitted he was infatuated with me. I was beginning to see his point. I'd asked him for sex with no strings. But I had to ask myself if I could do that. I wasn't certain I wouldn't always want him. Even if he didn't fuck me, part of me would always compare other men to him. I had no doubt I'd always find anyone else lacking.

Before I could ask what he was going to do, he

scooted down the bed and leaned over my sex. Wrapping his arms around my thighs to hold me open to him, Liam buried his face between my legs…

And I lost my ever-loving mind.

Chapter Six
El Diablo

One swipe of my tongue through Jezebel's weeping cunt, and I was completely lost. She gasped and jumped reflexively, her hands flying to my hair where she tugged. I wasn't sure if she was trying to pull me closer or push me away. Probably both. Her responses were so fucking innocent, everything inside me responded. Which meant there was no hope for her. She was mine. Always. I knew she'd grow to hate me for the way I'd control her, but there was no help for it now.

"Liam!" She screamed my name as her pussy flooded for me. Every swipe of my tongue was met with more of her honey. All for me.

"My little wanton," I murmured against her wet flesh. "You respond to me like a virgin. I wonder if you've already taken care of that little physical barrier." I looked up at her, her eyes wide and shocked. "Have you let another man touch you?" I tried not to sound or look hostile but wasn't entirely sure I pulled it off. Just the thought of another man touching what was mine threatened to let loose the demon in me. Not against her. Against any man who'd dared take her innocence, then left her with that fucker, Malcolm.

"I... no," she said softly. "No one."

"Not at the parties you crashed? Not even to satisfy your curiosity?"

"No. It didn't feel right." She shivered when I absently swiped my tongue through her folds. "Besides, I was supposed to be the little virgin Malcolm sold to the highest bidder." She sounded bitter, and rightly so. "But even if I'd wanted to, I never felt..."

"Never felt what, my beautiful Jezebel?"

"Never wanted sex. Not like this." She took a shuddering breath. "I wanted what I'd read about in books and seen in movies. Someone who made me feel..."

"Like you'd die if you didn't come right then?" I fluttered her clit with my tongue shamelessly.

"Yes!" She screamed the word on a keening wail. She was close, but I wasn't ready for her to fall just yet.

I believed her. Until tonight, I was certain she'd never been touched. Even her kisses were hesitant, begging for guidance, which I gladly provided. Now, with my mouth sucking her wet pussy, all she could do was gasp and scream with each sensation. Every time I flicked her clit with my tongue, she cried out, her hips jerking hard. I slid one hand up her body across her pelvis with my forearm over her hips, trapping her so she was at my mercy. I had none.

"Tell me what you need, Jezebel," I growled, smacking the flat of my fingers against her pussy. "What does this needy little cunt want?"

"You," she gasped.

"I'm right here," I said, pushing her when I had no intention of fucking her. I couldn't. She was too Goddamned young and innocent for the likes of me. But if I couldn't have her, she was going to suffer too. It made me a horrible person, but there it was. She was mine. I couldn't have her. I damned well wasn't letting anyone else have her. I was punishing her for things that weren't her fault. Yeah. I was a fucking bastard.

"I need you to fuck me," she gasped, stumbling on the word only slightly. Even as she said it her skin flushed a delicate pink. She wasn't opposed to swearing, but in this context, when she was asking for sex in a harsh, carnal way, her innocence shone through.

"Too fucking bad," I growled, then set back in to eating her delicious little pussy.

As I drove her higher and higher, sweat coated her skin, making her slide against me in an erotic glide. She screamed, begging me almost incoherently to take her. To fuck her. Finally, when her movements became so erratic and strong I had a difficult time keeping her still for my sensual assault, I put her knees over my shoulders and lifted her lower body from the bed. She rested back on her shoulders while I engulfed her pussy with my mouth. I stared down at her, into those lovely hazel eyes as the pleasure built and built inside her. Her breathing became labored, and her hands fisted the sheets. She reached out to find the tops of my thighs and dug her nails into my flesh through the material of my trousers.

As I flicked her clit with my tongue, I carefully inserted two fingers into her until I could go no farther. That was all the sensation she needed to orgasm. With a scream, she bucked and writhed, thrashing her head from side to side. All that lovely chestnut-colored hair spread out around her like a cape. Little tendrils stuck to her damp skin over her face and shoulders and chest. Muscles played under her skin, and the veins in her neck stood out as a deep flush crept from her chest to her face.

"Liam!" She screamed her pleasure, her orgasm seeming to go on and on as her pussy clamped down around my fingers. It taunted me with what I couldn't take. Oh, I wanted her. Wanted her with a fierceness I needed to get under control before I dared touch her again. The last thing I wanted to do was hurt her like this. Besides, I needed to think about what I'd just done. Make sure this was the course of action I was going to follow through with. Even though I knew it was a token gesture at best, I was still going to do it. I shouldn't even be contemplating this. She wasn't for me even as I knew she belonged to me. But I knew I was damned. Because I'd do anything to possess this amazingly sensual creature in my arms.

Jezebel was... *everything*. She'd be my world. Hell, I already couldn't make it through a day without touching her in some way. I couldn't let her move out of my suite. It took all my willpower to let her have her own room. Which would probably change sooner rather than later. For now, though, I could pretend I was giving her time to come to terms with this. Once I reached the limit of the time I could give her, I'd completely take over her life. I knew this about myself and accepted it. I just hoped she could as well.

As she came down from her orgasmic high, I gently released her and lay down behind her, pulling the comforter at the end of my bed around us. I was still dressed below the waist, having only removed my shirt and kicked off my shoes before climbing onto the bed with her in the first place. I pulled her close, letting her pillow her head on my arm. It wasn't long before she drifted off to sleep without a single coherent word, though she mumbled something right before she crashed.

My world had just changed. No. Not "just." It had altered the second I'd laid eyes on Jezebel. My beautiful little Jezebel. She was aptly named. A wicked woman. Not in spirit, but by nature. She was made for sex and sin. Hell, she could probably come close to taming the devil himself. El Diablo and Jezebel. I had to laugh to myself. We were the perfect couple if ever there was one.

Jezebel

Two days had passed since I'd fallen asleep in Liam's arms after the most spectacular orgasm of my life. We had ordered even more decorations, determined to make this work. The kids acted put out, groaning and vowing to "catch that mean old Christmas Bandit," but I could tell they were having the time of their lives. Nearly every child returned every day. At first, they were confused, wondering why the stuff they'd put up the day before was now gone. When Holly and Bella explained about the Christmas Bandit, there was no stopping the little hellions. The guys grumbled outwardly, but I saw the winks thrown the children's way when they growled at me or the other women. I found some of them giving piggyback rides and helping string lights and garland in the hard-to-reach places inside and out.

"I don't know how he did it," Esther was saying as she laughed. "One minute I was setting my foot down about standing guard, the next I was in our bed, Shotgun fucking my brains out." The other woman didn't stumble on the work "fucking" but her face turned crimson when she said it. I'd learned Esther was trying her best to break out of her shell and not be so uptight about certain things. Sex and language being the two most pressing. "When I finally crawled away from him and got back to my post, POOF! It was all gone."

When Esther and I had first been introduced, her eyes had widened at my name, and she'd actually asked if that was my real name. I hadn't taken offense, and I'd since learned her background. I suppose she wondered what kind of person would name their daughter Jezebel. But given that I was supposed to magically summon Malcolm's demons and control them with my virgin body, maybe I was named aptly, in a way. She'd been horrified. Not that my own father had named me Jezebel, but that she'd been so cruel as to react in such a judgmental way. I could see her genuine distress and hadn't held it against her. The girl was trying, and I couldn't blame her. I had similar issues, though I'd had the benefit of media to keep in touch with reality. I suspect she had gotten a baptism by fire in her real-world education.

I couldn't help but laugh. "Honey, if that man of yours couldn't distract you from guard duty, I'd be disappointed."

"Are you sure? I mean..." She waved a hand around us at all the new decorations helplessly. "You're buying out the city of all the extra decorations! Are you sure you can afford this?"

"Not me, honey. El Diablo." It felt strange to call him El Diablo instead of Liam, but everyone always got confused when I did. It was kind of strange because I hadn't known him that long, but he was Liam to me. I just couldn't wrap my head around this other persona he had going on.

"What? El Diablo's footing the bill?" Her eyes widened, and she looked around the room. "Do the guys know?"

I shrugged. "I didn't tell them. I have no idea if Liam told them or not."

"He's OK with this?"

"It seems to amuse him. For how long is anyone's guess."

Esther glanced around her, then took my elbow and moved me toward one corner of the room where there weren't many people. "What's going on between you two?"

My guard went up instantly. I didn't want the other women in the clubhouse thinking there was anything between Liam and me. "I have no idea what you mean," I said evasively.

"Oh, come on, Jez. You're living with him! The club girls say he's not taken any of them to bed since you got here. Are the two of you a couple?"

"Not at all," I said dismissively. "In fact, he made it perfectly clear to me he's not interested in me, and that he's not interested in a relationship with any woman." I shrugged. "I guess he's a free spirit."

Esther's laugh was merry and more than a little mischievous. "Then why does he come up behind you and wrap you up in his arms every time you're in a room together?"

"Beats the fuck outta me." I shrugged. "I've kissed him a couple of times, but he always stops, and he made it clear that sex with me is definitely not something he's pursuing." Kissed him a couple of times. Right. To say nothing of the mind-numbing orgasms he gave me two nights ago. No way I was spilling that, no matter how much I liked the other woman. As we talked, Celeste and Lyric approached with waves and friendly smiles.

Esther continued as the other two women joined us. "Did he say why?"

I waved her off. "It was all bullshit. I'm guessing it has something to do with our age and experience differences. I've lived in a gilded cage my whole life, and he's been out living his. Any appeal I have to him would fade the second he takes my virginity, and I'm not too naive to admit it."

"Who're you guys talking about?" Lyric asked, her expression curious. "You got a man after you already, Jez?"

"El Diablo," Esther said. "But I think Jez believes he's just toying with her."

Celeste frowned. "I'm sure it's not like that. El Diablo is really a good man. I doubt he'd ever admit it, but he is."

"Didn't you tell me he offered to marry you when Wrath was being a douche?" I asked Celeste.

She grinned. "Yeah. I think that was more about Holly, though. He wanted to make sure she was taken care of with her leukemia and all. He thought we needed a strong man to protect both of us and to make sure Holly got the care she needed." She shook her head. "I believe he'd have gone through with it, but I also believe he did it more to make Wrath get his head out of his ass."

"Maybe that's what he's doing with me. Though I have no idea who he's trying to make jealous. The men in the compound barely talk to me. When they do, they make sure one of you girls or the children are with me."

Lyric gave me a knowing smile. "That's because El Diablo gives you 'the look.'"

I frowned. "What look?"

"The one that lets every male with any modicum of sense know you're his." The girls burst into giggles, and I smiled.

"I doubt that's the case," I said. "Anyway, I've got guard duty tonight. I probably should get some sleep, so I don't fall asleep on the job."

Liam chose that moment to appear in the doorway, scanning the room until his gaze landed on me. His grin was more than a little wicked. The woman giggled.

"Looks like you're going to have to fight more

than sleep," Lyric said with a laugh. "In fact, I'd say you'd have better luck fighting sleep than keeping that man from seducing you tonight."

"Trust me," I said, "he's not going to seduce me."

"Uh-huh." Celeste grinned. "Keep telling yourself that." They all three waved and sauntered off to help the kids decorate.

I frowned at Liam. "Are you trying to be cruel, or can you just not make up your mind?"

"It's a process," he answered with a smirk.

"Well, you can just process the fact that I'm done with this. What the fuck?"

"That's not what you were saying a couple of days ago."

"Yeah? Well, that was before you left me high and dry for two days." A stab of pain hit me, and I actually put my hand over my chest. "Have you been avoiding me? Because I already told you I wasn't asking for permanent. I wasn't even asking for anything more after that one time. I mean, surely you could have stood to be in my company one fucking night."

"Trust me when I say I look forward to being in your company. I found it exceedingly enjoyable." His smile was positively wicked. "But I hear you have a job?"

"I do," I said, putting my shoulders back. "I'm making sure none of our decorations disappear."

He gave me a knowing look. "I see. Well. If anyone can stop this Christmas Bandit that has the children so wound up, I'm certain it's you." He leaned down and brushed a kiss over my mouth. I shivered in reaction even as I pushed him away.

"Oh, no you don't! Go away," I said, making a shooing motion. "I'm done with all that!"

"We'll see, beautiful Jezebel."

Before I could get away from him, Liam pulled me into his arms and pressed his lips to mine. For a man who didn't want sex with me he was sure pushing for sex with me! The problem was, no matter how much my brain tried to tell me to push him away, my heart tried to pull him closer.

I enjoyed the feel of his arms around me and his lips on mine. I wanted more of all of it. But I also had some pride left. It wasn't much, but it was enough for me to finally push at his chest and duck my head.

He groaned. "My little Jezebel. What am I going to do with you?"

"Nothing," I said, my voice shaking slightly. "You're not doing anything with me." I took a breath, gathering my courage to meet his gaze. "I think it's time you found me another room. I don't think it's appropriate for me to stay in your suite." He opened his mouth to say something, but I cut him off. "I don't need anything fancy. Just a place with a good kitchen. Cooking is the one thing I can't do without. I have to be able to cook and bake."

He gave me a knowing little smile. "As you wish, my beautiful Jezebel. We'll discuss it." His smile widened. "After you get off guard duty."

That really shouldn't have sounded sinister. But the look he gave me said he had other plans besides the obvious one he'd agreed to. My traitorous body responded. My nipples hardened so fast I gasped. Just like that, my pussy wept for his touch. The bastard had me panting for him, and I hated it. Even as weak as I felt around his superior experience and the fact that he could make me want him so easily, I found Liam to be the most exciting individual I'd ever been around. When I was with him this way, when he was expertly and effortlessly seducing me, I'd never felt more alive. God help me, no matter what I said, I still wanted him. He knew it too.

I shook my head, backing away from him. "I'm taking a nap."

"Good," he said without hesitation. "You'll need your strength later." He winked. "Guard duty and all."

"Fucker," I muttered. Liam only laughed, the sound filling me with warmth and making a smile tug at my lips.

As I wandered around the room one last time, I noted how happy and cheerful everyone was. There were even a few of the men around either helping the children or teasing the women. It was obvious they were going to win the game of wills they had going on with the women. None of them could resist the ruggedly handsome men in the club no matter how hard they tried, something I knew about firsthand.

El Diablo…

What the hell was I gonna do with him? I was done throwing myself at him, but could I resist if he continued to come for me? I *craved* his touch so much I was afraid I couldn't. And I needed to. If for no other reason than to let him know he couldn't continue to expect me to just fall into his arms when he decided he wanted a taste. I couldn't even say he was using me for sex. Because he wasn't! Which was part of the problem. After a lifetime of an existence without human affection, I desperately needed his touch. No matter how weak it made me feel, every time he came up behind me and wrapped his arms around me, I melted.

After making sure everything was well under way and that no one needed anything, I made my way back to our suite. I didn't see Liam anywhere and hoped he'd let me sleep even as I prayed he wouldn't. I wanted him to come to me. To play with me like he'd done before.

But what then? No way I was content to have a one-time thing with him. And I wasn't sure how I'd react if I ever did see him with one of the women in the compound. I was pretty sure I wouldn't be the warm, inviting soul I'd been when getting them to bring their children and nieces and nephews to help decorate for Christmas. They'd never look at me the same way again, and I genuinely liked most of them. After a lifetime of never having friends, I needed the relationships I'd built in this place. All of them.

God, I was tired. My mind couldn't take much more. It wasn't the work I was doing. It was the mental stress I was putting on myself with regard to Liam. For someone I knew was unattainable, I was putting more of myself into him than I should. Even someone as sheltered as me knew this.

With a sigh, I stripped down to my panties and pulled on a tank top to sleep in. Crawling under the covers, I knew I'd feel better after a couple hours' nap. Then I'd shower and head down to the great room to stand guard. The Christmas Bandit was no match for me. I grinned at the thought just before drifting off to sleep.

Chapter Seven
Jezebel

I woke as a powerful orgasm washed over me. The scream forced from my throat was ragged and long. It took a moment to realize I wasn't alone in my bed. Oh no. El Diablo was with me. In fact, he had stripped me of my tank and panties and currently had his face between my legs, sucking and licking me to the most powerful orgasm I'd ever imagined.

And it was definitely the Devil in my bed.

He looked up at me, his lips and chin glistening with my juices. "Did you have a nice nap, beautiful Jezebel?" His words were a purr from between my thighs as he continued to lick lazily at my throbbing clit.

I gasped and sucked in breath after breath, my throat raw from my previous screams. "I've -- o-only been -- asleep -- an hour."

"It'll have to do," he said. Then attacked my cunt again.

The last time he'd done this had been wonderful. This time…

This time, I wasn't sure I'd survive. Even though I'd just come, El Diablo was ruthlessly driving me up again. I screamed, reaching desperately for his head to push him away. Instead, I found myself clinging to him, holding him to me. What if he took that wonderful mouth away like I thought I wanted? No. I couldn't live with that. I'd given myself orgasms watching Internet porn, but nothing had prepared me for the sensations this man was giving me now. Even the pleasure before paled in comparison to this. It was like he'd just decided he was giving me everything he had, and I was helpless to do anything but take what he dished out.

"That's it, my beauty," he praised as I gasped. "Your honey is so fucking sweet..."

The man was brutal in his oral assault. My clit took most of his attention, but he licked up and down the creases between my legs and my outer pussy lips, as well as my labia and opening. There wasn't a place left untouched.

When he inserted a finger inside me, I tensed. It didn't hurt, but I was afraid it would. His fingers were thick, and when he inserted the second finger it burned, and I whimpered.

"Ah, there it is. My little wanton virgin." He licked all around his fingers before settling on my clit. "When you come again, I'm going to claim your innocence and you'll be mine, Jezebel." His voice was a sensual rasp against my clit, vibrating through my sensitive flesh. It was nearly too much stimulation, but I had no idea how to voice it. I could feel another orgasm building and was afraid of what was about to happen. Not because I was scared of Liam. I was scared of El Diablo and what he would do to my heart. I hadn't understood before. I did now. El Diablo was a man who could take my heart and tear it to shreds. He was ruthless in getting what he wanted, and he wanted me.

With a cry, I embraced the orgasm tearing through me. My body clenched and rippled with the pleasure that was only amplified by the nearly painful over stimulation. Before the wave could fully crest, El Diablo was over me, sliding inside me. The brief pain did nothing to tamp down the raging waves still taking my body. I clamped down on his cock, which was now fully seated inside me.

El Diablo looked down at me, studying my face

intently. He was focused solely on me. Not on his pleasure, or anything other than my reaction. I gasped and panted, clinging to his broad, muscled shoulders.

"Liam," I whimpered. Then, "El Diablo."

His lips curled up on one side. "So, you see the difference."

"El Diablo's your ruthless side. The predator."

"El Diablo is the man who'll keep you safe and destroy any threat to you. His demands are your body and soul. You begged Liam to take your body. Will you do the same for El Diablo?"

I shook my head. "My begging days are long past," I said, meaning it. "I'll never again throw myself at you or any other man."

"You don't have to throw yourself at me. I can't keep my hands off you. But you absolutely will not go to another man. If you did, he'd die. That simple."

"I don't understand you." I wanted to hit him with something, but I was completely pinned down by his big body. "You don't want me, but you don't want anyone else to have me?"

"Oh, I want you. I have from the moment I first saw you in that suite I took you from." He stroked my hair away from my damp forehead. "Your fate was sealed even then. I tried, but even then, I knew you were lost."

He flexed his hips above me and I groaned, letting my head fall back to the mattress. Then he began to move slowly but steadily. Long strokes in and out of me. I clung to him, gripping his hips with my thighs because I couldn't help myself. It was instinctual. I needed to hold him to me. To keep him from leaving me yet again.

"Oh, God," I panted.

"God has nothing to do with it, Jezebel."

El Diablo shifted his pelvis just that little bit, hitting my clit in the exact right way. I came on a harsh, ragged scream, my body not my own. He was possessing me mind and body, even my very soul. He seemed to know exactly what I needed when I had no clue.

"Ah!" He cried out, gripping my hip with one hand while fisting my hair with the other. Taking my mouth, he captured the rest of my cries and gave me his own. His cock throbbed inside me and he stayed still inside me, not moving while I clamped down on him. "So fucking tight!"

"Liam!" I screamed his name, clinging to him like my only lifeline. "What are you doing to me?"

"Claiming you," he growled, trailing little nipping kisses down my throat. "Possessing you."

"Fuck me!"

With a brutal yell, he complied with my demand.

My body shook in a steady rhythm from the fucking he delivered. He surged inside me over and over. Harder. Faster. Taking my body to heights I'd never known existed. Every time I thought I'd reached the pinnacle of pleasure, he pushed me a little further, and it all shattered around me to be replaced by an even higher, more dangerous peak.

When I tilted my pelvis to meet his thrusts, Liam raised his body from mine, circling my neck with one hand and slapping the outside of one thigh sharply with the other.

"Don't move," he snarled. "You take what I give you, when I'm ready to give it to you."

The little bite of pain his smack had caused, combined with the utter helplessness I felt with his restraining hand around my throat, my life literally in his hands, was yet another sexual stimulation he gave me. I knew I should be scared, or angry, or any number of things other than what I was -- horny beyond belief. And I'd already come more times that I could count.

Instead of fighting him, I stretched my neck, giving him better access. That was my permission for him to proceed as he would. And I dearly hoped there was more of this rough, carnal side, the El Diablo side, of Liam that he'd show me. It was all scary and shockingly thrilling. I was drawn like a moth to a flame. And I wanted this experience more than I wanted to breathe!

Every move he made sent muscles rippling beneath his tanned, olive-toned skin. He was darkly mysterious with tribal tattoos snaking up his sides and over his chest and abdomen. His shoulders and arms were free of ink but thickly muscled and powerful. Faint scars crisscrossed his chest, making me wonder what kind of warrior he really was. His was a purely masculine beauty, honed in the fires of hell. Made into the man they called El Diablo.

I spread my legs as wide as I could, lying passively beneath Liam as he took my body. This seemed to be exactly what he wanted, because he grunted before lowering his body to mine once again. We were mashed tightly together, his arms going around me, holding me firmly to him as he continued to fuck me. He latched on to the side of my neck, sucking strongly until he'd left behind a stinging mark of his possession. It was primitive. Raw. Carnal. Sexy as fuck. And I loved every fucking second of it.

Just when I'd thought he'd wrung out the last orgasm I could possibly give him, he shifted his hips once again, once again aligning my clit with his body perfectly. Even though I thought I was ready for it this time, the orgasm still overwhelmed and overpowered me. I screamed long and loud, my throat burning from the many screams he'd already taken from me.

"That's it," he praised. "Squeeze my fuckin' cock! Milk my cum from me!"

"Liam!"

"Yes, yes, yes!" He roared his release. I felt his cum filling me. Running out of me to the bed sheets. His dick throbbed and pulsed inside me, giving me yet more. Filling my body.

"Liam," I gasped, my orgasm refusing to let me go even in the midst of what I was sure was panic. "I'm not on anything."

He just growled and bit down on my neck, silencing me as he continued to empty himself deep inside me. He even picked up my hips, forcing gravity to work to keep his seed inside me.

"You'll take my cum, Jezebel," he snarled. "Take it and keep it!"

"But --"

"If I breed you, so be it. You're mine now, anyway. Warned you."

I gasped out several shocked breaths even as I clung to him. Even when his cock stopped throbbing, he didn't pull out of me. He just clung to me, my ass resting on his bent thighs so that my pelvis stayed elevated.

I'm not sure how long we stayed like that, but gradually, his cock softened and slipped out of me on its own. Liam growled again in displeasure.

"Fuck," he bit out. "Wanted inside you longer."

"Liam," I whispered.

"I know exactly what I did, Jezebel," he said before I could voice my concerns again. "I told you I'd control you more than Malcolm ever did."

"But why?"

"Because I'm a ruthless bastard," he admitted. "The more ties I have to you, the harder it will be for you to keep distance between us."

I pushed at him, wanting to look at him. When he raised his head, I gave him what I was sure was a frustrated look. "I've not been the one putting distance between us. You ate my pussy like there was no tomorrow, then didn't talk to me for two days! Now this? Are you crazy?"

"Undoubtedly," he said without hesitation. Then he stood and scooped me up. When we were in the bathroom, he sat me on the vanity. "Don't move." Then he turned to a big sunken tub and started filling it before turning back to me. "Spread your legs," he murmured. "Let me look at you."

"I'm a mess," I said, not wanting him to see. "I can clean myself."

"I know you can. But I'm the one who made the mess. I'll clean it up."

I did as he asked. When he bent down to inspect my pussy, I felt a little like a bug under a microscope.

"You bled a little," he said before looking up at me. "Did I hurt you badly?"

I shook my head immediately. "It pinched, but I was so caught up in what you were doing it only added to the pleasure," I admitted. Faintly, I realized that giving him too much information about how I liked the little bites of pain he showed me, and how much I loved his dominance of me, wasn't the best idea. But I wasn't going to let him think I'd been in pain when he'd taken my virginity.

He nodded once before cleaning me with a warm, damp cloth. That task done, he picked me up again and headed to the tub, climbing in and setting me in front of him as he turned off the water and turned on the jets. I groaned in bliss as the water fizzed and bubbled around us.

Liam just held me, one arm around me, the other lazily petting me. We stayed like that a long time. The hot water and the massaging effect of the jets relaxed me so much I dozed off. When I woke, Liam was wrapping himself around me in bed. The sheets smelled fresh, so he must have changed them. Not that I cared. I was completely spent. Once he settled, my head pillowed on his arm, his warm body tightly against mine, I sighed once, then let sleep have me.

* * *

El Diablo

As I stared down at Jezebel's sleeping form I came to two stark realizations. *Nothing* could harm this woman. Of the two main problems she had, Malcolm was probably the least of her worries. Malcolm I could easily kill. It was just a matter of finding him, and I was pretty sure I had him. Killing him would be no more than an afterthought.

The second problem was me. I was a killer. Straight up. She'd seen my ruthless side tonight, and I wasn't sure how much she embraced and how much repelled her. She hadn't fought me, but I was sure she'd have a few words to say about me trying to get her pregnant.

Fuck! Just the thought of her growing big with my babe made me hard as stone and proud as fuck. I missed everything of Magenta's childhood. I'd never allow anything to make me miss this child's. And there I went assuming her being pregnant was a foregone conclusion.

Clenching my fists, I turned and left my bedroom. *Our* bedroom. From now on, this was where she would sleep. Well, once I killed that son of a bitch father of hers.

I stabbed Shotgun's contact number into my phone. He answered on the first ring. "Tell me you have that bastard," I growled, the devil in me clawing his way free to go on the hunt.

"Great timing. I was just about to send my information to Giovanni for corroboration."

"Tell him I want it verified tonight. If not, I'll scout it myself."

There was a pause. "You and the rest of the team. Right?"

"Did I say the rest of the team?" I snapped. "This is personal. No one from Black Reign gets involved beyond intelligence. We will be sending a message, and it will come straight to me. No one else."

"All the more reason to send someone with you."

"Shotgun," I said, clenching my teeth. "I'd hate to make your lovely woman a widow before she's actually your wife, but I will. Don't push me."

"Understood," he said. "I'll contact you the moment Giovanni confirms."

"Tell him he has until seven local time. We leave at dark." I hung up without waiting for an acknowledgment.

I didn't bother to call El Segador. I'd left him out with Shotgun on purpose. It was how we worked. No trail connecting us. I didn't visit him. I didn't call or text. It was Reaper's job to know when I needed him and when it was time to go. He'd never let me down. I didn't expect this time to be any different.

I spent the time before the deadline readying myself, checking equipment, my bike, and my armament. I had no intention of shooting anyone. Any kills I made would be at close range. But guns were a necessary evil, and I believed in always being prepared.

By the time I was packed and prepped on my end, it was time to check in with Shotgun. Before I could call my intel guy, however, my phone rang, his name popping up as the caller.

"It checks out," he said a little breathlessly. "Giovanni flew a drone or something over the place and positively identified Malcolm."

"Who identified him?" I asked. The source was as important as the information.

"Azriel."

"Well," I said, confident I had them. "Can't get more sure than that. Let Giovanni know I'm requesting he keep an eye on the place until I get there. I don't want anyone slipping out and disappearing."

"He's already on it. Sent some kind of message through several different sources to avoid backtracking the sender. I think it was that Jezebel had been found and the transporter was in deep cover, unable to be contacted. Malcolm had given word the girl was to be brought to him at the location he's at now."

"How many invitations were sent?"

"Two, just like you expected. Malcolm went to his trusted men, loyal to the Brotherhood. We intercepted both messages and killed the targets. They never got their orders, though Malcolm thinks they did, thanks to Giovanni and Azriel."

"Good work. Send me the information."

After looking over the location, the structure, and the surrounding area, I knew it would be hard to get in without raising an alarm. Hard, but not impossible. At nine that night, I set out for North Carolina and the safe house Malcolm had turned into his temporary base.

A couple hours after I left the Black Reign compound, El Segador pulled up on my left flank. He didn't acknowledge my presence, and I didn't acknowledge his. We just rode on in silence. Riding to kill a killer.

Jezebel would get over being mad at me for parting from her like I had. At least, I hope she would. If not, I'd have saved her only to lose her.

* * *

Jezebel

While El Diablo is making his plans…

A wonderfully cool breeze wafted in through the open window, fluttering the sheer curtains in a room I'd never been in before. Blurry-eyed, my body deliciously sore, I sat up in the enormous bed where I'd been cocooned in a down-filled duvet on a mattress soft as a cloud and a pillow to match. The sunlight was muted where it hit the window at an angle. I had no idea what time it was.

The previous night came rushing back, and with it the reason I was sore. There was no way to keep the goofy smile off my face. I had been well and truly fucked. And it. Had. Been. *Blissful!*

I sat straight up in the bed, looking around for Liam. Next to me where I vaguely remembered him pulling me into his body and wrapping his strong arms around me, the bed was cool, like he'd been gone for a while. I glanced at the clock and gasped. It was after noon!

I jumped up and ran from the room. The suite was empty. I didn't see a note or anything, but then I had no idea what to expect this morning. Liam had said some pretty radical things. He'd come in me and same as told me he intended to get me pregnant. It was a whole other level of crazy and erratic behavior that couldn't in any way be healthy, but, for some fucked-up reason, I was OK with it. The second he'd taken me from my suite at Malcolm's, I'd thrown my lot in with him.

I hadn't wanted to acknowledge it at the time, but if he had tried to send me off with one of the others or hadn't intended to bring me back with him to the Black Reign compound, I'd probably have stayed where I was. Something inside me recognized Liam as the one person in the world who could not only keep me safe from Malcolm but would protect me from any and everything. Sounded cheesy, but I didn't care.

I was also crazy attracted to him. I knew that wasn't necessarily a good thing. He'd told me as much. Though he'd negated nearly everything he'd warned me about last night with his treatment of me so far. Unless he intended to keep me in addition to his other harem. I just didn't know. That was something I needed to figure out. You know. Before I lost my heart to him.

Hurrying to my own bedroom, I headed to the bathroom and brushed my teeth. Then I dressed, readying to head back to the great room... Where I'd totally ditched guard duty.

I groaned. "Motherfuck."

Racing downstairs, I found all the women standing in the middle of the great room. Not a glitter of tinsel anywhere.

"Oh, man..." I groaned, sitting in a nearby chair. "I'm so sorry," I said, looking up at the grinning faces of Lyric, Celeste, and Esther. Holly and Bella were stomping around the room "looking for clues." Several of the men looked on from the bar innocently, nursing a beer.

"Good morning, sunshine," Celeste said with a giggle. "Sleep well?"

I sighed, then giggled. Next thing I knew we were all laughing, the girls hugging me and offering well wishes.

"Who was it?" Lyric whispered. "Was it El Diablo?"

"Yes, it was Liam. Or, rather, El Diablo. I saw the difference last night. Believe me, there's a definite difference."

"I'm so excited!" Lyric jumped and clapped her hands. "He's so good to everyone here he deserves someone of his own."

"Hold on there, cowgirl," I said with a laugh. "No one talked about happily ever after. We had sex. There's a difference."

Lyric waved that off. "Trust me. Everyone is talking about how different he is since you got here. I think there was a pool going on about how long it took him to publicly claim you."

"Well, it doesn't look like we're off to such a good start. Have you seen him today? Because he was gone when I woke up with no indication where he was going."

Celeste went white, then swallowed. "Oh, God," she said, covering her mouth with her hand. She dashed off.

Esther frowned, then looked at me and Lyric. "I better check on her," she said. "Excuse me."

"What happened?" I asked. "Did I say something wrong?"

Lyric sighed. "When Celeste and Wrath were first getting together, Wrath took off on club business and didn't tell Celeste what was going on. It looked like he'd gone to a high-profile city charity event without her." She frowned. "Actually, that's exactly what he did, but he was on club business. They were expecting enemies, and he was afraid he might be in a fight and didn't want to put Celeste in danger. Unfortunately, he didn't tell her. El Diablo was furious with him." She shrugged. "Maybe she just had a flashback or something? Anyway, I'm sure he's around somewhere."

I figured he was busy. After all, Liam had more to do than entertain me, I joined the team, taking my ribbing good-naturedly like everyone else had. Turned out, none of the guards had fared any better than me last night. Two club girls -- Iris and Deema -- had been carted off by two more club members. Both of them smiled as happily as I had when I'd first woke and remembered what had happened. Even if it was causing all kinds of extra work, the men carting off the women for sex was putting everyone in a good mood. The children weren't getting sick of it yet, so all was well.

Everything seemed to be going smoothly until around eight-thirty. The children had either been picked up by a parent or bussed back to their shelters or homes, and the girls were just finishing putting away boxes and doing a final clean of excess tinsel when El Diablo strode through the room. El Diablo. Not Liam.

He was dressed in dark leather from head to toe, complete with leather riding gloves. He walked with Shotgun and Samson, both men intently focused on their leader, taking instructions and answering questions. Several of the women squealed and headed in his direction. It occurred to me that this was the first time he'd been in the common room without first coming to me. In fact, he didn't even look my way.

Most of the club girls had decided El Diablo was off-limits. Though he hadn't said anything, and neither had I, it was suspected I was with him. Hell, after last night, I'd thought I was with him. Unfortunately, there were several women who still had their sights set on the president of what was apparently a very powerful club in the city. One of them, Goldie, had been in the group decorating and helping with the children. When she glanced over her shoulder at me, she smirked, and I realized how cutthroat the club girls could be. This was why they were always kept separate from family, and why none of the men would ever take one as his woman.

"El Diablo!" Goldie exclaimed as she bounded in his direction. "Liam!" OK, that hurt. No one called him that but me. Lyric had told me very few knew his real name until I'd used it. Now, the club girls were using it to get familiar with him.

He turned to look at the woman. She was in front of him when he turned his head, so I didn't get a look at his expression. Next thing I knew, she was up in the air, climbing his body like a jungle gym.

The pain stabbing through my heart was so great I nearly cried out. My hand flew to my chest, and the breath left my lungs. Lyric gripped my arm, murmuring at me to hold it in and keep it together. Showing weakness would be blood in the water to this bunch. Just like that, my magical, wonderful Christmas shattered into a thousand pieces.

I started walking toward El Diablo, my pace quickening as I went. I shoved my way past club girls and bikers until I reached the man himself, Goldie still wrapped around him.

"Good morning, Sunshine," I bit out. "Nice to see you so early this morning."

"Jezebel," he said patiently. "Now's not the time."

"Well, when is the time? Because there were some serious things happening last night that I never questioned. Now, maybe it seems that I should have."

"We'll discuss this when I return, beautiful Jezebel. Time is of the essence."

"Make time," I snapped.

His gaze fell on me, his eyes flat and cold. With a harsh shove, he set Goldie aside and stomped toward me. "I don't have time to explain to you what must be done, and, quite frankly, I don't have to. I'm president of this club, and there are things I must do to safeguard *everyone*." He emphasized the last word, and I got it.

"I realize I've brought Malcolm to your front door, but it wasn't my fault. You brought me here. You kept me here!"

"Would you rather be back with him? At his tender mercies?"

"Would it be any different than being at yours?" I was yelling now, confused and hurt. "Seems to me there's a very real possibility you changed my entire life last night. Or have you forgotten your caveman gesture of ownership?"

That must have been the exact wrong thing to say, because El Diablo lunged for me, gripping my upper arm in a bruising grip, and dragged me out of the common room. He took me to our suite and slammed the door when we entered. I'd never seen him look so angry. Strangely, I wasn't intimidated. I wasn't scared when I could see in his eyes he was a straight-up killer. He had to be if Malcolm was wary of him in the least. Instead of giving me pause, his show of temper fueled my own anger.

"What the hell's wrong with you?" I yelled. "You

fucked me, came in me, told me you meant to 'breed' me." I made air quotes. "Then you just... what? Go on with your life? Because, let me tell you, I may not know a whole lot about relationships, but I know when you tell a woman you want her to have your baby, you don't just up and leave at the first opportunity without talking to her!"

Instead of arguing with me, El Diablo attacked. He wrapped his arms around me and lifted, fusing his mouth to mine as he carried me to the bedroom. His bedroom. I tried to fight him, but really, what was the use? The second he claimed my mouth, my brain took a hiatus and my cunt took over.

Tossing me onto the bed, he reached for my pants and yanked them down with my panties. Like he'd done the first time he'd eaten my pussy, he brought my panties to his nose and sniffed even as he opened his pants and freed his dick.

Using the only remaining ounce of self-preservation I had left, I tried to crab-walk backward on the bed to get away from him, but El Diablo just grabbed my ankle and yanked me back to him with a vicious snarl. Once he had me on the edge of the bed, he shoved my legs apart and rammed his cock deep inside me. I cried out, my orgasm already hovering on the edge.

He didn't say a word, just grunted and growled as he fucked me. Our bodies slammed together, slapping loudly in the room. My whimpers were lost in his kisses as his tongue swept inside to tangle with mine. He coaxed me as much as he simply took what he wanted. The sex was explosive. Almost violent.

El Diablo stood at the edge of the bed, gripping my thighs while he plowed into me. He was still fully clothed, while I was naked from the waist down. He bared his teeth when I gripped his thick wrists, a silent warning not to try to pry his hands from my thighs. I wasn't going to. My only thought was to find something to hang on to. I picked him.

Finally, when I was nearly sobbing, begging for relief, El Diablo shifted his hips. He seemed to be the master of knowing exactly where I needed the friction of his body most. The second he did, pleasure exploded within me, centered at the place where our bodies joined. El Diablo pounded into me even harder and faster, his building roar growing louder with each rapid thrust. When my pussy clamped down on his dick, he yelled a savage, brutal shout, pumping me full of his cum.

We stared into each other's eyes for long moments, neither giving an inch. Finally he reached for me, pulling me into his embrace as he walked me to the bathroom, his dick still firmly embedded in my pussy.

He set me down and his cock finally slid out, letting a massive load of cum spill out of me and onto the vanity. Without a word, El Diablo got a wet cloth and cleaned me gently before stripping off my shirt and giving my nipple one sweet suck before picking me up and carrying me back to bed.

Sliding in beside me, he pulled me into his body so I was draped over his chest before pulling the covers over me. He lay on top of the duvet with his feet off the edge slightly so as not to get the bed dirty. Still, he held me, stroking my hair, not saying a word. I wanted to cry. I had no idea what he was doing or what his plans for me were other than knocking me up so I couldn't leave him. He'd said that, once he committed his life to a woman, he'd never stray. But he'd also said he had no intentions of keeping a woman permanently. He'd planned on using any child we might conceive as a weapon to keep me with him. Did that mean he intended to make me his in the eyes of his club? If so, what did that mean for us? Was he still planning on bedding women like Goldie whenever the mood struck him?

Those were questions too big for me to contemplate right now. I couldn't voice them without breaking down into tears so I kept quiet. It wasn't long before I took one final breath, then fell into a fitful slumber.

Chapter Eight
El Diablo

For someone who regularly busts my men for mistreating their women, I knew I'd royally fucked up. The ride to North Carolina gave me plenty of time to replay our last encounter over and over in my head. She was angry I hadn't told her what was going on, but how the fuck was I supposed to tell her I was on my way to kill her father? She might not be upset about it now, but when she had time to think about it? Yeah.

We had to stop several times for gas in the nearly seven-hundred-mile trip but never spoke. It was just our way. At about the halfway mark, El Segador approached me. "If you were one of your men, you'd be kicking your own ass right now."

"I know," I said, not taking my eyes off the gas tank as I filled my bike.

"You hurt her."

"Badly."

"She yours?"

"If she'll still have me."

El Segador snorted. "Or even if she won't."

"Even if she won't," I confessed.

"We've got eight days to Christmas. Seven to Christmas Eve. Do you want my advice?"

"Why do you ask me questions you already know the answer to? Of course, I don't want your advice. You're worse at relationships than I am."

As expected, I got no emotional response from Reaper. He knew me better than I knew myself sometimes. He simply did what he always did. Gave me what I needed rather than what I wanted.

"On our way back, you need to get her a ring."

"Already have it, brother," I answered without

hesitation. That got a response from him.

"Fuck me," he said. "You finally got one over on me. When'd you get it?"

"I actually picked it up a couple of days ago. But I got the stone the day after I brought her home."

"Ah. The representative from Moussaieff Jewelers in London."

"Yes. He wouldn't let me buy the gem she deserves, but he had one I can give her and still hold my head high."

"So he had the Moussaieff Red with him."

"He did. Or rather, he was on his way to New York to pick it up from the Smithsonian." I shrugged. "I have to admire the man. He wouldn't even take my offer to the board. He said they'd be too tempted to sell."

"Let me guess. He'd prefer it belonged to a museum?"

I shrugged. "I got a blue diamond instead."

"Well, if that doesn't help fix your fuck-up, you can always try a different approach."

"I'm not giving her the ring for her to forgive me. I'm giving it to her to prove I'm serious about her being mine."

"Ever think maybe she wants you to be hers as well?" El Segador gave me a stern look. The same look I often gave my brothers. "You need to apologize to her and promise to never shut her out again."

"I did pretty much tell her I'd never take a woman for myself because I believed in commitment and would never be able to fully commit myself to one woman."

"'Cause you're just as ass-stupid as the rest of the lot," El Segador said. Then he walked back to his bike. Man had a point.

By the time we reached Bug Hill, North Carolina, it was seven in the morning. It was still dark, but the sun would be rising in another half an hour or so. Not enough time to make it inside the place they'd set up as a safe house. It was a cabin in the woods. Not huge, but not a little hunting shack either. We set up camp and immediately started surveillance of the place. At about noon, we'd established there were four men inside the two-bedroom cabin. Two of them were highly trained. The other two were questionable.

"I recognize Malcolm," I told Reaper. "The other three are new to me."

"One of them is a man named Samuel," he said. "He's deceptive in that he looks like he can't handle himself. The man is as deadly as they come. The guards will be his personal guards. I can't imagine the other men are any less dangerous"

"Are we outmatched?"

El Segador looked at me and raised an eyebrow. "Do you honestly think I let you come without backup?"

I grinned, knowing who was on the way. "When will they be here?"

"Any time now."

Sure enough, an hour later, a pair of old friends tramped into camp. "El Diablo, you son of a bitch!" I had no idea how old Chief was. He always complained about getting old, but the truth was he was fit as they came. He just hid it under baggy clothes.

"Always a pleasure, Chief," I drawled. Looking to the other man, I grinned. "Loki, old friend. Good to see you out. Thank you for joining us."

Loki shrugged. "Reaper made it seem like it was life or death. I may be in mourning, but I'd never let a friend fall because of my own sentiment." His voice was soft and smooth.

"I was sorry to hear about Lividia. She was an honorable, kind woman."

"She was my world," Loki said softly. "She gave her life to spare our child only to have the baby die hours after birth."

"I thought sure Giovanni's people could help her," I said softly. "And the baby."

"Some things are just not meant to be," Chief said. "Doesn't make it easier to accept."

"I appreciate you coming to my aid," I said reverently.

Loki shrugged. "I had nothing better to do." The corner of his mouth turned up. It was the first spark of the old Loki I'd seen since his wife and daughter passed a few months earlier. I'd once asked him how long he'd be in mourning, and he'd replied with "as long as it takes for me to not feel so dead inside." Now, I understood. If something happened to Jezebel, I'd be dead inside, too.

We spent the rest of the day resting in shifts and planning the coming raid. When night fell, we waited until after midnight, then it was on.

With the combined skill and cunning of the four of us, the two guards were no match. There was a brief scuffle with Malcolm and Samuel, mainly because I wanted them alive for the time being, but we finally got them subdued. Seated in chairs, both men glared up at me.

"Do you know why I'm here?" I asked softly, looking at first one man, then the other.

"Because you're a son of a bitch?" Malcom asked with a sneer. I ignored him.

"Because of what you did to Jezebel," I said as calmly as I could.

Malcolm shrugged. "She was necessary."

"How did you convince her mother to go along with this?"

"How do you think?" He scoffed. "Money, of course. Didn't matter, though. She died shortly after Jezebel's birth. So sad." Malcolm shrugged as if it were no consequence at all. "It doesn't matter. I took care of Jezebel. Gave her a home."

"You made her a pawn to be used and discarded by the Brotherhood," I bit out.

"It's not all my fault, you know. The whole plot was Samuel's idea. Raise the perfect wife. Then I sell her to my biggest rival and solidify our hold on the Brotherhood."

"That why you came?" I asked Samuel. "To make sure she was recovered and still able to be used as you wanted?" I narrowed my eyes. "You'd planned on killing her out here in the middle of nowhere if she wasn't a virgin when she returned. Didn't you." It wasn't a question.

Samuel shrugged. "Not necessarily. I figured it depended on who kidnapped her. Since it was you? Well. She did her job admirably."

I cocked my head to the side. This wasn't what I expected. "Explain," I snapped.

"She was meant to seduce our greatest rival. To be sold as a measure of assurance we'd always have a direct tie to the one person who could depose us." When I stared at him without speaking, he spread his hands wide and nodded to me. "You, El Diablo. You're the one person in all the world who could successfully stage a coup on the Brotherhood. You're legendary among us. The only assassin to never miss a mark. The only assassin to stand up to the powers that be when a sanctioned kill hadn't been thoroughly vetted and the target was innocent. One of only two people to ever escape the Brotherhood. Even though you still took jobs, you did them on your own terms. Apparently, this new generation respects that rather than blind obedience."

That caught me off guard. Jezebel was meant to seduce me. I'd bet my life she'd had no idea who she was supposed to get close to. "What about Cypher?"

Samuel sighed. "Cypher is exactly what his name says. He's a puzzle. Your weakness was women in distress. When you offered to take jobs if we freed our... cash crop of women," he said with a little sneer, "I knew we had your weakness. You hid your daughter, Magenta, well, or we'd have capitalized on her and made you a better assassin. You'd have been forced to follow orders to the letter instead of inserting morals into a profession that had none."

"Fine," I said. "You got me. I'm completely smitten with Jezebel. In fact, I've been trying to breed her in order to make a permanent tie to her." I could see both men's faces light up with glee. "Unfortunately for the two of you, it changes nothing. I came here to kill you, and I always follow through."

"You can't kill us," Malcolm laughed. "At least, you can't kill *me*."

"Oh, that's rich," Loki muttered.

"He was never the brightest," Reaper responded with a chuckle.

"Do you honestly think Jezebel will ever look at you the same if you kill me? I'm her father. Love me or hate me, she'll still never forgive you. Not completely."

"Then she'll really hate me if she finds out how you died. Because you've earned a very hard death."

"Think what you will. I loved that girl. I took care of her. Saw she had the nicest things and lived in luxury. She had anything she ever wanted."

"Except her freedom," I said softly. "You offered her only a life of slavery from birth. With no way out. Also," I said, shaking my head. "Why name her Jezebel if you loved her? Did you name her thusly to remind her what her worth was? She's more than a woman meant to seduce your enemies. She's highly intelligent and as kind a person as ever there was."

"I named her that because she was supposed to tame the devil." He gestured to me. "You."

I shrugged. "She did her job. Now it's time for me to do mine."

"She won't forgive you," Malcolm reiterated. "It will be there between you two forever."

"Maybe. But I will live happily knowing I've removed the threat to her and avenged her lost childhood."

Their deaths were slow. We stood them on blocks just tall enough that the tips of their shoes could support a fraction of their weight on the floor when we removed them. Then we hung them with strong, thin wires. It took them several hours to die. Each moment I watched the fight draining out of them brought joy to my heart. Samuel succumbed first, and I took great delight in making Malcolm understand Samuel had died. We even held Malcolm's weight for precious seconds so he could confirm Samuel was actually dead before we slowly lowered him back to his toes. Had we dropped him, he might not have regained his balance, and it would have been over for him. So I made sure he had his weight as much as he could before I released his body. Then I watched another half hour while he slowly strangled to death.

It took us several days to clean up everything. Not only did we want our traces gone, but all traces that anyone had ever been here. Demolishing the house and burning it in small piles so we didn't draw attention took the bulk of our time. By the time we finished, it was three days to Christmas, and Reaper and I still had nine hours of hard riding.

We drove an hour before finding a small town with one motel used mostly by locals as apartments. It was a town full of hunters, as it happened, so we just pretended to be on a hunting trip. After staying one night, we headed back to Palm Beach as quickly as we could. I had no idea what kind of reception I'd get from Jezebel, but I knew I needed to see her. Even if she hated me, I still needed to know she was still in my world.

* * *

Jezebel

"Fuck this and fuck my life!" I was so over this fucking Christmas Bandit! If I found out who it was, I'd probably kill the fucker myself.

"Ease up," Esther said, putting an arm around me and leading me out of the great room. "It's all right. Really." She brought me outside to the pool, and we sat at a table with an umbrella so the sun was out of our faces. I was a fucking hot mess. "The kids are still having a good time. Most of the club girls are behaving, and the others have been banned by Rycks. Don't worry about this anymore, OK?"

"The party is tomorrow night. What the fuck am I gonna do? There's not gonna be any decorations. No presents? What happened to all those presents we put under that massive-ass tree yesterday? How the fuck did someone even get it out of the great room?" I was about to lose my shit. I hadn't slept since El Diablo had left, never to return. A whole fucking week! Fucker.

"Don't worry about it," Esther soothed. "Let me, Lyric, and Celeste take care of things today. You go rest. Have you even slept in a couple of days?"

I sighed, the anger leaving me in a rush to be replaced by a deep sadness fueled by intense loss. He was gone. He left me without a word. Just fucked me and left. "I'm sorry," I said, tears spilling over before I dashed them away. "How's Celeste?" I asked, changing the subject. "I feel so bad I didn't check on her yesterday." Though it had been a week since her first episode, Celeste had been plagued with bouts of illness over the last few days. I'd always made a point to check on her even though Wrath had her well in hand. Yesterday I'd completely forgotten.

"You think Wrath isn't taking care of her? He is. He's pampering her nicely. And she knows you care. She also knows you're busy with Christmas and upset over El Diablo's swift departure."

"Did she go see Fury?"

"Oh, yeah. That wasn't even up for discussion." Esther grinned. "Turns out there's a very good reason for her illness. You know, the one that seems to happen mostly in the morning?"

My eyes widened. "She's pregnant?"

"Uh-huh! Isn't it exciting?" Esther rubbed her own little baby bump.

Then El Diablo's words came back to me. *If I breed you, so be it.* Fuck him.

"Well, I need to get back to work. I kind of feel like Sisyphus," I sighed.

"Go rest," Esther said again. "No work for you tonight."

"You know," I said, tears welling again. "I loved him. I loved him so much." I dissolved into tears. Esther moved to put her arms around me, trying to comfort me when there was really nothing she could do.

"I know you did, honey. Men are dicks at the best of times. Just don't give up on him yet. I swear to you he's not a bad person. I think maybe he has demons in his past regarding women. I have no idea what, but no man gets to be as protective as he is without a reason." She stroked my hair and held me tightly until I got myself under control.

But it was impossible. Today was just the last bit of pressure the dam holding back my emotions could take. Esther helped me to stand and walked me back inside. We had to go through the great room before heading to the suite I shared with El Diablo. I no longer thought of him as Liam. Liam might have been a little rough around the edges sometimes, but he was kind. El Diablo was not.

When we entered the room, the club girls were out in force… and all congregated around El Diablo. All of them were vying for a position close to him, hanging off him. One caressed one cheek while she kissed the other. I couldn't really process him. His face or any emotions. It was like my mind knew I couldn't handle it if he was smiling down at them in welcome and just blurred the image so I couldn't see.

I stopped dead in my tracks, my ire building once again. Tears still flowed freely, but I knew I was getting ready to lose my shit and hit someone. Who I hit depended on which bitch got between me and El Diablo. How hard I hit him depended on how many club girls I had to beat off him.

Either I shrugged Esther off or she let go of me, because I left her behind and marched ever faster in El Diablo's direction.

"You fucking son of a bitch," I shouted. At first,

the girls ignored me, clinging to him adoringly. The men, however, covered smiles or cleared their throats.

Samson, the bastard, started moving club girls away and said, "Uh, boss, you might, uh, want to, uh…" He nodded in my direction.

El Diablo's gaze found mine. I still couldn't process the look on his face and couldn't make myself focus and try to see him.

The first club girl I reached, I shoved backward. Hard. She looked startled, then angry, but was gone soon after. I think one of the men snagged her, but I wasn't sure. The second one I came to, I snagged by the hair and yanked her backward. She fell on her ass with a startled cry. After that, most of them either moved away on their own or were snagged by one of the men surrounding El Diablo.

The one kissing him -- or trying to, as he seemed to be trying to set her aside, turning his face this way and that to avoid her -- clung tightly, not being shaken off by either one of the patched members or El Diablo himself. When I reached her, I gripped one pierced nipple, clearly outlined by her thin T-shirt, between my thumb and forefinger, twisting hard and pulling her away. "Get off him or I'm taking this barbell with me, you little cunt. Possibly your nipple with it."

I thought I heard some snickers, but a quick glance around showed everyone studiously looking someplace else. The woman -- fucking Goldie again -- looked like she was in agony as she let go of El Diablo. I don't think she made a conscious decision to let go. I think it was the shock factor of the pain in her tit.

When I let go, she struck out at me, going for a slap. I jerked back, but she still managed to catch part of my cheek. Which was when I lost my whole damned mind.

Chapter Nine
El Diablo

Jezebel launched herself at Goldie. The other woman was taller, but she wasn't as scrappy. I knew from experience my beautiful Jezebel could pack a punch. She tackled Goldie to the floor and just started to whale on her.

I let it go probably longer than I should have, but Jezebel was the one dishing out the beating, and Goldie knew better and deserved everything she got. When I finally pulled Jezebel off the other woman, she started on me.

"You bastard!" she screamed. "You fucking bastard!"

"I know, honey. I was a complete bastard, leaving you like that."

"Why?" She sobbed, the tears hurting me more than the slaps she rained down on my face. "Why? I gave you everything! I told you I wouldn't cling after it was over, but you said I was yours forever!

"I know, baby. I know. I have no excuses for you. I would have still gone, but I should have explained where I was going and why."

"And you never stopped that fucking Christmas Bandit and the Christmas Eve party is tomorrow, and we have no decorations! And the presents are all fucking gone! There were hundreds! What am I gonna tell the children?" She sounded even angrier about that than my treatment of her. "Then you come in here and, again, I find club girls all fucking over you! I'd blame them, but you never gave them any indication you were off-limits! So the only thing I can assume is that you expect me to stay with you while you're with other women! And I'm telling you right now, that ain't happening!"

"No, it's not, baby. I'm yours, and you're mine. No one else for either of us."

"Like hell! Stick a fork in me, cause I'm *done*!"

She started struggling again, this time kicking even more viciously than she had the day I met her. Having learned that lesson, I hefted her over my shoulder and swatted her ass. Which felt so right I nearly sighed.

"Put me down, asshole! You don't get to go all caveman on me! I told you we're done!"

Repeating her words, I muttered, "Like hell." Then took my time walking across the room. I took my time because I needed her to settle down so I could explain something to everyone. When she stopped struggling and just sobbed, I let her down only to scoop her back up in my arms bridal style. As I walked I tried my best to soothe her. "Don't worry, my beautiful Jezebel. Christmas will be saved because once I have you settled, if the Christmas Bandit hasn't put back up every single decoration, every single tree, every piece of tinsel and garland, and have this place lit up like the fucking Griswolds', I will flay said Christmas Bandit alive."

She was quiet on the way to our room, just sobbing softly into my chest. At least she clung to me now instead of pushing me away. When I took her straight to our room and laid her on the bed, she stiffened and rolled away.

"No," she said in a shaky voice. "I'm not letting you seduce me into forgiving you. I couldn't live with myself."

"Then let me tell you what I've been doing. Hmm?"

Surprisingly, she looked back at me, a curious

expression on her face. "Say that again," she demanded.

"Say why, my dear?"

"The sentence you just said."

Confused, I repeated myself, hoping I got the sentence right. "Let me tell you what I've been doing."

She sat up and crossed her legs tailor fashion, her brows knitting together. "OK."

I opened my mouth to start my confession but stopped. "Wait. Why did you want me to say that sentence again?"

She shrugged. "Because your accent changed."

I blinked. "I beg your pardon?"

"Your accent changed. When you're upset or angry or feeling any kind of sharp emotion, your accent changes from that smooth English to a mix of something else. Middle Eastern? Hispanic? It's hard to tell."

That surprised me. "You noticed that?"

"Well, yeah. The first night we met, but when we have sex, too. And whenever you're upset about anything. It's subtle, but there."

I shook my head, chuckling. "You are truly my match, beautiful Jezebel. No one but you has ever noticed that, that I'm aware of. And Reaper would definitely let me know if I had a tell."

"I learned early in my life to notice little things. It's because I'm observant I was able to figure out how to circumvent Malcolm's security and leave the house at will."

I cleared my throat. I suppose that was as good a lead-in as I was going to get. "I need to talk to you about Malcolm, my love."

She winced at the "my love" part, but didn't say anything, just looked at her hands. "What about him?"

"He's dead."

Her gaze snapped to mine, her eyes wide. "He is?" Then her mouth opened in realization. "Oh," she said. "That's where you've been."

"Yes. I'd say I'm sorry, but it got him off your back permanently. Him and anyone thinking to use you as a pawn."

She stuck her chin up. "Tell me everything." It was a challenge, a direct test of what I'd told her before.

"Be sure you truly want to know, beautiful. Because I will tell you everything. In as much detail as you want. You're my woman. You remember what that means. Yes?"

"I do. Tell me everything."

So I did. Through the whole thing, she was stoic. Never interrupting. Never asking questions. When I was done, she reached for my hand.

"I'll never be able to repay you for that, Liam," she said softly. "Not only for the deed, but for the cost to you."

"Baby, it didn't cost me a damned thing. Getting rid of that scum was one of my greatest pleasures. It freed you, but it also severed my last tie to the Brotherhood. It got them out of my city, since Samuel was running this end of it. We're not sure, but we think Malcolm was the new head of the Brotherhood. If that's true, there will be a power struggle. One big enough that it might break them apart for good."

"So, Malcolm's dead." She took a breath and let it out. She still held my hand in hers. "Now what?"

I hesitated, then said, "I should say you're free to live your life. Shotgun got you a birth certificate and a social security number. You have a bank account with enough money to get started. I could have put more, but I didn't for the same reason I didn't want to say you were free to go." I tried to smile to take the sting out of my words, but I'm sure it didn't help.

"So, if you're not saying I can go, what are you saying?"

"That I want you to stay here. With me. For the rest of our lives."

With a sigh, she leaned in and kissed me. Something inside me finally settled. "I'll stay," she said. Then she laid a silencing finger on my mouth. "But only if you swear not to ever shut me out again. I realize you thought it was for my own good, but I'm stronger than you think. Just give me a warning if you think I might have issues, but don't shut me out. And never, ever leave me like you did ever again!"

"Never, beautiful Jezebel. Never again."

"When you left, then I didn't hear from you for a whole week, it was the most miserable I'd ever been in my whole life. Because I finally knew what it was like to have someone I truly cared about and you just... left me."

"I swear, precious. Never again. Never, never again." I'd swear to anything if it meant she'd give me another chance. And I meant every word, because that was what I'd have to do to keep her. She was a strong woman, one who could leave here and make it on her own without me in her life. I was the weak one. Because I'd never survive without her.

When I leaned in to kiss her, she stopped me, a genuine smile on her face. Without a word, she got up, my hand still in hers, and led me to the doorway. Pointing up, she said. "It's the only decoration I managed to keep the Bandit from stealing." On the door frame was a clump of mistletoe.

"Then since this is our first kiss as a committed

couple, it's only fitting we have it under the mistletoe." I wrapped her in my arms, bent my head and kissed her gently.

Try as I might, there was no way to keep it gentle. The second my lips touched hers, there was a gnawing need to take her and make her mine all over again. But I tried. I tried for her, because she deserved everything. After my treatment of her, the way I'd fucked her so savagely, then left her without a word of how I felt about her, she needed gentle. If she needed, I provided.

Until she bit my bottom lip.

"You're holding back on me, Liam," she accused. "Don't."

"I thought you might need gentle."

"I need *you*. If you're my gentle, caring Liam, great. If you're my rough, raw El Diablo, I'm right there with you, baby." She grabbed my T-shirt and dragged it over my head, exposing my bare chest to her. Leaning in, she took my nipple between her lips and sucked... before nipping it sharply.

"Little wench," I growled before kissing her once again. This time, I swept my tongue inside her mouth, taking what I desperately wanted. Her nails bit into my shoulders as I made short work of her clothing. Then she hiked her leg over my hip. I couldn't get my pants unbuttoned fast enough, the leather not giving an inch when my dick was growing thicker by the second.

With a grunt, I finally managed to free my cock. Jezebel immediately found it with her soft palm and stroked firmly.

"I want you inside me, El Diablo," she said. Rarely did she call me that. I was beginning to learn that when she did, she was either in need of a hard fucking, or I was being an asshole. Naturally, I was hoping to shit it was the former. "Right fucking now!"

I stroked my fingers between her legs, shoving two fingers inside her. "So hot and slick. You want me to fuck you under the mistletoe, too?"

"Right here. Right now," she confirmed.

I pressed her against the doorframe and lifted so she wrapped both legs around my waist. Finding her wet little cunt was second nature, and I slid home with little effort. I groaned, savoring the feel of her tight little quim milking me already. She cried out, biting down on my neck.

"That's it, baby," I growled. "Mark your man. Mark me so none of those bitches ever come near me again."

She did. This time, I cried out in pain, but the gesture only made my cock throb more, and before I had a chance to process, I was doing everything I could muster to not come in her yet.

"AH!" I yelled, then swatted her ass and pressed her against the frame harder. "Beautiful little bitch," I bit out. "I'll take your punishment as well as your mark." I started moving, found a rhythm, then pounded into her as hard as I could.

"That's it!" she screamed. "Give it to me! Fuck me hard!"

"I'll fuck you hard." My snarl was animalistic. How the fuck did she have me going from a reasoning man to a raging animal in the blink of an eye? "I'll fuck you till you scream!"

She did, her orgasm triggering my own. I thought I had myself under control, but fuck if she didn't make me lose my Goddamned mind! Jet after jet of hot cum exploded inside her. As her muscles milked my cock, I truly thought she might strangle it to death. She milked every ounce of cum from me, taking it into her greedy body. It seemed to settle her, because she sighed and rested her head on my shoulder, kissing the bite mark I knew she'd left there.

"Fuuuuuck," I groaned. She giggled, settling against me.

I carried her to the bathroom and cleaned us both, stepping out of my pants before carrying her to the bed. Once we were cuddled together, I turned her face up to mine and kissed her gently.

"I love you, Jezebel. I think I have from the moment I first saw you."

"I love you, too," she smiled. "Even if you're an unthinking asshole sometimes. Amazing that a man so in control can lose it so catastrophically." She giggled.

"Brat," I said, kissing her again. "Where you're concerned, I suppose I do. I can't promise I won't lose it ever again, but I can promise to never shut you out again."

She shrugged. "As long as it's not you stomping off and staying gone for a week, I kind of like it when you lose your shit. Mainly because the sex is spectacular."

"I've created a monster."

"Maybe," she said with a yawn. "But I'm *your* monster."

"That you are, beautiful Jezebel. That you are."

* * *

Jezebel

The Christmas Eve party was a tacky, gaudy, commercialized, magical fairy tale. The Christmas Bandit hadn't been caught but every single decoration and present he'd stolen had been returned and then some. When the buses began arriving with the children, I was nearly as excited as they were when they got a look at the front part of the compound. They were only given access to the great room and courtyard but the whole compound was lit up. Just like the Griswolds.

"You ready, my sexy little Elf?"

Liam was doing Santa. I'd wanted to be Mrs. Claus, but he'd said he thought Santa's personal Elf would be better. Next year, he promised, I could be Mrs. Claus.

"Absolutely!" I was practically bouncing with excitement.

Children and puppies were everywhere. Again, there seemed to be several more Saint Bernard puppies than there should have been. The club girls were on their best behavior around me, and the ones who'd caused the trouble in the first place had all apologized. Well, all but Goldie. Apparently, I nearly did rip her nipple off. Oh well. Sorry, not sorry.

The guys helped with the presents and occasionally snuck kisses under the mistletoe from some of the women. Holly, the little hellion, had managed to put something in Jax's shampoo and turned his hair red. Like bright, Christmas red. He tried to hide it under a hat, but Holly just snuck up behind him and jerked it off, running away with a giggle. Jax stomped off angrily, but I caught the way his lips turned up briefly at the corners. All in all, everyone was well-behaved. Everyone ate and had a great time.

When it came time for the kids to get their picture taken with Santa and tell him what they wanted for Christmas, Liam was *the best*. He listened intently to every single child. Once they'd finished, he gave them their gift. Always, it was exactly what the child had asked for.

"How'd you do that?" I asked when we were nearly done.

"I'm Santa, my beautiful little Elf. Granter of Christmas wishes."

"I hear there was a trust fund set up for every single child here. You wouldn't know anything about that, would you?"

He gave me a wide-eyed, innocent look. "Why is it you just assume it's me? Could have been anyone," he said, his English accent somehow more pronounced than usual. "Someone really rich must have thought they deserved a chance at higher education if they wanted it. Or a chance to start out life with a little nest egg. It would take someone with money to burn to be able to pull that off."

"Uh-huh. Or someone who just eliminated the biggest crime syndicate in the region."

"Well, there is that. Shotgun might have stumbled onto some private accounts with ties to a club we'd recently... encouraged to leave the state. If that money happened to fund something good, well, who am I to judge?" he said with a shrug.

"Christmas wishes," I said.

"Christmas wishes."

"Fine. What about my Christmas wish?" I asked cheekily.

"Don't you worry your pretty little head about that. Santa has your present. If you're good the rest of the night, I'll give it to you." He winked at me with a wicked smile, and I had to wonder how the hell I was gonna make it through to the end of the night.

"Last one," Samson murmured as he led a little girl to Santa. She looked to be about four, with pale skin and curly dark hair as black as a raven's wing. When the lights shone down on her little head, I could see blue highlights gleaming in all that dark hair.

She stood next to Santa shyly before finally crawling up in his lap and promptly sticking her thumb in her mouth. The child was obviously nervous but determined to go through with this.

I stroked my hand down her gleaming locks, trying to soothe her. "Don't be shy. What's your name, sweetheart?" I asked.

She took her thumb from her mouth. "Dawn," she said softly. Her hand went to her dress, and she twisted the material nervously.

"Well, Dawn," I said, smiling as I knelt in front of her and Liam. "What do you want for Christmas?"

For a long moment, I wasn't sure she was going to say anything, then she looked around, like she expected someone to be listening. Then she motioned us closer before whispering. "I want a mommy and daddy."

I thought my heart would break in two right there. Some of these kids were dirt poor. Others were orphans or wards of the state. I wanted to give them all good homes and good places to live with parents who loved and cherished them for the treasures they were. But I couldn't. Even for this one little girl, it was the one gift I couldn't give.

"I see," Santa/Liam said. "What about a computer or a puppy?"

She sighed, then shrugged. "That'd be OK, I guess." Then she slid down and trudged to the Christmas tree and sat under it, picked up a rag doll and a tattered blanket and started playing with them, wrapping the doll in the blanket and cradling it like she was the mommy and the doll her child.

Liam motioned to Wrath, a lawyer and an assistant DA in Palm Beach. When the big man was close enough, Liam said quietly, "I want that girl." He pointed at Dawn sitting in the corner under the tree. "Run the process through as quickly as you can and make it final. Do whatever you have to do, but I want that child here permanently tomorrow. She wants a mommy and a daddy, and I'm giving it to her. She'll be mine and Mrs. Claus's."

My mouth fell open. Then I snapped it shut. "You don't have a Mrs. Claus," I said dryly. "You have a personal Elf."

Liam chuckled, pulling me into his arms and dancing to Silver Bells as it played over the speakers.

"I do have a personal Elf. And she's beautiful."

"Yeah, well, a personal Elf ain't a Mrs. Claus."

"And that's something I intend to remedy." Stepping away slightly from me, he went to one knee. My heart nearly stopped beating, and my hands flew to my mouth. "My beautiful Jezebel, my little Elf, will you do me the greatest honor of being my Mrs. Claus, my beautiful wife?"

In his hand was a tiny box. When he opened it, there was the most beautiful ring I'd ever seen. It was a deep blue stone, maybe two carats, in a ring of diamonds in a platinum setting. When I just gaped at him, he took the ring from the box and gently took my hand in his, slipping the ring onto my finger.

"Oh my… is that… sapphire?"

"No, my beautiful Jezebel. Only diamonds will do for you."

"What?" I felt the blood drain from my face. I'd watched a lot of TV. That included educational stuff on Discovery and other channels. One thing I knew was that colored diamonds were rare. The rarest were red. Right behind red was blue. The ring he'd just given me was worth a fortune. I tried to take it off, but he stayed my hand, giving me a stern look.

"You'll not take that ring off, Jezebel." His words were harsh, but I could see the hurt in his eyes.

"I'm not rejecting you, Liam. Just… the ring. It's too much! I could probably buy a house for what this cost!"

"And a nice house at that. But, baby, that ring is nothing compared to your worth to me. I only wanted to get something for you that at least came close to your beauty." He gestured at the ring on my finger. "That at least comes closer than anything else I found, though it still isn't nearly enough."

I sighed like a sap. How could a girl say no to that? "Fine," I said, rolling my eyes to try to keep from crying. "I'll marry you."

No sooner had I gotten the words out than the whole place cheered. Liam stood and lifted me into his arms, then lifted me into the air and swung me around. He gave me a gentle but lingering kiss as we continued our dance along with everyone else.

"I love you so much," I said, batting away one errant tear of happiness.

"I love you too, my beautiful, beautiful Jezebel."

After the music stopped and another song began, Liam took my hand and guided me to the corner next to the tree where little Dawn sat. We sat with her and talked with her a while. She was shy, but quickly warmed to us.

This is going to be my daughter, I thought. *Our daughter*. Was it something we should have talked about first? Oh, most definitely. But this was Liam. El Diablo. We hadn't been together that long, but he knew me, just like I knew him. He knew I had it within my heart to love a little girl in need of loving. If that meant he had me tied to him with this one more tie, so be it. It wasn't like I would ever willingly leave him.

As if sensing my thoughts, Liam looked at me and winked.

Then we continued our discussion with Dawn. Tomorrow, her life would change. Mine already had. And I was so much better for it. Liam might also be El Diablo, but he wasn't the Devil. He was my angel. And always would be.

El Segador (Black Reign MC 8)
Marteeka Karland

Swan: I'm barely in my twenties, but I'm dying. Bone cancer. The treatment could be worse than the cancer itself. When my mom died shortly after my diagnosis, I made a bucket list and started working on it. All was going well until a big, tattooed guy found me on the beach. Well, the kid and the huge dog found me first, but… semantics.

El Segador: They call me The Reaper. I've lived my entire adult life in the shadows so I could be the deadliest asset El Diablo has. Together we've brought death to more men than I can count. But then I meet *her*. Swan. I may be a sucker for a woman in trouble, but I'm not stupid. There's no way her real name is *Swan Lake*. Except, apparently, it is. When she tells me about her bucket list, I'm in. Now, I'm thrust into the light with Swan at my side going to… romantic dinners? My only goal is to clear her bucket list before it's too late. But what if one item on that list is to fall in love?

Chapter One
Swan

I woke up to the music of seagulls and crashing waves on the morning tide. A fresh, warm breeze came off the ocean, caressing my skin with a fine saltwater mist. The sun was just peeking on the horizon in beautiful pinks and blues as clouds wafted lazily just in front of the rising ball of fire. How had I gone twenty years without witnessing something so spectacular? For my first morning in Lake Worth, this wasn't turning out to be as awful as I thought it would.

Stretching in my nest of quilts in the white sand, I gave a contented groan. Yeah. If my life was going to be cut short, I was going to live what time I did have to the fullest.

Bucket list check: Wake up on the beach to see the sunrise.

A little beach house currently sitting empty was only fifty yards or so away. I could have slept on one of the lounge chairs, but the sand had been so warm from the day's heat, once it was dark out, I couldn't resist. The warmth spread through my nest, and the sensations were just magical. Now. I just hoped I hadn't picked up any sand crabs or other creepy crawlies. Surprisingly, I wasn't too stiff. My thigh still ached, but nothing more than usual. The more I walked, the more it hurt. But I knew my walking days were numbered anyway, so I was determined to push myself until the leg just wouldn't hold me anymore.

I sat with my arms crossed over my bent knees, a smile on my face and the wind in my hair. Time for another adventure today.

No sooner had the thought entered my head than I was tackled by the biggest, slobberiest, hairiest dog

I'd ever seen. My squeal of surprise quickly turned to giggles as the dog licked my face like it had found a long-lost friend. It was long-haired but well groomed. A big red collar was buried in all that hair.

"Where'd you come from, huh? You lost?"

In answer, the pooch licked my face again. I struggled to sit up with the weight of the big brute pressing me down. Once I did, the lovable giant plopped down across my legs, effectively pinning me in place.

"You know this ain't gonna work. Right?" I ruffed up his ears, and he closed his eyes in bliss. "I got shit to do today." I thought for a minute. "Though I've never met a Saint Bernard before. Maybe that could be one of my bucket list completions.

"Bucket list check: Get licked nearly to death by a Saint Bernard puppy." I laughed as the dog looked up at me as if I were his best friend. "I'd say that's just as important an experience as anything else." I continued to scrub his ears, and he continued to behave as if he were living his best life.

"Bruno!" A girl about six or seven. She had short, curly blonde hair and wore pink shorts and a white shirt with the word "Maddog" emblazoned in a bold, pink font across the front. "You're not supposed to be on the beach! What are you doing?"

I waved a little sheepishly at the girl. "I'm sorry. I didn't invite him over, but he seems to have made himself at home."

"Yeah. He does that. Of all the dogs at home, he's the neediest. If he doesn't get petted, he runs off to find someone who can devote all their time to him." The girl was tiny in comparison to the dog, but she walked up to him and snapped a leash onto his collar. The dog whined and laid his head down, obviously pouting.

"Really? Your name's Bruno and you're acting like this? You're almost as big a lame-o as Wrath started out being."

"Holly!" The bellow came from off in the distance in the same direction the girl had come from. It was male and didn't sound happy.

"Uh-oh," she said, wincing a little. "I'm gonna get it now."

I looked up to see a large man in running shorts, running shoes and nothing else jogging in our direction. He was huge! Muscles everywhere and a scowl on his face that almost looked like worry. But I couldn't be sure.

"He's not gonna hurt you, is he?"

"Him?" The girl, obviously Holly, hiked her thumb in his direction. "Nah. He's harmless. My mommy, on the other hand… yeah. I see a scolding in my future."

I took another look at the man as he got closer. Lord, the man was fine! Muscles. Tattoos. A short beard and shaggy hair… What's not to love? Maybe I needed to add "Have sex with a hot runner" to my bucket list.

"He belong to you?" I asked the girl, indicating the big guy headed in our direction. "Are you Holly?"

The girl sighed. "Yeah. But you can ignore him if you want. He tries to be all scary and stuff, but he never is. Me and Bella put pink glitter in his hair last week, and he just growled at us."

The man in question trotted next to us. He gave me a passing glance then dismissed me before speaking to Holly. "Your mother told you not to run off."

"I had to get Bruno. *He* ran off. Not me."

"You followed him. Which means you ran off."

The man scowled at the little girl. She should have been intimidated -- I know I was -- but she just shrugged.

"If I hadn't gone after Bruno, he'd probably have mauled my new friend here. Then I wouldn't have had a friend. That would be horrifying!" I wasn't certain if her not having a friend or me getting mauled was the horrifying bit.

"Right," the big guy said, shaking his head. "Well, you've got the mutt now. Let's get him and you back to the clubhouse. Your mom's worried, and you know Wrath doesn't like to see her upset." The word clubhouse caught my attention. Not many people used that term, and it was prickling my Spidey senses. I had a feeling this was a man I didn't need to be around. There were motorcycle clubs all over the area. Though no one really said negative things about them, weren't all MCs up to no good? At least, that was my perception. If this guy was a biker, though, he didn't quite fit my mold of dangerous person who'd kill me to death.

"Daddy Wrath doesn't like to see me upset either. Think how upset I'd be if my dog ran off, and my friend got mauled!"

The guy gave me a measured look. "Your friend, huh? What's her name?"

Holly glanced at me, obviously expecting an assist. The kid was good.

"I'm Swan," I said.

When I said nothing else, he raised an eyebrow. "Last name?"

I winced, dreading what was about to come next. "Lake."

"Swan Lake," he said. He sounded like he either didn't believe me or was struggling not to laugh.

Which got my back up.

"It's not my fault, you know. I didn't pick my name."

"Nothin' wrong with your name."

"Swan was just about to come back home with me for breakfast," Holly said. "She likes pancakes with lots of syrup."

"I see," the guy said. "Well. I guess I better put in an order with Archangel. He's cookin' breakfast for you and Bella."

"Oh, boy! He makes the best pancakes!" She handed the leash to the man and tugged my hand, trying to get me up. "Come on! You don't want to miss out!"

"Yeah, but I think I'm gonna have to pass. I appreciate the offer, Holly."

"You're not comin'?" Now Holly looked like she was on the verge of tears. I glanced at the man, and he gave me a hard look. Yeah. Not accepting her invitation was not an option.

"Well, maybe for just a little while, then." I smiled, trying to take the sting out of my earlier blunder. It must have worked because Holly jumped up and down.

"Yea!" She took my hand as I carefully got to my feet, lifting my backpack over my shoulder. Holly then tugged me along with her. I didn't know the guy's name, but I had the feeling I didn't want to know. I was pretty sure what I needed was to run. Fast. Except I wasn't sure I could run. My thigh, while not hurting a horrible amount, made the night on the ground known with every step. I was sure I limped at least a little.

Holly chatted all the way to our destination. Which I thought was a hotel instead of a "home" or a "clubhouse."

"Holy shit!" I gasped. "I thought you said this was a clubhouse."

The guy shrugged. "It is."

"Come on," Holly said, tugging me harder. "We're gonna be late for breakfast!" She frowned. "If that asshole, Jax, gets there before we do, he'll eat everything."

"Language, Holly. You know your mother doesn't like it when you call Jax an asshole."

"Well, he is," she groused prettily. The guy chuckled and winked at the child.

Holly led me through one building across an open area in the center of the place to another building. There seemed to be a whole herd of Saint Bernard puppies, and they'd missed their buddy. Before I could get inside, I was surrounded by at least five of the beasts. They didn't jump or knock me down, but they were in the way, not allowing me inside without pushing my way through them.

"Off with all'a'ya," the man said, waving his hands and shooing them all away. Surprisingly, all but Bruno obeyed him, bounding off to get into their own mischief. Bruno leaned against me, looking up as if to say, "Please pet me, Mommy." I did.

"You too, Bruno." The dog whined and hung his head, but he slinked off, tail between his legs like he'd been kicked, to lie down beside the door. "Come on," the guy said, grabbing my arm, and guiding me inside.

"Wait!" Before he could push me any farther into the interior, I had to know his freaking name.

"You never told me your name."

"Holly didn't tell you?" He looked amused. "I mean, since you're friends and all."

"Hey, she said that. Not me. Cute kid, though. Nice dog."

He chuckled. "Likely, she thought your presence would keep her out of the trouble she's in with her mother and father." He stuck out his hand. "I'm El Segador. Most everyone calls me Reaper."

Oh. Fuck. I was in so much trouble...

"Well, that's not intimidating or anything." The statement slipped out before I could stop myself.

Reaper chuckled. "It's just a name, Swan. I didn't choose mine either."

That caught me off guard. "You didn't. Who did?"

"Not really sure." He'd paused and got a puzzled look on his face. "I've had that name as long as I can remember."

"Well, I'm not sure it suits you. You don't look like a Reaper."

Instantly, his mein changed. "Looks can be deceivin', girl."

He probably meant to look and sound dangerous, but he just looked... hot. Intense. Wow.

"Need to add to my bucket list," I muttered. That entry would be "Fuck a biker."

"Bucket list?" He looked like he'd never heard of bucket lists.

"Yeah. You know. A list of stuff I want to do before I die."

"Ah. I see. Well, I have no idea what you're putting on that list, but I'm sure you'll have plenty of time to get it done."

Right. If only. "Yeah. So, are we eating?" I wanted to change the subject. I didn't like to think about it, but I knew it wouldn't be long before I would be limited in what I could do and what I had to give up on. Which was why I was getting as much traveling done as I could now.

"Of course." Reaper ushered me inside the kitchen. Instead of a big dining table, there was a little breakfast nook and a long, island bar. The adults gathered around the bar while the children sat at the table, happily chatting away while they drowned their pancakes in syrup.

"Smells great!" I grinned as I entered. "Is that sausage, too?"

"Yep." The guy manning the pancake griddle grinned at me over his shoulder. "Pancakes and sausage. Just a little bit of syrup." He grinned as he held his thumb and finger an inch apart as he glanced at the kids. "I'm Archangel."

"Swan," I said. Then grinned. "Yeah. Have a few pancakes with the syrup, huh?"

"You got it, darlin'." The man was charming, and I found myself blushing at his attention. Which meant there were two guys giving me palpitations. Yeah. Definitely needed to add "Fuck a biker" to my list.

"Watch it, Angel," Reaper snapped.

The other man just laughed. "You keep that one in line, darlin'. He can be a tad cranky when he's bored."

"Might have to help with that bucket list of yours," Reaper said as he handed me a plate and proceeded to pile on the pancakes.

"Stop!" I laughed as he put a fourth cake on the stack. "No way I can eat that much!'

"You're gonna try," he said firmly, giving me a dark look.

"Sorry, big guy." I started putting pancakes back on the platter. "Two is plenty. After that I just get a sugar rush from the syrup."

As I was pulling my plate back, he tossed on three pieces of sausage. When I gave him an exasperated sigh, he raised an eyebrow. "It will counteract the sugar."

"I can't eat all this."

"When was the last time you ate a complete meal?"

"Hum… Define complete…"

"Something not out of a vending machine." He crossed those tattooed arms over his brawny chest. And really, why had he put on a shirt in the first place? A body like that should be naked. At all times. If he was, I could just eat him up.

"Thinkin' that one's hungry for something not on my menu," Archangel said as he flipped another pancake.

"I -- what?" Shit. They'd caught me fantasizing about Reaper and called me out on it.

"If that's the kind of stuff you've got on that bucket list of yours," Reaper said, "I'll definitely be able to help you out." The bastard had a shit-eating grin on his face.

I ducked my head, concentrating on eating the food on my plate. It was way more than I was used to eating in one sitting. Maybe I ate that much throughout the whole day, but I doubted it. I just wasn't hungry most days. Mainly, it was that, if I stopped to eat, it meant thinking about my situation. When I did, I lost my appetite and got depressed.

"Aww, didn't mean to embarrass you, darlin'."

"You didn't." When he snorted, I amended. "At least, not much. Anyway, if I ogle a guy that hard, I deserve to get called out."

"I'm just sayin' if you want to add me to your bucket list, I'm willing to make the sacrifice."

My head snapped up so I could look at him then. "Sacrifice?"

"Well, yeah. I mean, it's hard on a man my age to naked wrestle with a girl your age. But I'm willing to sacrifice my body for your cause."

God, I wish I'd had more experience with men. I had no idea how to take this guy. Was he making fun of me or was he sincere?

"I think maybe it's time I go," I said as I laid the fork in my plate. "I have a lot to get done today."

"You're going?" Holly turned from where she was eating at the table with the other kids. "But you just got here!"

"I know, sweetie, but I really do need to get back."

Holly looked puzzled and scrunched her nose. "To the beach? Or were you living in that house next to where you were sleeping?"

I started to answer no, but thought better of it when I saw Reaper. His gaze was glued to me, as if my answer were extremely important to him. "I like to walk the beach in the morning. Bit later than I usually go, but I like combing the beach for seashells."

"Oh, boy!" Holly said. "We can go with you! I know where there's a perfect spot for getting seashells," the girl said with enthusiasm. "No one gets to pick 'em up but us!"

Reaper grinned. It wasn't a reassuring sight. He looked like he was ready to eat me up. And I wasn't all that broken up about it. "Yeah. I can take you to the stretch of beach Bane owns. Samson!" He called out the name loudly. I didn't see anyone else, but there must have been someone close by. A moment later, a bald man with tattoos creeping up the sides of his neck walked in with a smiling woman. She had her arms wrapped around his waist as they walked side by side. He dropped a gentle kiss on top of her head before answering Reaper.

"Yeah?"

"Give Havoc a call. See if Thorn'd mind if we used the beach this morning."

Samson nodded. "I can do that. Anything special in mind?"

"Yeah," Holly said, bouncing up and down in her chair. "Me and Swan're gonna hunt for seashells!"

Samson glanced at Reaper in confusion, then his gaze landed on me. "Swan, huh? Where'd she come from?"

"She came from the land of It's None of Your Business," I said sweetly, my smile firmly in place. "And she doesn't like to be talked about like she's not here."

Archangel barked out a laugh while Reaper grinned, dropping his arm over my shoulder.

"Lottie, did you not teach your man there any manners?"

The woman with Samson laughed, burying her face in his chest. "Well, I tried. Obviously, it didn't take."

"Look, I appreciate you making me feel welcome and all, and thank you, Holly, for inviting me over for breakfast, but I really do need to get going." Because I could really see myself falling for this entire club. They didn't seem like anything I'd ever thought about when I envisioned biker clubs. The people I'd met so far were friendly and open. Maybe the guys flirted a little too much, but I couldn't honestly say I hadn't enjoyed the banter.

"You can go after we find the perfect seashell," Holly said, getting up from her place at the table and throwing herself into my arms. "Me and you and Bella are all gonna be best friends!"

My heart melted. If it hadn't been for Holly, I'd have brushed everyone off, waved a jaunty goodbye, and left without remorse. But I just couldn't. There was something about the little girl that tugged at my heartstrings. She had the look of someone who'd seen a lot in her young life. Maybe I recognized something of myself in her. Whatever the reason, I found myself hugging her back and agreeing to stay.

"Fine," I said. "But only until we find the perfect seashell."

"Hooray!" she whooped. "I'll go get Bella. Better wear your swimsuit under your clothes," she said. "We can play in the water while we look for shells."

The girl hurried off. I smiled after her and, before I realized what was happening, I was surrounded by several of the big men. They didn't get close enough to intimidate me, but it was clear they wanted answers.

"How long you known Holly?" Samson said. Lottie had moved to the bar to grab her own pancakes while Archangel joined the men in grilling me.

"I just met her before I came here." I glanced up at Reaper. "I got the impression she thought she was in trouble. Probably thought to use me as a diversion."

"That's right," Reaper said to Samson. "I came on them both together when Celeste realized the little imp was missing."

"You here to spy on us?" Again, Samson asked the question. It wasn't cruel or accusing, just a bit abrasive.

"Spy? Why in the world would I do that? No. I'm not spying." I backed a couple steps away from everyone, only to back up against Reaper. I jumped and turned abruptly stumbling and falling against him. His arms closed around me automatically. Grinning down at me, he tightened his hold on me and didn't immediately let me go.

"Relax, honey. We're not accusing."

"Sure sounded like it."

"Samson's just overprotective. He's our vice president and takes his job very seriously.

"Well, I'm not a spy. If you're going to let me go with Holly to the beach, I need to change. If not? You get to tell Holly why. That kid has a story I don't need to know, but I'm not gonna be the one to break her heart."

That got me more than one raised eyebrow and several grins.

"She's all right," Archangel said. "Back off her, Samson." Archangel smiled at the other man, but I could see he meant business.

"Fine," he said, pointing a finger at me. "But I'll be keeping an eye on you. Anything funny turns up, and I will confront you about it. No matter how many of these pussies you've managed to charm." His words were gruff, but he winked at me, and I thought that might just be his personality. But honestly, I didn't blame him. I *did* have secrets, and I was a stranger chatting it up with one of their children. I'd be suspicious of me too.

"All right, all right," Reaper said, chuckling. "Back off the girl. Surely to God we can handle one little female."

"Uh-huh. Like Shadow was able to handle Millie? Venus even said the girl could kick his ass. Hell, Shadow even admitted it. You sure this lil' bit ain't got Millie's mad skills going on?" Archangel smirked.

"Well, no," Reaper admitted. "But, honestly. How many women like that could we be unlucky enough to run into?"

"I'm not sure I like that remark," I said, needing to butt in on behalf of all womankind.

"No?" Samson said, raising an eyebrow. "Kick his ass. Prove to me why I need to make him keep you around."

"No one said I wanted to stay around. And I'm sure I'm not capable of kicking anyone's ass, let alone someone as freakishly huge as Reaper. I'm here because Holly asked me to come for breakfast, likely as a deflection on her getting in trouble for running off. Breakfast is done." I shrugged. "I'm happy to leave."

"Like bloody hell," Reaper muttered. Then he cleared his throat, glancing at the other men around us. "Holly wouldn't like it."

Samson barked out a laugh while Archangel snickered openly. "Callin' bullshit on that one, brother. El Diablo know 'bout this?"

Reaper shrugged. "Not his business at this point. Later? We'll see."

"OK," I said, trying to put some distance between me and the men in the room. "You guys are starting to make me feel unsafe. I'm leaving."

"Who's making you feel unsafe, my dear?" The masculine, accented voice from behind me made me gasp and whirl around. He was dressed impeccably, even in casual clothing. The woman at his side was just as elegant, but in a different way. She looked like she had it in her to be as hard as the guys surrounding me, but it wasn't her default setting.

"All of them," I blurted out. "They're crowding me."

"Back off," the man said in a hard voice. "We don't intimidate innocent women, and we don't gang up on them for any reason."

Samson raised his hands and backed away. "Just

testin' her out for El Segador, boss. Won't happen again."

"Well?" the boss man asked.

Samson smirked. "She passed."

"You're all crazy," I said, trying to find a hole to slip through. "I'll just be going now."

"You know you promised Holly," Reaper said.

"And you tested me for what reason?" I wanted to let that slide but found I just couldn't. The nerve of these guys!

"Not a thing," Reaper said, glaring at Samson. He reached for my hand. For some stupid reason I let him have it. I wasn't exactly telling the truth that I felt unsafe. Yeah, they made me nervous -- especially Samson -- but Reaper, despite his scary name, had been nothing but nice to me. And he did seem to have Holly's well-being in mind. He'd seemed almost panicked when he'd been looking for her earlier. "Let's go. I'll take you to a room where you can change and leave your things until you're ready to go. If it's late enough, you might want to consider staying. Jez is cooking tonight so you'd be in for a treat." Reaper glanced back at the woman at "Boss's" side.

"Jez?"

"Yeah," she said with a cocky grin. "Short for Jezebel." The woman managed to look vulnerable and proud all at the same time. I was sure the man at her side was her man. I was equally sure she'd seen this scenario play out many times before, to the detriment of anyone making fun of her name.

"Well, considering my first name's Swan and my last name is Lake? Yeah. I ain't making a comment about your name."

Jezebel laughed and lunged for me, bringing me in for a hug. I was so startled I hugged her back. "You and I are gonna be great friends." She pulled me out of Reaper's grasp as easily as if we were already best friends. "Come on. I'll set you up with a space next to Liam and me."

"Liam?"

"Yeah." She hiked a finger over her shoulder at the sophisticated man behind her. "Liam. Only he goes by El Diablo so that's how most people know him. He's the president of Black Reign. I'm his ol' lady. His woman."

I blinked. "You actually use the term ol' lady?"

Jezabel shrugged. "The term is before my time. As long as it means the club girls know he's taken, I could give a shit what term they use."

"Just for the record," Liam said, moving in beside Jezebel, "I did ask her to marry me." He lifted her left hand, showing me a beautiful, very expensive-looking ring. "I'm only waiting because Celeste and the other women need time to pull together an appropriate wedding. Otherwise, I'd have had Archangel do the deed the first night we met."

Jezebel snorted loudly. "I wouldn't have had you that first night. And you were still riding the fence. Then there were the club girls I had to pull off you after you'd left me for two whole weeks without even saying goodbye. Or calling. At Christmas!" The more Jezebel lined out Liam's sins, the angrier she became.

Liam grinned. "So, maybe the second day."

"Oh! Come on, Swan. My advice? Stay away from all of them."

"Riiiight. I see that worked out so well for you."

She gave me an exasperated look. "Whose side you on, anyway?"

"I'm on the side that gets me out of here in one piece. They look like they're having too much fun baiting us both, and you look like you're eager to get your man in private so he can make up with you properly. So yeah. I'm on my own side."

"Think I might just fall in love with that one," Archangel said with a chuckle. "She's got brains and spunk."

"The hell you will," Reaper growled. I looked back over my shoulder, and Reaper followed me and Jezebel down the hall. When the other men laughed, he simply flipped them the bird and continued to follow.

Chapter Two
El Segador

Stick a fork in me. I was done. In all my years, never had I met a girl so beguiling. She had wit in the face of a scary situation, courage to stand up to all of us, and intelligence to know none of us would really hurt her. Otherwise, she'd have run screaming instead of allowing herself to be led off by Jezebel. She occasionally glanced back at me as I followed at a reasonable distance. When I winked at her, she blushed but gave me the grin I was hoping for. My ass Archangel was gonna fall in love. From this moment forward, Swan Lake was mine.

When they stepped inside the room next to El Diablo and Jezebel's, Jez gave me a superior smirk before closing the door firmly in my face. Yeah. I got it. No boys allowed. The thought made me chuckle. That was fine. Soon, I'd lure the lovely Swan into my room. Into my bed.

I waited patiently. It wasn't long before the women came out with laughter and smiles. Both had on shorts and bikini tops with flip-flops on their feet. Not that I noticed much past Swan's bare torso. She was covered, but still teased me with all the glorious skin she revealed. Creamy, delicious-looking, glorious skin. A bounty set before a starving man.

They passed me, both giggling softly like the joke was on me. Likely it was, though I didn't care. Swan was in my house now. With my club. Even in the short hour she'd been here, they all knew she was mine. That fucker Archangel had likely realized it the second we walked in.

Both women were gorgeous, but my gaze focused squarely on Swan's perfect, perfect ass. With every step forward, her hips swished. Was it my imagination, or could I see the curve of her cheek under her short shorts when her leg moved forward? I tilted my head for a better view. Yeah. I could see it. And the sight of it made my cock throb inside my jeans.

I followed them to the beach. Black Reign didn't have as large a section of beach as Salvation's Bane, but then it wasn't used for amphibious training. We just used it for fun. And I was looking forward to having fun now.

I reached the beach behind the girls a few moments before Wrath and Celeste arrived with Holly and Bella. Wrath spotted me and headed in my direction.

"What's going on?" Wrath indicated Swan. "Archangel says you're pussy-whipped, but I didn't believe him. Mainly because I'm pretty sure you ain't had the pussy yet."

"Unbelievable," I muttered.

"What? I'm just saying. Besides, ain't often the hard-ass of the club gets called out." Wrath looked entirely too smug.

"Good thing Holly's here or I'd kick your ass."

Wrath shrugged. "You could try. Seems to me you've got just as much to lose. I mean, maybe more. 'Cause Holly still thinks I'm kind of a lame-o. Swan? Well, she's still making up her mind."

"Asshole," I muttered. But I didn't have time to beat his ass right now. The girls were walking down the beach. Celeste had joined Jezebel and Swan and brought Bella with her. Rycks's and Lyric's daughter wasn't as exuberant as Holly, but she was close. Both girls showered Swan with attention, picking up and discarding seashells by the dozens.

Swan smiled and laughed with them. The carefree way she acted warmed my cold heart. Even through the playing and the laughter, though, there seemed to be something I was missing. Watching her closely, I tried to take her in completely. Well, past her obvious beauty. She was pale and a little skinny. It was more than the fact she was just thin, given the sharp way her cheekbones stood out from her face and the dark circles under her eyes. If I didn't know better, I'd say she was sick. Maybe she was recovering. It couldn't be that bad. She was out and about, playing on the beach. I squinted a little, realizing I'd nearly missed a slight limp. She seemed to be favoring her right leg. Not much. Just slightly.

"Hey, Reaper!" Holly called out. "You should see the seashell Swan found! It's the perfect seashell!"

Swan grinned at the child, ruffling her hair. Absently, she rubbed her hip. I noticed that, whenever she stood still, she put her weight on her left leg.

"I'm going for a swim," Swan called. "Don't wait up."

"Are you kidding?" Lyric said. "We can all go. I brought lifejackets for the girls."

Rycks and Wrath went to the women and helped them and the girls into their lifejackets. I noticed Swan didn't put one on and expected the other guys to say something. Instead, they just glanced at her with raised eyebrows but let her head to the water. When I met Rycks's gaze, he gave me an impatient look.

"Well?" he called. "You gonna do somethin' about that, dumbass?"

Swan was laughing as the waves crashed around her body. She was waist-deep and playing like a child. It almost made me smile. Until she went under briefly, knocked off her feet by a breaking wave as it crashed over her.

"Swan!" She resurfaced quickly enough but went under again a few seconds later. When she didn't immediately resurface, panic seized me. I never panicked. And why would I panic? This girl was nothing to me. A vagabond on the beach. Maybe it was that, by allowing Holly to invite her into the club for any reason, I felt responsible for her. But honestly, Swan had gotten under my skin in a very short amount of time. She was an enigma I couldn't figure out. I was drawn to her and had no idea why, exactly when it started, or how it happened.

I was in the water at the same time as Rycks. It couldn't have been more than a few moments. Just as I reached the spot where she'd gone under, she resurfaced a few feet away before going under again. Taking a deep breath, I dove under the waist-deep water. Her hand brushed over my outstretched arm, and I grabbed blindly for her. The silt and sand stirring up from the undertow and our movements made it difficult to see, but the second I had a firm grip on her, I pushed up the short distance to the surface. Rycks was right by my side, snagging her other arm until he was sure I had a solid hold on Swan so she couldn't be pulled away from me.

"Fuck!" I gasped for breath and wiped my hand over my eyes to clear the water. "Swan, are you OK?"

"I-I'm fine. Omigod! That was intense!"

"Intense? Are you fuckin' kiddin' me? You almost drowned!" I knew I sounded angry and probably scary, but I couldn't reign it in easily.

"Yeah," she said softly. She clung to my shoulders, looking up at me with wide eyes. "You saved me."

"Of course, I saved you! Rycks too! You think

we'd simply let you drown?"

"Well, if I had any doubt about what kind of people you guys are, it's been resolved. Thank you." Then she looked away a little wistfully.

I snagged her chin and turned her head back to face me. Looking into her eyes, I realized there was something there I never thought to see. Mixed with relief and gratitude, there was also a wistful kind of... resignation? Disappointment? That couldn't possibly be right.

"What's going on with you, girl?" My whispered question made her eyes go wide.

"Nothing," she said. Her voice was so soft I nearly didn't hear her.

"Don't lie to me," I said, gripping her shoulders. "You scared me nearly to death. I think I have a right to know what just went through your head. Because it wasn't only gratitude for us saving your life."

She sighed, closing her eyes and wincing slightly. "You only gave me a stay of execution," she muttered, still not meeting my gaze even though I'd all but forced her. "I don't want to die, Reaper. But it's inevitable."

"You're gonna have to explain what that means. It's inevitable we all die, honey. It's the circle of life and all."

She looked at me then. "That's right." She smiled then tried to pull away.

"Swan," I gave her what I hoped was a threatening look. In reality, it might have been a pleading one. I had to know what was going on. Not just because I'd decided she might just be mine, but because something was hurting her. And it was more than physical.

With an exasperated sigh, she took my hand and placed it high on her outer thigh near her hip. Even through her shorts I could feel a slight prominence. It was rounded and uneven. Not too large -- it probably wouldn't be readily visible unless you were looking for it.

"What's that?" My fingers traced the edges of it. It was hard. Not malleable. "Does it hurt?"

"Yes," she said, though she didn't push my hand away. I was careful as I continued to examine it with my fingers.

"What is it?"

"A tumor attached to my bone. The doctors called it a high-grade osteosarcoma. They took every image they could think of. Chemo had no effect, and it continued to grow."

"They try removin' it?"

She shook her head. "I wouldn't let them."

That struck me as odd. I'm sure I looked at her like she'd lost her mind. "Why the fuck not?" I know I sounded angry, but I couldn't help it. Here was a beautiful, young woman with some type of bone cancer, and she wasn't treating it as aggressively as she could?

"Because I don't want them removing my leg. They told me they thought my cancer would be classified as regional, which means it had already spread into the lymph nodes and surrounding areas. The survival rate was a little over fifty-fifty over five years, but they still weren't sure. As high up as it's located, they'd probably have to take part of my pelvis, too. Where does that leave me then? Will they go far enough I have a colostomy? Will I have a urinary catheter the rest of my life? Can I even have sex after that kind of surgery? I certainly wouldn't be able to have children." She shook her head. "If I'm going to die, it's gonna be on my own terms. I'm not spending the rest of my life feeling like a freak of nature. Something that lived that shouldn't have."

"Honey, do you know that's what will happen? Did the doctors tell you that?"

"They didn't have to, Reaper. I could see it in their eyes." Then she tilted her head to the side before chuckling. "That's pretty good." She continued to chuckle as she moved away from me toward the beach. I didn't let her out of my grasp, but followed her.

"What's pretty good?"

"Your name. Reaper." She looked back at me, meeting my gaze full on this time. "Perfect for a girl like me."

"Fuck," I swore, scrubbing my hand over my face. "Where are you staying, Swan?"

She shook her head. Once we were on the shore, she spread her hands wide. "Anywhere I fucking want. I slept on the beach last night. I woke up to see the sunrise. It was on my bucket list."

"That's right. You're marking things off your bucket list."

"I am. I'm not sure how much time I have, but my leg hurts worse every day. I'm trying to get to the stuff I'll need the full use of my legs for first. After that, I'll do the smaller stuff."

When she started away from me, I snagged her hand, continuing beside her. "Fine. Show me your list, and I'll help you."

"I -- what?" She looked up at me in confusion. "Help me?"

"Yeah," I said gruffly. "And one of those items on that fuckin' list better be to kiss a biker. Ain't doin' shit like this for nothing less."

She grinned. Then laughed, throwing herself into my arms. I wasn't fully prepared for the feel and smell of her. Though she'd just been thoroughly dunked in the ocean, she still smelled of sunshine and oranges. She pressed womanly curves against me, seemingly heedless of what it would do to a mere mortal male. Instantly, my cock sprang to life, and I wanted nothing more than to hook her leg around my hip so I could grind against her sex. With those skimpy shorts and what I was sure was a very small bikini bottom, I bet I could slip my cock inside her with little to no effort.

"That would be the best thing in the whole wide world!" She pulled back, a huge smile on her face. A smile I couldn't reconcile with such a young woman who'd just told me she was dying. "I've got a notebook filled with things. I'm sure some of it's impossible, but that's OK. I just want to do as much as I can."

"Honey, let me see the list when we get back to the club. Do you have it with you?"

"Everything I own is in my backpack. The notebook with my bucket list is in there."

"Let's go. I want to see it. We can start planning right away. Anything I can help you do here we will while the others see to any logistics we need for any traveling."

"The others?" She scrunched her nose as if not processing what I was saying.

"Yeah. Once they know the situation, they'll all want to pitch in. We'll do everything in our power to make it all happen. In the meantime, would you object to me getting a couple of our doctors on board?"

"You have doctors in your club?"

"We do. Fury is a doc, but I'm thinking more about a club in Palm Beach. There's a guy there called Doc. His name is Donovan Muse. He's board certified in pediatric oncology as well as emergency medicine. You're not exactly his specialty, but with his background in oncology, I'm sure he'd be helpful."

"I'm grateful for any help, as long as he understands I can't pay him. My mom had insurance on me up until she died. That was just a couple days after they made the tentative diagnosis, wanting to do more tests. The docs said it was broken-heart syndrome, and I believed them. My mom and I were pretty tight. I imagine my diagnosis was more than she could take." She took a breath, sighing. "Anyway, I had the remainder of the month on her insurance, and I told them to do what they could in that amount of time. After that, I'd have to reevaluate. I'm a college student just out of high school. Didn't have a job, and my prospects with a new diagnosis weren't great. I mean, who wants to hire someone they know is gonna be missing a lot right off the bat?"

"What about your dad? Can you get on his insurance?" I was grasping. Mostly wanting her to be comfortable with the plan, because now that I'd found her, I had no intention of giving her up so easily. Though my interaction with her had consisted of only a few hours, she was now thoroughly and completely sunk into my skin. I had no idea why. Maybe it was her attitude. Maybe it was the way she was with Holly and Bruno when I'd first come across them. Maybe it was just the beautiful fucking smile and contagious laughter. All I knew was this was the woman I wanted for my own. No matter how much time I had. But I was greedy for as much time as possible. If there was a way to help her, Doc would at least be able to tell me. Besides, she was right. My name was El Segador. The Reaper. I'd done some bad shit in my life, earning my name. It was only fitting she be given me as her protector and the person she went to for comfort during this period in her life. And I knew I was up to the fucking task.

"He left when I was a baby. I never knew him."

That made me grind my teeth. Why did men do that shit? "We'll figure something out. Besides, Doc won't care. I'm only thinking about if he thought there was an intervention less invasive than a radical surgery like you described."

"As long as it's not horribly unpleasant and doesn't make any extra time he buys me miserable. I realize it's gonna hurt. But I don't want to be constantly sick from the chemo or lose all my hair. I got lucky with the two rounds I did before. Probably because we stopped before going further, since the tumor was growing instead of stopping or shrinking."

"I hear you. Now. Tell me the truth. Does it hurt for you to walk on it?"

She sighed. "Sometimes. Like when I've been on it too much or when I've been in one position for too long."

"OK." I turned around. "Up you go. Piggyback ride." I bent over slightly at the waist and squatted.

"Piggyback ride?" She laughed but put her hands on my shoulders and hopped up. "I haven't done this since I was a kid." She continued to giggle as I approached the others.

"Everything OK?" Rycks asked as he stood up from where he was helping Bella and Holly sort seashells.

"Mostly," I said. "Need you to reach out to Salvation's Bane. I want to talk to Doc. Blade as well."

Rycks looked from me to Swan. "Anything Fury can help with?"

"Possibly. But Doc Muse will be the most qualified. Fury could give him a head start if he's not readily available, though."

"Sure," Rycks said. "I'll have him give you a call." He raised an eyebrow. "You guys headed back?"

"Yeah. We got some stuff to discuss. Also, I need to talk to El Diablo. We may need an all-hands effort soon. Got some plannin' to do."

"Well, that's not cryptic or anything." Rycks and Wrath both stepped closer. "What's goin' on?" Rycks glanced at Swan again. "Everything all right?"

I felt her shrug. "As all right as it can be, I suppose."

"I'll explain later," I said. "Just have Doc give me a call at his earliest convenience. We're headed back to the compound."

"Bye, Holly. Bella." Swan took one arm from around my neck and waved at the girls. "That was so much fun! We'll have to do it again."

Holly smiled. "That'll be fun! You find the best seashells!"

"What can I say? I'm a shell-finding expert."

The girls giggled and waved as we moved off. Swan laid her head on my shoulder and inhaled, her nose close to my neck.

"Don't be shy about it, girl." I chuckled. "Take what you want."

With a groan, she swiped her tongue up the side of my neck. "Mmmm," she moaned. "Been wanting to do that for a very long time."

"That all you want to do?"

"Nope," she said without hesitation. "'Kiss a biker' definitely needs to be on that list. Along with a few other things."

"Oh? Like what?"

"Like tracing that biker's tattoos. With my tongue."

"Yeah? I could probably arrange for that."

"See that you do. That's going to be a very important item on my list."

"I can guarantee you, having you trace my tattoos with your tongue will be the easiest thing on that list you accomplish. And that kiss the longest."

"You need to hurry up, Reaper. Time's wasting!"

Chapter Three
Swan

Had I been a normal person, the thought of what I was about to do would have been horrifying to me. Hooking up with a stranger definitely wasn't the safest thing in the world, to say nothing of taking any kind of trip with this guy. But I was far from normal. I was dying anyway, so I really had nothing to fear there. Besides, if this guy wanted to hurt me, he wouldn't have saved me.

Instead of taking me to my room, he brought me to a different one.

"Where are we?"

"My room." He set me down and turned around. "Come here." Reaper pulled me into his arms. "Not waitin' any longer for that kiss." Then he took my mouth in a sweeping kiss.

I'd been kissed before, but never like this. Reaper took me like he had a right to anything he wanted, like I was his and he was making sure everyone -- including me -- knew it. In that moment, he wasn't wrong. I'd surrender to anything he wanted. Hell, I was there for sex. He knew that and was reinforcing the idea. Making sure I enjoyed myself? Maybe. I didn't know enough about men to know for sure. All I knew was how my body responded to that kiss. And I was completely lost in it. In Reaper.

His tongue swept inside my mouth over and over, tasting me. Learning me. Letting me learn him. Surprisingly, he didn't grope me or pull at my bikini top. He just kissed me over and over and over... I was dizzy with them. Craved more. Craved Reaper.

When he finally lifted his head, I was pretty sure the only thing holding me up was his arms around my body. I blinked up at him uncertainly, confused.

"Why did you stop?" I was pretty sure there was a little bit of hurt in that question. "I thought…"

"What? What did you think was going to happen, little Swan?"

I tried to think, to push past the lust haze in my mind, but Reaper was too close. Too… real. "I thought we were going to have sex."

He leaned in to lick a path from my neck to my ear. "No one said anything about sex. I believe licking was involved, though that's your job."

"Oh. Well, yeah." He grinned at me as I looked up at him. I knew I was in way over my head with this guy, and that anything he did with me would likely be a pity fuck, but I wasn't sure that I cared. I mean, if it meant I got to enjoy that muscular body of his before I died, I'd take it. Did that make me desperate? Pitiful? Maybe. But life was just too fucking short for me to give a shit. If he was willing, I wasn't going to pretend I was too good to take whatever he offered. Or too proud. "So why are you still dressed and not naked on the bed? I'd like to start immediately."

That got a laugh out of him. His eyes seemed to light up with merriment. "I figured you were a demanding creature. I like a woman who knows what she wants."

"Well, consider this your notice. I want it all. I want sex in every form imaginable. Every single night. If you don't want to sign up for that, find me someone who does."

"Oh, no, little Swan. You're mine for the foreseeable future. In fact, I think I'm gonna insist that you be mine for the rest of your life."

"Right." I rolled my eyes. "Will likely be a short time, but you're not thinking this through. I'm probably not gonna just, you know, die. It will be a process. Probably not a very pretty one either. Cancer never is."

Instantly, he sobered, his gaze so intense I sucked in a breath and would have taken a step back except he had me backed against a wall. "I know what I'm getting into, Swan. I wouldn't say I want you to be mine unless I meant it. When I say until you die, I mean it. From this point forward, you're not alone. I'll be with you no matter what." He cupped my face with one big hand. "You get me?"

"No," I laughed. "I don't get you at all. But I'm not too proud to take what you're offering and be grateful for it." I gave him what I hoped was a cocky grin. "But I'm still expecting sex, or your ass is outta here, buster."

"Oh, that can definitely be arranged."

This time when he kissed me, he lifted me, urging my legs around his waist. He tugged at my bikini top until the strings were loose and the only thing holding it in place was our bodies pressed together. When he laid me gently on the bed, he shoved the scrap of material to the floor, never taking his eyes from my bare breasts.

"Baby," he said, his voice husky. "How the fuck did you get such perfect tits?"

His voice and the way his gaze locked on my chest, moving lower with each moment, had me squirming. His hands followed his gaze. He didn't immediately cover my breasts, though. His big hands urged my arms above my head and skimmed down to my chest. Then he caressed my sides, only his thumbs brushing over my nipples on his way down.

My whole body tightened. Sweat erupted over my skin, and I couldn't help but cry out. I arched into his touch, needing everything he was willing to give me.

"That's it, my beautiful Swan. So eager."

Reaper took his time. He seemed to be gauging my responses to everything he did. For my part, I was completely lost in the sensations. I wanted to focus on him, on what he was doing, but all I could do was either look up at the ceiling and gasp or squeeze my eyes tight and try my best to hold back my screams. Just his touch on my skin was overwhelming. Combine that with the kisses he'd already given me, and I was a squirming mass of sensation.

"Easy, baby," he murmured against my belly. "Love the way you respond to me." He brushed his face with that tantalizing beard tickling me in the most erotic way. He absolutely knew his way around a woman's body. Likely could tell how inexperienced I was. "How far you want me to take you today, hm?"

How the fuck did he expect me to answer him? I could barely function! "I --"

"Come on, honey. Tell me what you want."

"Y-you s-said we c-could have s-sex," I stammered. "I want th-that!"

He chuckled, the sound vibrating through my belly where he kissed my navel. Fuck! I wanted this like I wanted my next breath!

"You want me to fuck you, little Swan?"

"Yes! Oh God, Reaper! Yes!"

"Hm... I could definitely do that. But first, I want to play with you. See what I can coax your beautiful body into doing."

I had no idea what that meant, but I was pretty sure it meant he wasn't going to fuck me right away. While I wanted that with everything in me, I also knew he wasn't going to leave me hanging out there with my body on fire.

The next thing I knew, Reaper had latched onto one of my nipples and sucked gently. I thought I was gonna lose my everlovin' mind!

"Reaper! Jesus!" My hands went to his head automatically, tunneling through his thick hair. I gripped hard, not sure if I wanted to draw him closer or push him away.

"Mmm," he hummed around my nipple, before taking it between his teeth. I squealed, my body jerking in response. His hand went to my other breast, pulling and tugging the straining nipple as he teased the other with his lips and teeth.

My mind was gone. I couldn't decide if I wanted to continue or stop this before I plunged over the cliff into madness.

"Little Swan," he whispered. "Are you close to coming? You think I can make you come just from sucking these luscious nipples? I bet your pussy is soaked right now." His voice was sin dragging me into hell, and I was going willingly. "If I get rid of these little shorts and that bikini bottom, will you give me your cream?"

"Please," I whimpered before I could stop myself. I raised my hips, using my other hand to try to shove off my shorts.

Reaper chuckled. "Eager. I like it." He sucked my nipple again, hard this time, stretching it out until it slipped free of his lips with a *pop*. "But we're not doing that just yet. I have questions you're going to answer before we get to that. First, I'm gonna make you come. As many times as you can."

He slid one hand down to my mound. I still had on my shorts and my bathing suit bottom, but the material was thin, and I was sensitive. Then I tensed up, and the most intense orgasm of my life pushed through my body like a battering ram. I screamed, arching off the bed, my head thrashing along with the rest of me. I thrust my pelvis at him, needing harder friction. Needing penetration.

"REAPER!"

"Oh, yeah, baby. Give me your cum. Give it all to me." His wicked whisper was gruff and fuel to the fire that raged inside me. "Tell me what you want."

"You! I need you on top of me," I said frantically. "Pressing me into the bed while you fuck me!"

"You like the thought of me dominating you? Of me using you how I want?"

"Fuck! Reaper, please!" I was begging, uncaring of how desperate I sounded. I needed this man with everything inside me. I had no idea how much time I had left, and I didn't want to waste a moment. He said he had questions, but I didn't want to wait. I wanted everything he had to give, every single day we were together. No matter how long or short. I didn't want to miss out on anything.

"Come for me again," he said. This time, he pulled my tiny shorts and bikini bottoms aside and rubbed a finger through my sex. The second he settled on my clit, I exploded again, screaming his name over and over.

When the spasms lessened and the sensations faded, Reaper moved up onto the bed and pulled me with him. He wrapped me up in his arms and held me against him tightly. It almost felt like I mattered to him. Like he was holding someone he cared about after a fantastic round of sex. My breathing was still ragged, and I clung to him, trembling with aftershocks every time my clit rubbed against the ridge of my shorts.

"That's my good girl," he praised. "We're gonna

have so much fuckin' fun together."

"Why didn't you fuck me?"

"Because I wasn't ready. I don't know your experience level, and given your situation, I'm sure you'll want me to use a condom. Ain't got any here, but I'll fix that today."

He was right. I didn't need to get pregnant on top of my cancer. Even if I made it until the baby was born, I wouldn't be around for the child.

"I guess the last thing you need is a kid to worry about after I'm gone."

He jerked like I'd hit him. Then he gripped my chin and turned my face up to his. "Baby, I ain't the kinda man who'd ever bail on my kid. I'd take care of him or her and be thankful I still had a part of you with me. But that's not what I meant. It would worry you even more if you had a child to think about, and I ain't havin' that. You're not gonna worry about anything other than gettin' as much of your bucket list done as you can and having fun doing it. You get me?"

I couldn't help but laugh. "Not at all! I don't get anything about you, Reaper. You're way too good to be true, and I'm just taking you one moment at a time. When you're done, you're done." I smiled up to take the sting out of my words. "I know what you said earlier, but the only thing I'm holding you to is letting me lick your tats, and the sex. I want and expect both. Other than that, if it happens it happens." I yawned and stretched before settling back against him.

"All right, baby. I get you." God, that voice of his should be illegal. "For now, just rest. When you wake, we're gonna have a talk. I've got to meet with my brothers, but I'll be back soon. Take a nap."

"I can do that," I said. "See you later, then?"

"Wild horses couldn't drag me away,

sweetheart."

* * *

El Segador

I held Swan until she drifted off. When she started with the cute little contented snore, I chuckled lightly, then unwrapped myself from her. As I gazed down at her I marveled at all the ways this was a huge fuck-up on my part. I wasn't sure how old she was, but the story she told me put her at eighteen or nineteen. Which meant she was way the fuck younger than me. More than twenty years younger. Instead of sexing her, I should be protecting her. I mean, I was gonna do both, but I should really keep my hands to myself. Which wasn't happening. I just needed her experience level. If she was a virgin -- which I suspected might be the case -- then I'd ease her through that before taking her to the more carnal delights I knew. If she wanted it, I was going to show her everything there was to know about sex in whatever time she had.

"Christ," I swore, scrubbing a hand over my face. Nothing seemed to faze her. She seemed to have gotten past the shock of it, the unfairness, and the horrible hand she'd been dealt and was concentrating on living as hard as she could.

I left my suite, heading down the hallway to hers. I needed her notebook when I went to El Diablo. I needed to know what I'd just committed us to. Not that it would matter. I was gonna complete every Goddamned thing she'd written down and help her make more.

The more I thought about it, the more it settled within me. By the time I found her bucket list, I was preparing to take her on a fucking cruise around the fucking world to every single fucking country we could safely get to.

Her wants weren't all that complicated. In fact, we definitely needed to add a few more long-range things. Places away from here she wanted to go. She had mostly simple stuff.

Romantic dinner for two
Ride every roller coaster at Disney World
See the sun set from the beach

She'd marked that one off.

Climb Mount Everest (Haha!)

She might not be able to climb Mount Everest, but I bet I could get her to base camp. Let her see the mountain up close.

Take a cruise
Go to Hawaii
Take a hot air balloon ride
Have fantastic sex

That one I could help with easily.

Laugh until I pee

Well, I might not actually make her pee, but...

Get a sunburn

She'd marked through that one, as well.

Sing karaoke
Get drunk
Get high

The girl was killing me.

Fall in love

Fuck. Yeah. I could help her with that one, too. At least, I thought I could. I'd meant it when I'd told her she was mine until she died. I was keeping her for as long as I could. If Doc knew a way to get her better, to heal her, I'd take it and be grateful I got that much more time with Swan. I'd thrown myself into this girl for no apparent reason other than she intrigued me. And tugged at my protective instincts more than anyone, other than the kids at Black Reign had in years.

Since I'd met him, El Diablo -- Liam -- had been my focus. He had a job as the top assassin of the Brotherhood. It was a job no one lasted long in. Any failures to take out a target, any innocent who was harmed in the fallout, were the responsibility of the lead assassin. El Diablo. He'd earned his name because he was ruthless in an almost unimaginable way. But also because I was there to double- and triple-check everything. Liam's woman, Jezebel, had named me the one who never was. I was a ghost. The one no one ever saw or even knew existed. I did that because Liam had saved my life. So I saw it as my mission to keep him safe. Then his woman. Even I had to admit, my job as his bodyguard was well over. The club as a whole protected the pair of them better than any one man alone could. Even me.

Maybe that was the problem. With Swan, I was back to having someone who needed me. If that was the case, I was ready to admit I needed her as much as she needed me. But it wasn't all about having a white-knight complex. I wanted Swan to have the best life possible. If that meant condensing a lifetime into a few years -- or months -- I was ready and willing.

With a sigh, I headed down to El Diablo's office. He needed to know my intentions and what I was asking of him and the club. Of course, he likely already knew. It was his way, and I long ago stopped questioning it.

"Ah! El Segador! How's little Swan? I heard she had a mishap at the beach."

"She did, but she's fine. At least, she didn't drown and is showing no ill effects from her tumble under the water."

That raised his eyebrows. "Implying there's something else wrong with her?"

"Yeah. Says she's got some kind of bone cancer. Got a mass high on her thigh close to her hip."

"I see. What does she need?"

I sighed, scrubbing the back of my neck with my hand. "Couple of things. First, I've asked Rycks to reach out to Doc at Salvation's Bane. I'd like him to at least examine her and look at her medical records."

"Good idea," El Diablo said. "He's an oncologist. He may deal with children mostly, but he can probably help point you in the right direction. What else?'

I laid the notebook on his desk, opened to her bucket list. El Diablo ran his finger down the page, taking in every single entry. "Black Reign can help with some of these. I'm assuming you're taking care of the emotional entries?"

"Absolutely," I said without hesitation. "I've already started, but I need to find out her experience level. I doubt the girl is twenty years old yet. And the way she responds to me…"

"It's possible she's a virgin," El Diablo finished. The man didn't look in any way like he disapproved of my decision. In fact, he looked pleased. "I have no doubt you will take good care of her in that regard. My only concern is this one." He pointed to "Fall in love."

"Yeah," I said. "I can make her fall in love with me."

"But what about you? If she's destined to leave you so soon, falling in love with her isn't the greatest of ideas." El Diablo frowned and continued to look at the list.

"I know. But if she's falling in love with me, then I'll fall in love with her. No way to prevent it, so I might as well embrace it. Better to know it's happening than to realize it after she's gone."

El Diablo looked up at me, a determined look on his face. "So you're claiming her as your woman."

"I am."

"Good," he said with a curt nod. "I'll start planning the trips. She'll go in nothing but the height of luxury. It will take a day or two to get things together, but, while I'm doing that, you can take her out to dinner. Let the girls take her shopping for a dress and all the accessories. And you, my friend, need a suit."

I grimaced. I knew that, but I hated them. "At least it's not a fuckin' tux."

"Don't count it out yet. May come to that before it's over."

"Fucker," I muttered, even as I knew I'd do anything for Swan. If that meant dressing up in a fucking tux, I'd put it on and never say a fucking word.

"I doubt she has time to fully prepare for dinner tonight, so I'll get you reservations at Mortons or the Four Seasons for tomorrow night. Her choice, so let me know this evening."

"On it." I knew El Diablo would take over this once I handed it to him. It was what I'd been hoping for. While I was certainly capable of organizing her list into something I could work with, I was too close. My focus needed to be on Swan. "Thanks, Liam. I owe you for this."

"No, Reaper," El Diablo leveled a serious look on me. "This might come close to making us even for all your help over the years, but you do not owe me. Besides, if it makes little Swan happy, it's worth anything I could do to make this work. You focus on her and making her as happy and comfortable as she can be. Have you talked to Fury yet?"

"Thought I'd tell him when we told everyone else, but I can go to him now if you think it's best."

"Do that. She might need something for pain."

I nodded, then sent Fury a text, asking him to meet me in his office. It wasn't but just a few seconds later my phone rang.

"Gonna need her medical records." Fury wasn't the most sociable man on the planet. Fortunately, I was used to his abrupt manner.

"Ain't got 'em," I said. "If she's got 'em, I'll have her bring them."

"Do you at least know where she was treated?"

"I'll ask her. She's asleep. Last I checked she looked too peaceful to wake. Probably needs the rest. She's got dark circles under her eyes, and it's been an eventful morning. She's only been asleep an hour." Then I thought of something. "Hang on a second." On a hunch, I went to her room and found her backpack. A quick inspection, and I found a folder with a bunch of papers in it. "OK, yeah. Found at least some things for you, including the name of the facility and her doctor. No disks or images, but there's X-ray reports."

"Great. I'll see if I can pull some strings -- or get someone to hack into the hospital's system -- to get whatever Doc wants. Giovanni can do some digging. In the meantime, if she needs something for pain, let me know. If she doesn't mind, I'd like to do an exam. See if the tumor has any obvious growth since her last physical exam."

"I'll have her come down after she wakes."

"She eating much?"

"Not sure. She didn't eat much breakfast, but didn't complain about being sick or anything. But I've only been with her a few hours. I have no idea of her habits or overall general health."

"Bring her down when she wakes. If she's willing. If nothing else, I can get her some supplements that will help build her up."

"Fury." Rycks entered the clinic, nodding at me. "Doc is out of town. Said he'd be back in two days. He wanted you to work with Blade and go through any records we can get on Swan. See if anything jumps out at you."

"Make sure Giovanni gets us her imaging. Me and Blade might not be able to make much sense of it, but when Doc gets back, he'll need it. Did he mention anything else he wants before he gets back?"

"No. Said she'd waited this long. She could wait a couple more days. He didn't want to jump into it before he reviewed everything."

"Sounds like a plan," I said. "We've got things to do tomorrow so anything you do will need to be this afternoon. I won't have her stressed at all tomorrow."

Fury raised an eyebrow. "So it's like that, huh?"

"If by 'like that' you mean she's mine, then yes. She's mine. Spread the word, because there absolutely will be no misunderstandings. I'd hate to have to kill some son of a bitch for hittin' on her. But I will."

Rycks and Fury both chuckled. "Welcome to the club, brother," Rycks said. "We all check our man cards in our woman's panty drawer before meetings."

I couldn't help but bark out a laugh. "Yeah. I get you." Shaking my head, I tried to absorb the meaning of everything I was doing. I was committing my life to this girl. And I knew it was the rest of my life. "I've known her hours, man. *Hours*. Yet, she's gonna be with me the rest of my life. No matter how long she lives."

Fury gripped my shoulder. "One day at a time, brother. Don't give up on her until Doc's had a chance to look at her. And whatever you do, don't let her go.

Any woman who can make you feel like this deserves your whole heart. No matter how short a time she's in your life."

Chapter Four
Swan

I woke as a vicious orgasm crashed through me. My legs were spread wide, my knees bent. Reaper was between my legs, his mouth latched on to my pussy as he drank from me with a groan. When he flicked my clit with his tongue, I exploded again. The pleasure I got from this man wasn't like anything I'd ever thought possible. If I'd known anything close to this was possible, I'd have given up my virginity at the first opportunity. But I suspected any pleasure I got was more because of the man than anything else. Reaper was experienced in pleasuring a woman, and I wasn't experienced in receiving. Naturally, he'd be a little overwhelming. But I loved every blistering second of it.

"Reaper," I sighed. "God!'

"You awake now, baby?" He chuckled, crawling up my body, trailing kisses in his wake. He'd stripped me completely so that my body was bare before him. He was shirtless, but still had on his boxer briefs. All that yummy, inked skin was on fine display. Heavy muscles played beneath his skin just beckoning me to touch.

My hands went to his shoulders, and I rubbed them over his upper arms before moving back up over his shoulders to his chest. "You're beautiful," I whispered. "I've never seen a man like you before, Reaper. Never knew a man could be so wonderfully built."

"You like what you see?" Could he look any cockier? Probably not. But, fuck, the man had a right to be proud of his looks.

"Absolutely." It came out a purr as I hooked my

hands behind his head and pulled him down for a kiss. I met him halfway, needing to kiss him as much as I needed to breathe.

Reaper swept his tongue into my mouth, and I opened willingly. I tasted myself on him, and it was the most erotic taste, a heady mixture of me and him. Each caress of his tongue sent a shiver through me. My hips thrust at him, and I slid one leg over his hip, digging my heel into his ass.

"My little Swan is greedy for me," he growled. "Wanting my cock, are you?"

"Yes, Reaper," I gasped. "It feels so fucking good!"

"Imagine how much better it will feel when I fuck you. Slide my cock inside your tight little pussy and fuck you with it. Will you scream?"

"You know I will!" I was barely holding it together as it was. It was entirely possible I could come just from listening to him talk dirty to me.

He chuckled. "Yeah. You're not a quiet lover. I love that you never leave me wondering if I've satisfied you."

"Are you going to fuck me now?"

He flexed his hips, rubbing his cock over my pussy through his boxers. "Not yet, baby. We've still got a talk to have. But I'll make you come again." As if to emphasize his commitment, he rocked against me over and over, putting that much-needed friction on my clit again.

Pleasure built inside me. The kind I had no hope of fighting off. Like I'd want to! Reaper was introducing me to a whole new world. One I was loath to leave under any circumstances. It made me wonder whether my decision to stop treatment and just live the rest of my life had been the right one. I mean, if I had continued treatment, I wouldn't have met Reaper, and none of this would ever have happened. But what about now?

Just as I was having the epiphany of my life, an orgasm ripped through me, and I could no longer think. I clung to Reaper, shuddering in his arms as I cried out. My body seized, my hold tightening on him. I never wanted to let him go. Never.

"Reaper." I gasped out his name. "Please don't leave me." I hadn't meant to say that out loud, but once I'd voiced it, I knew I meant it. I'd beg him to stay even though it was the most selfish thing I'd ever done. He shouldn't have to witness my decline. I knew from the hospitals I'd visited when my diagnosis first came down that cancer was never pretty. Especially on the young. My body was strong, my heart and lungs not affected. There would be no quick death. My body would fight for life as long as it could. I was under no illusion Reaper was so naive he didn't know what he was getting into. The man was larger than life. Anyone could see he was world-wise. He still shouldn't have to stay with me through all that. Yet, I'd just asked him to do just that.

"Never, sweetheart," he said without hesitation as he kissed me, bringing me down gently. "I said you were mine. I meant it. That means I take care of you. I soothe your fears. When I can't, I hold you and make sure you're not alone."

"It's a shit detail, Reaper," I said, needing to make sure even though I knew I'd do anything to get him to stay with me through this. "It's not going to be pretty."

"I know, baby. I'm not going into this with blinders on. The rest of the afternoon, I need you to talk to Fury. He's our club doctor, remember? He wants to examine you and try to determine if the tumor has grown. He admits it's not going to be very accurate, but it will help later when Doc gets here. So, we're going to think about it for the next couple of hours, then we're going to plan the first thing on your bucket list. We've got full days ahead starting tomorrow, and I won't have it interrupted with thoughts of the future. You get me?"

"But I haven't shown you my bucket list yet."

He grinned, a cocky smirk that would have set me teeth on edge if I were a stronger woman. Instead, it curled my toes. "Baby, you told me where it was, and I violated your privacy and rifled through your backpack. I took that fucking notebook and started making plans."

I laughed. "You know there's no way to do all that shit. Most of it was just stuff I'd written down as a wish list. Something to keep from going crazy."

"You leave it to me. We'll go through as much of it as we can." He kissed me again. Gently. Comforting. All the while, one brawny arm held me tightly as he rolled us to our sides so his weight no longer pinned me to the bed. He didn't let me go, though. Just continued to kiss me, to praise me softly, telling me not to worry about anything. He'd take care of it all.

I must have truly surrendered to him then, because the weight I'd been carrying for the last few months seemed to lift. I looked up at Reaper, and he smiled. There was no reason to believe he meant what he said. That this wasn't all some kind of cruel joke to him. But I was taking a chance. I was going to embrace him and take everything he said at face value.

"Do you promise to tell me if it gets to be too much and you need out? I'll understand when it happens, but I'm not sure I could take it if you just ghosted. Just… just tell me when you need to leave."

Did I imagine it or did he look disappointed? "Baby, I ain't gonna leave. It's not going to be too much. And if it is, I'm not a big enough bastard to leave you to it by yourself. I'll need you as much as you need me. I understand you can't believe me yet. But I swear, I'll get you there. You're mine. I'm yours. Accept it."

For long moments, I just stared into his eyes, unsure what I was looking for but needing something. There was a quiet resolve on his face. He meant what he said. Whether or not he could follow through remained to be seen, but I had no doubt he intended to.

"OK," I said. "I'm going to choose to believe in you. Mostly because it feels good to not feel so alone and scared. I mean, I'm still scared, but it's somehow easier to know I can cry on your shoulder if I need to."

"Now you're getting it." He grinned. "Come on. Let's get a shower and go see Fury. The quicker we can get that over with, the quicker we can make plans for tomorrow. El Diablo needs your input, and I don't want to be interrupted once we start talking."

"Well, that's not mysterious or anything."

"Hey. It's your list. You wanted a romantic dinner for two? That's being worked out first."

"What?" My heart raced. "A romantic dinner? You're really going to do this? Because I don't want to go out with anyone but you, Reaper."

"As if I'd let one of my brothers have the privilege. Already told Fury and Rycks to pass along that you belong to me. 'Cause I will bust a motherfucker up if he tries to make a move on you." That got me giggling. I have no idea why, but I loved it. "Are you laughing at me?" He gave me a hard look, but it was lost on me. It turned my giggling fit into full-blown laughter.

"Not at all! You're a big mean, scary biker! I'd never -- eek!!"

"Little witch!" Reaper proceeded to tickle me until I shrieked, squirming and fighting to get away. "Laugh at me, will you? I'll show you!"

"No! Stop!" I squealed when he dug his fingers in my ribs.

"Not until you tell me you're about to pee," he growled. "You wanted to laugh until you peed? Well, here you go."

"Reaper!" I continued to laugh, not giving in because it just felt too damned good to actually laugh uncontrollably.

He let it go for a long time. My face was hot -- I was sure it was beet red -- and I was breathing heavily. Reaper rolled over, pulling me on top of him this time. His arms held me close, and I kissed the skin of his neck where my head rested on his shoulder.

"You didn't pee, but I think it was close."

"Yeah. Not saying I dribbled. Not *not* saying it either."

"I want you to always be happy, Swan. I want to always hear that laugh."

"You make me happy, Reaper," I said, still kissing his neck. "I never wanted to face this alone, but I hate that I've dragged you into it. Maybe it makes me a bad person, but I'm glad you're here."

"Honey, I wouldn't have it any other way. Now. No more talk about this. Let's get a shower and take care of business with Fury. Then you have a decision to make."

"Oh? What's that."

"Where to go to dinner tomorrow. Your choices are the restaurant at the Four Seasons or Mortons."

I thought my eyes would bug out of my head. "Are you shitting me?"

"Not at all. And if I have to wear a suit, you have to get dressed up as well. The girls will be taking you shopping tomorrow. No arguments."

"I can't do that! That's an outrageous amount of money!"

"Honey, you have no way of knowing this, but money is no object. We will fulfill as many items on that bucket list as we can and make more. Black Reign is very wealthy. Many of us are independently wealthy. So yeah. This is happening."

"Well. Shit. Fine. But I expect sex afterward. And I don't mean just me. You're fucking me when we get home."

"Honey, just try to stop me. After Fury's done, we're having our talk. Then I'll be more prepared."

"I don't want you holding back, Reaper. I want it all. Just because I'm not as experienced as you doesn't mean I can't handle it."

"I have no intentions of holding back. I just need to know how far I have to go to get you there. And I will get you there. I'm not going to hurt you in any way, but I'm going to make sure you get the full experience. I just intend to be careful doing it."

I needed to think about that. I'd never heard of anyone being this patient. Didn't men like to shock inexperienced women? Sure, he'd shocked me, but not in a scary way. He was bringing me into his world in stages. Even I could recognize that. The whole thing about not having condoms, while it might be true, wasn't the entire truth. He could have gotten condoms at any time he wanted. He was giving himself an excuse to make me crave him so much he didn't hurt me. I knew it the same as I knew my own name.

He led me to the shower. Thirty minutes and three orgasms later, we exited. I was weak in the knees but had a goofy grin on my face. Reaper just looked smug.

The walk to Furr's clinic was done with me riding piggyback again. Reaper apparently saw me favoring my leg and just took matters into his own hands. Strangely enough, I wasn't opposed to him making the decisions. Even little ones like this. And what did it really hurt? I was in pain. He could fix it.

When we arrived, Fury greeted us with a woman at his side. "Swan, this is Noelle. She's my woman. We thought you might be more comfortable if she was here with you."

"It's nice to meet you," I said, holding my hand out to the other woman. She had flame-red hair and a slight build. Her frame was strong, though. She wore a tank top and shorts. Her arms were muscled, showing her strength. I thought it fitting that a man named Fury had a woman who looked like Noelle.

"I hope we'll become friends," Noelle said with a smile. "El Diablo said you'll need the other women and me to help you pick out a dress tomorrow. Lyric has already planned a spa day to get you ready. We're going to have so much fun!" The other woman's smile was bright, and she looked genuinely pleased, though she didn't look like the type to enjoy spa days.

"I think this is the part where I'm supposed to protest and tell Reaper he's spending too much money."

"And I'd follow with telling you it's my fuckin' money. I'll spend it when and how I want, so you're not winning those types of arguments."

I shrugged. "However, I'm not winning those types of arguments, so I'll refrain." Everyone chuckled.

"All right. Lie down on the table here. I'm not going to poke and prod. I just want to get an idea of how big an area we're talking about." I did as Fury instructed. "Just going to pull your shorts down over your hip. Are you OK with that?"

"Yeah. I'm good."

Fury did, looking at the slightly raised area from different angles before actually touching it. The lump was painful, but I tried to be stoic through the whole thing. It wasn't as bad as it had been when the docs were constantly doing stuff to it, but it was still tender.

"Does it hurt all the time?"

"No. Only when I'm on my feet too much or when it's being touched excessively. What you're doing is uncomfortable, but not nearly as bad as when everyone in the world was examining it."

"Good. So. I've looked at your records. I've also looked at all the imaging you had done. I see nothing mentioned about a biopsy or any kind of lab sample to determine exactly what it was. Only imaging documentation."

"Yeah. I didn't let them. They wanted to do chemo first, which I went along with, because they said it would make the excision easier. There was no talk of just doing a biopsy and leaving it as it was. When the chemo didn't affect it at all, I didn't really see the point. The procedure they described had the potential to get pretty invasive."

"I see." Fury stood and looked at the affected area as if he really wanted X-ray vision so he could see exactly what was going on. "Well, my guess is Doc is going to want lab samples. I'll let him make that decision, but knowing for sure is really the key."

"I thought I already knew."

"Well, they *think* they know. It's like the old

saying, if it looks like a duck, walks like a duck, and talks like a duck, it's probably a duck. Things aren't always what they seem, though. I have a few questions I need to ask you. Questions I didn't see answered in any of the history and physicals in your chart."

"All right. Shoot."

"You started experiencing pain about four months ago. Yes?"

"That's right."

"Did you injure yourself in any way?"

"No. I just woke up one morning and my hip ached."

"Hum... what about... before that. Like a few weeks? A month? Two months?"

I thought back. "Well, yeah. I fell when I went hiking in the woods. Wasn't a big fall or anything. I just tripped over a tree root and landed on another one."

"Did you land close to where the tumor is now?"

I nodded slowly. "Yeah. Maybe? I'm just not sure. I think so?"

"OK. OK. We'll visit that later when Doc gets here. How's your pain level right now."

"Not bad. I've been walking a lot lately. That seems to make it worse. It aches now. It's more aggravating than anything else."

"OK. I want you to take some anti-inflammatories along with some painkillers. Nothing too strong. I'm also giving you a stronger pain medicine to take at night to help you sleep. Looking at you, I'm betting you're not sleeping well."

"Well, I've been sleeping outside mostly. It's not very comfortable and, I'll admit, not very safe. I tried to stay in good neighborhoods and such, but it wasn't very... relaxing."

"Right. I'm assuming that's all at an end?" He looked at Reaper instead of me. I had to grin. Normally, I'd be upset, but Reaper had effectively taken over my life. And I wasn't at all broken up about it.

"Yep. She's staying with me. Hadn't planned on letting her sleep too much, but if you say she needs it, I'll try to keep my hands to myself. Sometimes."

I giggled. Fury just shot me an exasperated look. "Don't encourage him," he scolded. "You need sleep. And nourishment. I'm betting you've not been eating regularly, or food high in calories or protein."

"I eat when I'm hungry. I've been worried, and I can't eat when I'm stressed."

"Something else that stops now," Reaper said. "I'm officially making it against the rules for you to stress over anything. You leave the stressing to me."

"Right," Noelle said, grinning at me. "Honey, you've got your hands full with this one."

"Tell me about it," I muttered, but I smiled just the same.

Fury rolled his eyes. "That will do for now, I suppose. I'm giving Reaper your medicine and some vitamin supplements I want you to try to take. You need your strength and, until Doc can put everything together, I think it best to just do supportive care."

"I can live with that," I agreed.

"Let me know if you need something stronger for pain. I don't want you any more uncomfortable than you absolutely have to be. Don't put it off until you're hurting so bad it's difficult to get on top of the pain. You hear me?"

"I got you." I looked at Noelle. "Are all the men here so bossy?"

"Every single fucking one of them, honey. And

they'll all bully you like this. I think they get off on it."

"Great," I muttered, but spoiled the effect by giggling.

"Too bad," Reaper said, turning and motioning for me to get on his back. "You're just going to have to put up with it."

I hopped up and wrapped my arms and legs around him. "Like it's such a hardship." I slapped his ass. "Hi Ho, Silver! Away!"

Noelle and Fury burst out laughing. Reaper just scowled at them before giving them the bird. "Just remember, I will tickle you 'til you pee. All I have to do is get you in the shower."

Chapter Five
El Segador

The next day was a special kind of hell for me. The girls took Swan off to a spa somewhere while I spent an hour getting fitted for a suit El Diablo's tailor promised would be ready in a couple of hours, which had to be some kind of record. El Diablo stayed with me, offering instructions while I stood there, my arms straight out while some uptight tailor fussed over the damned suit.

"If I get out of this in one piece, Liam, I may fuckin' kill you."

"Now, is that any way to treat the man helping you romance your girl? How can you make her fall in love with you if you don't sweep her off her feet?"

"Was kinda hopin' the bike would help with that. Chicks love the bike."

"Chicks." He snorted. "That right there is your problem. Your woman needs romancing. Wooing. The bike may fuel her lust, but you need to win her heart."

"Which is the only reason I'm still fuckin' standin' here," I growled. "Fuckin' ridiculous. No biker should have to go through this."

Then something happened I'd never seen. At least, not aimed at me. El Diablo's face turned hard. Angry. "You go through whatever you have to for your woman. Indignant or not," he snapped. "Now stop whining like a child and do what you have to do to be the man she needs you to be." El Diablo paced across the room. "Even the children wouldn't whine so much."

"I'm gonna be the man she needs, and I'm gonna make her fall in love with me. I'm all in with this, Liam. Don't mean I have to like the method."

"One question." El Diablo turned around, giving me a curious look. "Have you thought about what you'll do if Dr. Muse is able to heal her? You'll have yourself a woman. One you can't get rid of without breaking a promise. Or, likely, her heart."

"Not sure it matters," I said with a shrug, which got me stuck in several places with fucking pins. "She said this started several months ago. If she's gone this long without treatment, I'm not sure anything can help."

"I'm just saying, you need to be prepared for her to live longer than you've planned."

"Hey. If she does, great. I don't want the sprite to die. She's got so much life in her. I want nothing more than to see her thrive and live to be an old woman."

"And you're older than her by what? Fifteen years or more?"

I rolled my eyes. "Something like that." When the other man just glared at me, I continued. "Look, I got this. I'm giving her everything she wants. If we get a better outcome than we're expecting, it will just be more time to spoil her. I swear to you, Liam, I'm good with this. No matter how long or short." I frowned then. "OK, so that's not exactly true. I'm not going to be good with this if she dies. That I know without a doubt."

"OK, then." That seemed to satisfy my friend. "I just don't want you regretting anything if her illness turns out not to be as bad as she thought. It would hurt you both in unspeakable ways."

"If I have to give up everything I am to see her live, Liam, I'll do it. And I'll be happy till the end of my days. She's a good girl. If anyone deserves a break, it's Swan."

"That's what I wanted to hear. Now. Suck it up.

There's still a few hours to go before your date. I hope you've brushed up on your table manners, because I have it on good authority there is nothing at the Four Seasons you can eat with your fingers."

"Great. Thanks for reminding me."

"One other thing. Did you have a talk with little Swan about her experience and her limits?"

I glanced at the tailor, who was busy putting yet another pin in the damned suit. "Yeah. Her experience is practically nil, and her limits are surprisingly broad. You were right. I'll be her first in most things. But when she said she wanted to experience everything, she meant it. We went over procedures to stop should she be too uncomfortable, and she has yours and Jezebel's phone numbers should she find herself uncomfortable with me when we travel." That conversation had ended in another round of "make Swan come as many times as I can." Just the memory put a smile back on my face.

"Good. Looks like you've covered all the bases."

"Who do you have on the girls while they do their business today?"

"Rycks, Wrath, and Fury. Their women are with them along with Esther and Eden. Grady is on standby if he's needed, but I don't anticipate it. So far, Rycks says everyone is having a splendid time."

"At least someone is," I muttered. "How much fuckin' longer?"

The tailor was unperturbed. "Almost finished here, sir. The alterations will take approximately two or three hours. You should be ready on schedule."

"Good," I said. "I still need to get her a gift for our date."

"Might I suggest Tiffany's?"

"That will definitely make an impression." The

tailor made the comment happily, as if he were a huge part of the conversation. I glared at him, but we both knew El Diablo was right. His gleeful reply was probably his revenge for my attitude toward him.

"I'll leave the selection to you. That way when you fuck it up, I can have a good laugh." He smiled at me. We both knew that, although I tried to emulate El Diablo in mannerisms when necessary, I had horrible taste.

"Ha, ha. Very funny."

"Not yet." He grinned. "But I'm sure it will be."

Once the fitting was over, I hopped on my bike and headed over to the jewelry store El Diablo had suggested. I hadn't realized how much I needed the break until I was flying down the highway with the wind streaming all around me. I definitely needed Swan behind me on the bike. I had the feeling she'd fall in love the instant we took off.

Getting anyone at the fucking store to wait on me took effort and patience I never knew I had. What they wanted to do was call the fucking cops. To be fair, I was in faded blue jeans, motorcycle boots, and a tight T-shirt. I hadn't exactly tried to hide my tats either. While the women eyed me with appreciative gazes, the manager -- a man in his late fifties to early sixties -- was afraid I was there to rob them. Guess they didn't often get bikers as paying customers.

"Look," I said for the sixth time. "I just want to buy a gift for my girl. Is that so hard to grasp? I even have money." I waved a wad of bills at them. "If you're not comfortable with cash, I've got plastic and a photo ID." I raised my hands in a gesture meant to put the man at ease. "Whatever makes you happy, old man." Probably shouldn't have tacked on the "old man" bit, but the guy was seriously trying my last nerve.

Finally, the guy's greed got the better of his delicate sensibilities. "What did you have in mind, Mr..."

"El Segador," I said. "Everyone calls me El Segador."

The guy's eyes widened. "Uh... I see. Uh, Mr.... uh..." He stopped and cleared his throat, tugging at his collar. Yeah, he was nervous. Wouldn't surprise me if he spoke Spanish. Not unheard of in this area. In fact, it was very much an asset, especially if he had a shop in Miami as well as Palm Springs. "El Segador. Did you have, uh, something specific you were looking for?"

"Just something simple," I said, ignoring the man's obvious discomfort. "Tasteful. Something she can wear with anything."

The man pursed his lips as he thought for a moment. Apparently, the challenge of finding the perfect piece overcame his objections to me. Then his eyes lit up. "I think I know just the piece."

He motioned me to a table where he instructed me to sit. He left and returned with two boxes. He opened one to show me the contents. "Perhaps these would do?"

I grinned. "Perfect."

"Would you like this delivered or will you take them yourself?"

"I'll be taking them," I said. "Now, which method of payment would you prefer?"

Like I didn't know. I already had my card and license out. The guy took it eagerly, probably expecting to see my real name. If so, he'd be disappointed. My legal name was El Segador. Giovanni Romano had seen to it. He also provided me with an ID every so often, so it looked current. When the guy glanced back at me after looking at my card, I just grinned. It didn't take long for him to take my payment and send me on my way.

I tucked the boxes into an inside jacket pocket as I straddled my bike. I looked up at the early noon sun and grinned. A romantic dinner for two. Yeah. I'd suffer through figuring out the right fuckin' fork to use with what course to give her this.

With a chuckle, I started up my bike and took off. It wouldn't be long before I needed to get ready. Then I'd see my girl's face light up. And tonight, I'd make love to her gently. Until I couldn't. Then I'd take her as far as she was willing to go. Then maybe I'd push her a little further. Whatever happened in the next few weeks, Swan was going to be the happiest woman in the world if I had anything to say about it.

* * *

Swan

The day had been full, probably by design. The girls had taken me shopping and helped me pick out a stylish cocktail dress. After trying on what seemed like a hundred dresses, they finally found "the one." It had a crossover bust with an off-the-shoulder design. The chest tapered down, emphasizing my narrow waist. The front of the hi-low skirt stopped just above my knees while the back of it hit my calves. It was black satin with a lace overlay covering the top. They'd picked out strappy sandals with just enough of a heel to flex my calves without making it painful to walk.

"I feel like Cinderella getting ready for the ball." I laughed. "You guys ain't gonna rip my dress to shreds, are you?"

Lyric hugged me tightly. "Never! And I'll make sure the guys keep the club girls out of the common room when we bring you down to El Segador."

"Club girls?" I knew I had a puzzled look on my face.

"Yeah," Celeste said, rubbing her tummy, which showed her advanced pregnancy. Wrath, the dear man, barely let her out of his reach and only with much fussing over her before he left her. I wanted a man like that. I'd probably never see that dream realized, but if I could, and Reaper lived up to his promise, I was sure he could be like that with me. "Club girls can be a bit territorial when it comes to the unattached men. The club brothers and all of us realize he's yours and you're his, but the club girls are slow in accepting the message. They sometimes cause trouble even when they know better."

Lyric rolled her eyes. "Yeah. I think it's in their blood or something."

"Even if they know he's taken," Jezebel added. "If you have an argument and they smell blood in the water, they'll try to take advantage. The guys never go for it, but that's beside the point."

"You sound like you speak from experience," I said, not liking the sound of this.

Jezebel shrugged. "I do. But believe me when I tell you, they all know better now. And Liam knows better than to give them even the slightest opening. He shuts everything down hard before they ever get their greedy hands on him. And if I'm not satisfied with his effort --" she buffed her nails on her top -- "I take matters into my own hands."

Celeste snorted. "Yeah. I think there's a club girl still in the hospital. Holly has decided she's going to be just like Jezebel when she grows up."

"She did? I thought she was going to be like Noelle." Jezebel laughed merrily. The woman was absolutely beautiful. Had I been in my prime, I might have been jealous of her, but every day I looked in the mirror, I knew I was going downhill fast. There was no reason to be jealous, because I was never going to attain that kind of beauty ever again.

"Noelle's an MMA fighter," Esther said. "Fury told Shotgun she knocked out Shadow, and he's three times her size."

"Wow," I exclaimed. "And Holly would rather be like Jezebel than Noelle? That's impressive."

"I know, right?" Celeste's laughter seemed to make the whole place smile. These women were truly extraordinary.

"If I forget to tell you guys later, I had an awesome time," I said. "I've never had such wonderful friends as all of you. Thank you."

The women all huddled around me, pulling me into their embrace. We all stood there for long moments before Lyric broke us up.

"We'd better hurry," she urged. "We still have the spa to go to. I want Swan as relaxed as she can be before we help her dress. Nails. Toes. Massage. Hair. Then we head home."

"Did you get the makeup artist, Lyric?" Celeste handed out tissues around to a couple of the girls, myself included, as we dabbed our misty eyes.

"Yep. He'll be there in about three hours. So we need to hurry."

By the time they were finished with me at the spa, I was relaxed as a puddle of goo, yet I was excited and even a little nervous. The makeup guy said there wasn't much to do other than conceal the dark circles under my eyes and make my cheekbones look less sharp. He used color sparingly and covered my lips not with a ruby red like I'd expected, but a nude gloss. Celeste and Esther fluffed my hair a little and smoothed my dress, almost as nervous as I was.

"This is so surreal. I can't believe I'm going out on a romantic dinner date. And with a guy who seems more like a steamroller than a hopeless romantic."

"I can't believe it either," Jezebel said. "At least, not with El Segador. Me and Liam have a bet going. I'm betting he wears leather. Liam says he'll get him into a suit and tie even if it kills El Segador."

"I know, right?" I smiled, but I wanted to defend Reaper. Only problem was, I couldn't imagine him in a suit and tie, either.

"All right, Swan." Lyric rubbed her hands together. "You ready?"

I sighed, smoothing my dress once more as I looked in the mirror. "As I'll ever be."

The girls escorted me down the stairs and into the main room. There were bikers hanging out from one end to the other, but no women unless they were with one of the men. Even some of those were given the stink eye by one or more of my escorts. It was touching how these women looked out for me. I couldn't remember a time in my life where I felt so cared for and protected. And it wasn't just from Reaper. His whole club seemed to have adopted me. It struck me how much I'd isolated myself from people since my diagnosis. I'd done it to protect myself, to keep from caring about someone only to have them realize being with me was more than they could handle. I knew it didn't automatically follow that they'd abandon me, but it would hurt them. I didn't want to hurt anybody.

Then, like in a movie, a group of the guys parted, and Reaper stepped from their midst. He was dressed in an obviously tailored charcoal-gray suit, his large frame encased perfectly. He wore a lighter gray shirt and a burgundy tie. One tattoo peeked out from his collar, giving me a sexy glimpse of what I knew lay beneath the sophisticated wrapping. He took my breath.

"Wow," I whispered.

"Indeed," Reaper responded. He approached me slowly, his eyes intent on me. His gaze narrowed as he looked me up and down, taking me in more completely than anyone ever had. "Not sure I want to take you out, though. I've been told fighting isn't gentlemanly behavior, and I have a feeling I'll be fighting men off you left and right."

I couldn't help but giggle. "Well, if you get in a fight with men looking at me, I'll take it as permission to go postal on the women looking at you." That got some chuckles from the men. I wasn't sure what I expected, but I thought Reaper might get teased about our date. Instead, everyone looked at us with approval.

"Since I can't have my girl breaking a nail marking her territory, I'll have to keep it to scowls and murderous looks, I suppose." That got some more chuckles from the guys. He walked to me and held out a hand. When I took it, he brought my hand to his lips and kissed my palm. "I have something for you." Reaper pulled a flat, square box from his inside jacket pocket. He opened the box and turned it to face me, and I gasped.

"Reaper?" I looked up at him, unable to stop the smile on my face. "This is too much. So precious…" It was, but I still couldn't stop myself from reaching out to touch the beautiful necklace. One single, nickel-sized pearl on a thin chain of diamonds. Under the lights of the common room, the necklace sparkled like stars in the sky.

"It's not as precious as you, little Swan. But

maybe it's a start." He took the necklace from the box and urged me to turn around. I met Jezebel's gaze as Reaper fastened the necklace around my neck. The pearl sat in the hollow of my throat like it had been created for me.

He urged me back around and pulled out another, smaller box. When he opened it, the earrings inside made me gasp. They perfectly matched the necklace with a pearl surrounded by diamonds. Lyric came forward and helped me with them. We giggled as I fastened the backs on them before focusing on Reaper again.

He rested his hands on my shoulders. I looked back at him. My rough biker now had his shaggy hair tamed. He looked like a rich, powerful man. And for all I knew, he was. But he was also my tattooed biker. I just wasn't sure which one I preferred.

Scratch that. I knew I preferred the biker. This version of Reaper, however, was very intriguing.

"You like it?" He raised an eyebrow, acting as if my answer meant nothing to him. But I could tell it did. There was just something in his eyes. My reaction, how well I liked his gift, meant everything to him.

I gave him what I hoped was my best smile, then threw myself into his arms. "I love it, Reaper. It's so beautiful. It's perfect."

He clutched me to him in a tight embrace, burying his face in my neck. Then he did something wicked.

"When we get home tonight, I'm gonna fuck you while you're wearing nothin' but that fuckin' necklace." Reaper whispered his naughty idea in my ear. I had no idea if anyone else could hear it but figured they couldn't. Seems that several members of his club were paying out bets lost. On Reaper?

"What are they betting on?" I needed to deflect him. If I thought about the night after our romantic dinner for two, I might not make it through the dinner.

"On whether or not he managed to get you a gift of good taste, my dear." El Diablo stepped toward me, his arm wrapped around Jezebel. "I'm afraid I lost quite a bit of money because of your man there."

"I-I'm sorry. I didn't mean --"

"Relax, little Swan." El Diablo laughed. "I wasn't blaming you. I had great plans of laughing at my old friend here. El Segador isn't exactly known for his finesse. Apparently, he was paying attention all these years. He just ignored anything he didn't think was useful."

"Bastard," Reaper said without heat. El Diablo clapped him on the back before leading us outside.

"Cinderella, your carriage," he said, grinning at me. "Be back before midnight." He opened the door to a black limousine, stepping back to allow us entry.

"Wow," I exclaimed. "This is awesome!"

"Anything for you, baby," Reaper said, kissing my temple. He helped me inside, then nodded at El Diablo. "No promises on being back before midnight," Reaper said. "I'm gonna show Swan a good time, no matter how long it takes."

El Diablo looked pleased with Reaper, though I had no idea what about. "Call if you need anything. Tank said he'd be your chauffeur for the evening. Don't keep him out too late, or he'll be cranky." Everyone laughed.

Another big man in an expensive-looking suit approached the car, tugging at his collar. "I better get hazard pay for this," he grumbled. "Fuckin' thing's uncomfortable as hell."

"Don't worry," Reaper replied. "Everyone knows

suits are chick magnets. You'll have some hapless female undressing you before you know it." Laughter all around again.

"Off with you now." El Diablo chuckled. "Take care of our girl. Show her a good time. When you get back, I'll have an itinerary worked out on other activities for her."

"Other activities?" I squeaked out my question.

"Of course, baby," Reaper said, kissing my temple. "I told you we were making that bucket list happen. We're all working on everything we can to see it done."

I was incredulous. "There're things on that list there is no way I can do. I mean, the Mount Everest thing alone is physically prohibitive. Even in my prime, I wasn't a mountain climber."

"Just trust me, baby. All you need to worry about is having a good time and enjoying everything to the fullest. Now, wave to everyone."

I did, and someone closed the door to the limo. Taking a breath, I looked up at Reaper. His beard was neatly trimmed and his hair tied back. Though it was in a tail at the nape of his neck, his hairline was trimmed neatly. It was an unusual look for the man I'd gotten to know over the last day and a half, but he made it work. Hell, I was pretty sure there wasn't much he couldn't pull off if he wanted to. The man was seriously gorgeous. And tonight, I was with him. The goofy smile just wouldn't stay off my face.

"At some point tonight, I'm going to lose my composure and either laugh like a loon or cry. I'm apologizing now in case I embarrass you."

"Baby, as long as I'm not an asshole and hurt your feelings, I could care less. Laugh. Cry as long as it's from happiness. You'll never embarrass me." He laced our fingers together before bringing my knuckles up to his lips for a kiss. My breath caught. As romantic dinners started, I imagined this was as good as it got. Off the charts.

The Four Seasons didn't disappoint. We were seated in a private dining area overlooking the sea. Soft lights created a romantic moonlit atmosphere along with the distant crash of waves along the shore. I was so excited I was practically bouncing.

"This… is… the… tits!" I sat with my thigh touching Reaper's. He just smiled at me indulgently as if he expected this exact reaction and was being duly rewarded for his patience. "But, OMG! This has to be costing a fortune!" I turned to face Reaper. "We don't have to do this."

"We absolutely have to do this, and I ain't hearin' anything else. Now. Do you want to order or would you like me to do it for you?"

I glanced at the menu in front of me. "I have no idea what any of this stuff even is." I broke out into giggles, just as I knew I would. It was a combination of nerves and the absurdity of the whole situation. "This is way out of my league, Reaper."

"Half the fun," he whispered with a wink.

When the waiter arrived, Reaper ordered for us as if he did this sort of thing every day. An appetizer of king crab and mimosa eggs, then lobster linguine with bottarga, tarragon, and sundried tomatoes for both of us as the main course. The wine he picked out was exquisite.

"You've done this before," I accused gently, looking to compliment him more than dredge up any memories he might have of other women in this kind of setting. Lord knew I'd fall short on that account. I'd never been to a place like this in my life!

"Nope. Not even once. I did observe El Diablo on more than one occasion under cover of protecting him, though. I'm a fast and efficient learner."

"I can't wait to taste everything!"

"Taste to your heart's content. If you don't like something, we'll get something different. This is your night, baby."

"But it's so expensive," I whispered. The whole meal probably cost more than I wanted to know, because after I'd mmm'd and ahhhhh'd over the meal, he'd ordered me the white chocolate mousse for dessert. To top it all off, Reaper took every opportunity to touch my hands and kiss my fingers. Even when management checked to make sure everything was to our liking and the woman tried to flirt with Reaper, it was painfully obvious he only had eyes for me. Yeah. I was in heaven.

"So, for a romantic dinner, how'm I doin'?"

"Dude, you get an A-plus. This is amazing." I leaned in to brush a kiss over his lips, lingering for just a moment. "You're amazing. I can't thank you enough, Reaper."

The waiter chose that moment to bring the check. Reaper handed over his card before turning back to me.

"You can thank me when we get back to the clubhouse." He took one of my fingers into his mouth and swirled his tongue around it. "Got somethin' I've been wantin' to do since I first met you. Would've too. If Holly hadn't been around." He winked at me.

"Oh really? What exactly did you want to do?"

He leaned in to whisper wickedly in my ear. "Gonna fuck you tonight, Swan. Gonna give you all the pleasure you can stand. And make you beg me for more."

"Reaper…" My breath caught, and I turned to catch his gaze with mine. He was intense, daring me not to give him what he wanted. "Yes." I swallowed nervously. "Yes, let's do that."

"Come on." He pulled me to my feet just as the waiter approached once more. Reaper signed, then put his card back in his jacket pocket. "Let's go."

The ride back to the clubhouse was an exercise in patience. I wanted with everything in me to jump him right there in the limo. Reaper pulled me into his lap and kissed me senseless until we pulled into the club property. Our driver, Tank, didn't pull into the main parking area where we'd left from, though. He pulled around the back of the compound to a secluded bungalow.

"Where are we going?" I asked as I tried to slip off Reaper's lap. He was having none of it.

"Stop squirming. This is where we're staying for the foreseeable future," he said. "We'll have privacy but be close enough to participate in any parties or whatever we want. You'll be close to the other women if you want to do things together. We have our own pool and everything we need right here if you don't want people around."

"Wow. Reaper. This is… it's extraordinary! And far, far too much."

He tilted his head at me. "I'm sensing a but in there."

"Yeah. Well, it is way too much, but I'm just selfish enough to take it and just thank you for it. It's perfect."

"Good." Reaper opened the door, and Tank was there to help me out. Reaper growled when the big man leaned in to kiss my cheek. "Hands off, you big bastard."

Tank just chuckled. "Didn't have a hand on her. My mouth, on the other hand…" He winked at me when Reaper pulled me away from Tank and scooped me up into his arms.

"Get your ass back to the fuckin' clubhouse. I got this from here."

"You sure? I'm always willin' to help a brother out."

Reaper didn't respond. I slid my arms tighter around his neck, buried my face in his neck, and smiled to myself.

"You think this is funny, huh?"

"Maybe just a little," I confessed. "He was goading you."

"Know it, babe. Can't help my reaction. You're my woman. Not his."

Reaper carried me into the master bedroom, which appeared to already have been equipped with our things from Reaper's room in the main building. Once there, he set me on my feet, framed my face with his hands, and kissed me like he meant to keep me.

Chapter Six
El Segador

I'd wanted to hate every second of that dinner. It was everything I wasn't. Civil. Sophisticated. Elegant. Looking at the smile on Swan's face made it worth every uncomfortable fucking second. She'd cheerfully told me she had no idea what any of the food was -- other than the white chocolate mousse -- and ate every bite on her plate and some from mine. I'd never witnessed anyone enjoying their food so thoroughly as she did tonight. I'd half expected her to plea for mercy on the sex when we got back, but when I kissed her, Swan put everything she had into it.

It took some uncomfortable doing to get her out of that fucking dress. Not because it was particularly difficult, but because my hands were shaking so fucking much. I was going to take Swan and make her mine, and I wasn't letting her go. I didn't care what I had to do to keep her. I'd find a way to heal her. She'd be with me for the rest of my days.

By the time we were both naked, I was a mass of nerves. Up until now, I knew where I was stopping. It had been like a game to me. All part of making her want me. Now, I was having performance anxiety. What if I couldn't satisfy her?

No. That wasn't even an option. I could do this. If I couldn't make her come when I fucked her, I'd do it afterward. Either way, she wasn't leaving my arms until she was good and satisfied.

With that settled in my mind, I let my gaze wander over her naked body. As always, she was perfect. Yes, I could see signs of her illness, but I could see how beautiful she was despite all that. Just her smile and those big, wide eyes made my cock leak precum when I looked at her.

"I'm gonna fuck you tonight, Swan. Gonna start out slow. Do my best to get you ready." I brushed a lock of curly hair away from her face. "But this is gonna end in me takin' you hard. You know how to stop me if it's too much."

She nodded eagerly. "Yes. Red to stop. Yellow for you to slow down and take it easy."

"You got it, babe. Now, lie down and spread your legs. You ate your dessert. I want mine."

Swan sighed, giggling a little, but she did as I told her. Her pussy was freshly waxed and dripping wet. "Someone's been looking forward to this, I think."

"You know I have. You won't make me believe you didn't intend to get me worked up, either. All that touching and tickling my neck with your breath when you'd whisper something wicked in my ear? I know that was all to make me horny for you."

"Well, that, and because I figured if I was gonna have to suffer through it, so should you. I voted to skip straight to dessert, but figured you needed this thing ticked off that bucket list."

"Didn't I add 'Fuck a biker' to that list?"

I snorted. "Not sure if it was you or me. Either way, yeah. It's on there."

"So? Let's get it done."

That was all the encouragement I needed. I held her thighs open wide and lowered my face between them. Her glistening lips beckoned me to taste, but I knew from experience the second my tongue touched her, she'd go off like a rocket. I also knew, when that happened, I wouldn't be far behind her.

"So fuckin' wet," I whispered, blowing against her clit. "So beautiful. Did the waxing hurt you, baby?"

"Not as much as I thought," she said, smiling

down at me. "It did make me super sensitive, so you blow on my clit one more time, I'm liable to come before you want me to."

I chuckled. "Am I so transparent you can read my mind?"

"Yes," she said without hesitation. "But also because you're a guy. You've been playing with me for a day and a half and haven't fucked me yet. Unless you're getting it from the club girls, or whatever they're called, I'm getting way more action than you."

"God, you're priceless." The humorous way she tried to put it was unexpected. I could see the vulnerability in her face, something she probably had no idea she was feeling until she'd thought about me being with another woman. "No, Swan. I've not been with any other woman in any kind of sexual situation for any reason since I met you. Any relief I've taken has been with my own fist in the fuckin' shower."

"So, why haven't you let me take care of you? I mean, we were just in the shower together. You made me come three times. I tried to get you to let me suck you off, but you wouldn't." OK, now she sounded hurt. Which wouldn't do.

"You keep telling me what you're feeling, Swan. Always. Even if it's uncomfortable for me to hear because I'm not giving you what you need," I said, taking a lick on the crease of her thigh at her pelvis. Not anywhere close to where either of us wanted me to be, but close enough for her to weep more of her intoxicating honey. "That's the way we make it through this, baby. We talk to each other." I took a swipe on the other side. "I didn't let you suck me off because I knew there was no way I finished in your mouth if I did. When I come the first time, it's gonna be deep inside this pussy." I stroked my finger up and down through her folds. "So, yeah. Tonight I ain't stoppin' till my cock is throbbin' inside you, fillin' that fuckin' condom full of my jizz. You get me?"

"Oh, God," she groaned. "Yeah. I get you. And I love it when you talk that way! It's so dirty!"

"Yeah. Kinda figured."

"Now hurry up with the fucking condom and get up here already!"

I wanted to chuckle at her eagerness, but the truth was, I was eager too. Probably more than she was. "You think you're ready for this little pussy to be filled with my dick?"

"Yes! Fuck yes!" Her response was instant. No thinking about it or fretting over whether or not I'd fit or how bad it would hurt. She was completely lost in the moment.

"Good." I grinned up at her. "I'm still playing down here awhile."

"Fuuuuck…" As she moaned out the word, she fell flat on the bed. "You're gonna kill me."

"I promise you'll survive this," I said dryly before taking a swipe from her opening to her clit with the flat of my tongue. She cried out and arched her back, her hands flying to my hair. She tugged. Hard.

"No! Up here. Now!"

That time, I did laugh. "All right, all right. Scoot up the bed." I reached into the nightstand and pulled a condom out of the new pack I'd put in there earlier. Ripping it open, I glanced at her. "I'm gonna fuck you so good, Swan."

"I know," she said with a smile. "But more action. Less talk."

I raised an eyebrow as I rolled the rubber down my shaft. "Bossy little thing, ain't ya?"

"Well, you're taking entirely too much time."

"Ever think the longer I can drag it out the better it will be for you?"

"Sure. But we can do that later. Right now, I want to feel you inside me."

I hesitated, really looking at her face. Studying what I found there. "Are you sure, Swan? You don't have to do this with me. It's your first time. We can wait until --"

"Shut the fuck up and put it in me already! Jesus! I thought bikers were horny motherfuckers all the fucking time!"

That got a laugh. She was absolutely priceless. "Hey. I was trying to do right by you. You deserve to have exactly what you want for your first time."

"Oh, and you're prepared to stop and let me pick some other guy to be the first man to fuck me?" She raised her eyebrows, challenging me.

"Little witch," I muttered. "No. I'm not. I'd just eat you out until you were so lust-stupid you didn't give a fuck who fucked you. As long as you got fucked."

"Uh-huh. That's what I thought." She crooked her finger, beckoning me to her. "You're my choice, Reaper. You. I've never even imagined a man could treat me like you have. But don't mistake my virginity as some kind of gift. I'm doing this for me. You just happen to be the bastard good enough to get me to yes. I'm tired of talking about this. Fuck me. Now."

"Who am I to say no to that?"

I covered her body with mine, settling myself between her legs until my cock was just where I wanted it. I pressed her into the mattress like she'd described to me. She'd confessed to wanting to feel my weight on top of her. As I looked into her eyes, I gave her what she wanted, lying fully on top of her, wrapping my arms around her. When I was there and she still welcomed me, tunneling her fingers through the hair at the nape of my neck, I kissed her again.

Her lips were addictive in the extreme. I could happily kiss her forever and kill any man who'd ever had the pleasure of tasting her even for a brief time. She was all mine. No matter the circumstances, she was mine, and I'd keep her forever.

At some point, she pulled my hair free of the band I'd fastened it with to give myself the appearance of civility. She mussed it until I was sure it was all over the place, wild and untamed. Just like me.

"Much better," she said when I pulled back to look at her.

"You like the wild side of me better than the one that looks sophisticated?"

"Absolutely. Because the wild side is you, Reaper. I want you. Not what you think everyone wants you to be, or, rather, what you think I want you to be."

"You enjoyed the dinner, yes?"

"Oh, absolutely! I wouldn't have missed it for the world!"

"Then you needed that side of me more than this wild side."

"Oh, Reaper." She laid a hand on the side of my face. "No. I didn't need you to be that man for me. I would have been happy if we'd gone to some cheap fast-food joint and run everyone out of the kiddie section, put a white bed sheet over a table with a few candles, and shared a burger and fries. As long as you were with me, I was going to be happy."

I shook my head, giving her a little sigh. "What am I gonna do with you, baby?"

She grinned. "I already told you." She reached

between us and guided my cock to her entrance. "Fuck me. Make me come. Show me what it's like to belong to a rough, tough biker like yourself."

With a defeated groan, I slid into her. I saw her eyes widen when I pushed through her innocence, heard her gasp of surprise. There was a slight wince of pain but nothing else to indicate her discomfort, so I pulled back. Then slid back inside. I shuddered above her, groaning in ecstasy.

"Reaper." Her plea was music, the slight pain where her nails dug into my shoulders an erotic pleasure unlike anything I'd ever known. "You're inside me." Her voice was a husky whisper, a mix of awe and satisfaction. "You're really inside me."

"I am. You ready?"

Her expression turned eager. "Fuck me, Reaper. Do it!"

Not waiting a moment longer, I slid out, then back in, taking it slow at first. I waited until she tilted her hips at me, meeting me thrust for thrust, before I picked up the pace.

Working her body with mine was glorious. She responded to me just as beautifully as she always did. If ever there had been a woman made for me, it was Swan. She took my wants and desires and made them her own. Even as untried as her body was, she threw all in with me. Her cries and moans of pleasure sang throughout the room, letting me know she was on board. Feeling the same joy I felt.

There was so much I wanted to do with Swan. So much I wanted to show her. I knew I'd never last this first time. Not in any way. I was going to be lucky to last long enough to get her off.

"So good," she gasped. "Oh, God! Reaper! Why is it so fucking good?"

"Because we're meant to be, Swan," I said at her ear. I should have looked her in the eyes when I said it, but I couldn't. Not because I didn't believe it, but because I knew she'd see right through me. See that, somehow in the last thirty-six hours I'd known her, I'd already managed to fall in love. I wasn't opposed to her knowing, but I was going to make her tell me first. She wouldn't believe me otherwise. Wasn't sure she'd believe me even then. Either way, I had to at least manage to hold off that long. "You're mine, baby. I'm yours."

She tightened her arms around me, digging her heels into the small of my back, and met each surge of my hips with one of her own. "Yes," she gasped out. "I'm yours. You're mine."

"Always, Swan. For always."

"Reaper!" She screamed my name as her pussy clamped down on my cock. It pulsed and massaged my dick, her body telling me she wanted me to come with her.

"I'm comin'," I groaned, my movements frantic now. "Gonna come so fuckin' hard!"

"Yes! Please, Reaper!"

I turned my head to the side so I wouldn't hurt her ears and bellowed my release, unable to part our bodies long enough to arch my back and roar to the ceiling. My cock pulsed and emptied into the condom and, as satisfying as it was, I still wanted to fill her pussy instead of the fucking rubber. I wanted that. Wanted to fill her full of my cum. It was a primal instinct I found hard to control or ignore.

For long moments we lay there. I turned my head back to bury my face in her neck, kissing and praising her. "You're beautiful, Swan. So fucking beautiful." I nuzzled her neck, softly thrusting my hips.

"I -- I --" I felt her swallow where my lips were still at her throat.

"Yeah, baby?"

"I --" She cleared her throat. "That was amazing." I'd bet my last dollar that wasn't what she'd wanted to say. I had to smile inside. She was there. She just didn't want to admit it yet. That was fine. Things were happening fast. I'd just admitted to myself I was already in love with her and had sworn to myself not to say it until she did. How could I expect her to voice the same thing so soon when I wasn't willing?

"It certainly was. And there's plenty more where that came from. We've got all night. I'm gonna show you so much stuff, it's gonna blow your mind."

She giggled. "Is that supposed to shock me?"

"It's supposed to make you look forward to me recovering so I can put you on your hands and knees and take you from behind." I gave her my best cocky grin. "Gonna take that pretty little ass, too. Maybe not tonight, but soon."

"Oh, goodness." Her pussy contracted around my cock.

"I think my little Swan is very interested in that prospect."

"I didn't say that." She shook her head, her eyes wide, but her lips flirted with a smile.

"You didn't have to, baby. Your pussy said it for you."

She play-slapped at me. "You're horrible."

"Oh, yeah? I'm not the one squeezing my cock to death at the mere suggestion of it being in your ass."

Swan laughed then, throwing her arms around my neck tightly. "Thank you so much, Reaper. For everything."

"Nothing to thank me for, sweetheart. You deserve every little bit of happiness me or anyone else can give you. I'm just thankful it's me."

Chapter Seven

Swan

"Wait. We're going *where*?"

"Katmandu. You'll need some warm clothes. It's not real cold in the city, but Everest Base Camp will be pretty fuckin' cold."

I laughed. I was sure the sound was borderline maniacal. "I'm equipped for Florida, Reaper. I don't have anything even close to appropriate for extreme temperatures."

"Honey, that was a list for me. Not you. Everything will be delivered and already stowed away when we get to the airport."

"Airport."

"Well, yeah." He turned to give me a confused look. "We can't take the bike there, I'm sorry to say."

This wasn't computing. "We're going to Mount Everest Base Camp?"

He grinned. "Yeah, baby. That's what I said."

"This is insane!" I was laughing at him, but I wasn't joking. "We can't go to Nepal!"

"Why not? And I caution you about telling me how to spend my money."

"Well, for one, I don't have a passport." I grinned, knowing that would be a deal breaker.

"Good thing I know a guy who can make one and the finished product is official."

I blinked at him. "Are you fucking kidding me?"

Reaper barked out a laugh. "No. Not at all, baby. Now. Pack everything you need. We'll be gone about two weeks. It takes close to a full day to get there and a full day back. We'll fly into Lukla, then take a helicopter to Base Camp. El Diablo already has the permits and permissions and all that shit, so it's no problem. The only thing is the altitude. We're not used to it. If we walked up, no problem. Flying up there with only a day or so in Katmandu? We'd probably be fine since we ain't stayin' long, but I'd rather be safe than sorry. We'll likely be the only dumbasses there wearing oxygen, but Fury tells me it might be necessary if we stay any length of time given the speed with which we're going."

"We don't have to do this, you know." I wanted to laugh and cry at the same time. "I only put that on the list because, I mean, who doesn't want to see the tallest mountain in the world? I'm not in any shape for climbing -- or a lot of walking, for that matter."

"And you won't be walking much. Another reason for me to have oxygen is so I can piggyback you when necessary. But we're choppering in. We'll stay as long as you want, then leave. Another overnight stay in Katmandu, then home. It can be that quick. If you want to see some of the sights in the city, we can do that, too. Only thing we have to worry about is keeping you off your leg as much as possible."

"Reaper…" I didn't want to hurt his feelings or anything, but this was seriously too much. "I can't do this."

He stopped, his attention suddenly focused on me wholly. "You hurtin'?"

"No. It's not that."

He narrowed his eyes. "Then what is it?"

I sighed. "You know why. Reaper. No. It's too much."

Instead of arguing like I figured he would, Reaper just nodded a couple of times. "I see." Then he pulled out his cell, stabbed in a number, then put it to his ear. "Yeah. Need you out here ASAP." A pause while he listened. "Yep. I got everything else packed.

Just waiting on her and she's balking." Another pause. "Don't think so. It's the money." Pause. "Yeah. Thanks."

Reaper scowled at me. "You're gonna learn not to tell me not to spend money on you. I told you you'd never win those types of arguments."

"I'm not trying to tell you how to spend your money, Reaper," I said softly. "I just don't want you to put so much of an investment into me when I'm not gonna be here. In fact, as much as it pains me to say this, I really wish you'd find a woman who's gonna be here with you to spend your time and money on."

"Stop!" he growled at me, taking a step forward before stopping himself. He was about to say something when the door opened, and El Diablo and Jezebel stepped inside. No invitation required. I raised an eyebrow but said nothing.

"What's this I hear about you not wanting to accept El Segador's trip to Nepal? Wasn't climbing Mount Everest on your bucket list?"

"Well, yeah, but it was a token addition at best. No way I was ever gonna be able to climb a mountain of any kind, let alone Everest."

"She's starting to talk about herself like she's already gone, Liam," Reaper said. His face was tight, his expression closed off, but I could see I'd hurt him in some way.

"I just said you should put all this effort you're giving to me into a woman who'll actually stay with you. I don't have tomorrow to give you. It's all got to be about today."

"That may be," El Diablo said, looking carefully at Reaper before continuing. "But you're with him now. Let him spoil you as he sees fit."

"This whole thing is so surreal... Can't you see

how wrong this all is? He should be out there doing all this with a woman he plans on keeping. Not me. No one can keep me. I'm dying!"

"One thing at a time, sweet," El Diablo soothed. Jezebel moved to me and wrapped her arms around me in a hug. I returned it automatically.

"Honey, we just want you happy. El Segador does too. And, if you'll take time to really think about it, I think you'll find he feels something special for you. This isn't something he's doing out of pity, if that's what you're afraid of. He's doing it because he…" She trailed off and looked up at Reaper. "He's doing it because you're special to him. We're all helping in every way we can. I got El Segador's list ready with instructions for everything on that list to be loaded on the plane. Me and the girls picked out all the stuff for you. Fury made sure you had the oxygen and equipment for a trip at that elevation, and that El Segador knew how to use it. When you get back, we've got other things planned." She smiled at me, brushing away the tears tracking down her cheeks. Then she brushed mine away. I hadn't even realized I'd been crying. "You've made more than a few friends here, Swan. You're a very special woman indeed to get this bunch on your side so readily. They're usually suspicious of everyone, but you even won Samson over. I can't even begin to tell you how rare that is."

"I wasn't trying to win anyone over," I muttered. I looked over at Reaper. His face was still blank, but I could tell I'd hurt him. With a small sob, I threw myself into his arms. Without a moment's hesitation, he had his arms out and ready for me. When he held me to him, he squeezed me to him almost unbearably tightly. Not that I minded. My arms were so tight around his neck, I was probably strangling him. "I jjust want to not die!"

To my complete and utter horror, I broke down completely. I think it was the first time since my diagnosis I let the reality that I was going to die soon sink into my mind. I was scared of so many things. So many fucking things.

"I don't want to die, but I'm afraid of lingering. I don't want to hurt. I don't want to be a burden on anyone. I just... I want children and to see them grow up and have children of their own! Is that too much to ask? I'm not a bad person, Reaper." I sobbed, my words running together. My chest ached, and fear was so sharp I couldn't contain it.

"You could never be a burden on anyone, baby," Reaper said. His voice was husky. I thought I felt Jezebel and El Diablo surrounding me as well as Reaper, but I wasn't sure. "We're all here to help you. Me especially." Reaper kissed the top of my head. "I'll always be here for you no matter what."

"Us too, precious girl," El Diablo added.

"All the girls," Jezebel said. "We're all here. The whole club. Anything you need, we'll see that you have it."

I looked up at Reaper, cupping the side of his face with my hand. "I just don't want you to waste time on me when you could be with someone who'll be with you the rest of your life. I don't want to take away from your happiness."

"You're not," he said with a shake of his head. "Before you came along, I fucked a few women here and there, but I'd never met anyone I wanted to keep. You, I want. If that means it's for a few weeks or months or years, then I'll take it. It will gut me if you leave, but I'll take anything I can get and welcome the pain if I get to keep you in my life as long as possible."

I looked at him for long moments. I got the sense there was more he wanted to say, but I had no idea what. I sniffed, then tried to laugh a little. "I'm such a mess."

"You're perfect," Jezebel said. "You're absolutely perfect. Now. Let Reaper spoil you as he sees fit. Join the mile-high club. Let him show you the joys of sex while you go on a glorious, exotic vacation. If you hate it, at least you get to say you saw the highest mountain in the world, and you hated every fucking second of it." She grinned. "But I'm betting Reaper can make you enjoy at least part of the journey."

"Oh, I have no doubt about that," I said through my tears. El Diablo handed me a few tissues, and I wiped my tears and my dripping nose. "Gross," I muttered into the tissue.

"We're all here for you, but most especially El Segador. Let him."

"I'm so sorry," I said as I buried my face in Reaper's shirt once again. "I'm a hot mess right now."

"How many times have you broken down like this?" Reaper asked his question gently, but I got where he was going.

"None. This is the first time."

"Maybe you needed to."

"Not sure I ever let myself think about it long enough to. I was just so focused on not thinking about it. I didn't have anyone…"

"Well, you do now." Reaper kissed the top of my head. "You have me. You have Jezebel and all the other ol' ladies. We've got your back. But most especially me. I'm gonna be here with you through it all. I swear to you on my life, Swan."

"OK." There was nothing else for me to say. I looked up at Reaper. "When does the plane leave?"

He grinned at me. "That's my girl. We've got another hour, but honestly, this is on our time. We can leave whenever the fuck we want."

I gave everyone a watery smile, still wiping at my nose. "Well, we can't let everyone's hard planning go to waste. Let's go conquer Everest."

* * *

Swan

The flight to Nepal was interesting, to say the least. There wasn't much to do on the flight other than have sex, and Reaper and I did tons of it. He also told me about his past. At least as much as he could. He said there were things he'd never tell me, no matter how long we were together, because he never wanted that part of his life to touch me. I got the impression he'd killed several times and might even do so again. No matter what he thought, it didn't bother me. I was from the South, and we all knew that sometimes people just needed killing.

Once we got to Nepal, I was so mixed up with the time I just laughed and gave up. We landed at exactly eight-thirty P.M. local time, which was nine hours and forty-five minutes later than it was in Palm Beach. As if the time change itself wasn't enough, I now had to contend with the fifteen-minute shortfall. Ugh!

"Don't worry about it," Reaper soothed, amusement on his face. "It's not like we have a schedule to adhere to. Anything we choose to do, we do on our own time."

We stayed at the Hyatt Regency Resort in Katmandu. Three days and several small walks and rides around the city, and I felt like I'd been dropped in a magical land. While the city was busy, there were areas of great beauty. Buddhist temples and breathtaking landscapes had me thankful I hadn't turned down the trip.

"It's magical here," I said one evening as we watched the sun set. Mount Everest could be seen off in the distance. "With it being the middle of the summer, I wonder if there will be anyone at Base Camp when we arrive tomorrow."

"Couldn't say. If I had to guess, there's probably always someone there testing themselves against the mountain."

"True. I hope we don't disturb anyone with the helicopter and all. I'm not sure I could actually walk up there, though. The altitude's already brutal. It will only get worse, I'm sure."

"I got you covered. Besides, we only have to stay as long as you want. You get ready to leave, whether it's five minutes or an hour, we leave."

"You know" -- I leaned into Reaper, wrapping my arms around his waist as I nuzzled his chest -- "I bet if we exercise a little, we'll acclimate faster."

He glanced down as I looked up at him. I was grinning. "You do, huh? What kind of exercise did you have in mind?"

"The horizontal kind."

"How about the kind where I bend you over the rail and fuck you from behind."

"Yeah," I said. "I could get into that."

He scooped me up and I squealed, giggling as he took me back inside our room. "How about I get into you?"

"You're horrible!"

"You started it, squirt. I'm just ending it to my satisfaction."

He laid me down on the bed, stripping off his

shirt once I was settled. I stretched, smiling up at him. "I'm so glad you brought me here, Reaper."

"I'm glad I did, too. I think the clean air and sunshine is doing you good. You look more rested and have more color than you have since we met. How's your leg?"

"It hurts less than it has in months. Of course, you haven't let me do much. Who'd have thought you could find ways of getting me from point A to point B without me walking in a city of a million hikers! Literally everyone here is climbing a mountain somewhere."

"Not everyone. Just most of them. Besides, I see two mountains I want to climb right now."

"Oh yeah?" I grinned.

He stripped off my shirt, unfastening my bra as he went. "Yep." When he lay down on top of me, he took both my tits in his hands and pushed them together. "These two right here." He kissed each nipple before sucking them gently. "Gonna take the rest of the day, I'm thinkin'. After that, I might need to go spelunkin'."

I laughed. "You're crazy. Completely crazy."

"Yeah? I think you like my crazy."

I did. I really did.

* * *

El Segador

The next morning, we boarded a helicopter El Diablo had rented for us and headed to Everest Base Camp. It was the second week in June, and we'd been really lucky. So far, the monsoon season hadn't started, but it was only a matter of time. There was no rain forecast for today, but the pilot and his team were keeping close watch. At the first sign of anything, they'd call us back and head to Katmandu.

We actually had a better view of Everest from the air and in the city. This close to the mountain, other very tall mountains blocked the view. But Swan wandered around the camp, talking with mountaineers headed back to Lukla, the village where the trek to Base Camp traditionally begins for climbers. I could tell most thought she was some rich woman with little sense, thinking she could climb the mountain when she hadn't even bothered to make it to Base Camp without a helicopter. But she soon won over everyone she talked to. That was just Swan. She was no-nonsense and just a genuinely nice person. We stayed several hours until Swan was visibly winded and favoring her right leg more and more.

"All right, little bird. Time to go."

"But I'm not ready." She pouted prettily, but she was tired. She was practically drooping before my eyes.

"Maybe not, but it's time. We want to get back before dark. Besides, I'm an old man. I can't keep up with you young chicks."

She laughed. "You're in better shape than I've ever been. Like you're having a hard time." She sighed. "Fine. But I want it known I'm leaving under protest."

"Noted. You can complain to El Diablo when we get back."

"Uh, no. Not on your life. The man's nice and all, but he intimidates me more than a little bit."

"He's harmless to you. You know that, right?"

"Yeah. I know. Still. His name's literally the Devil. How safe could he be?"

"Well, my name's the Reaper, and you ain't scared of me."

"You're different. Something about having your

mouth between my legs all the time negates any intimidation factor."

"I don't have my mouth between your legs all the time. Like now. My mouth is not between your legs."

Swan giggled, leaning into me as we approached the helicopter. "Maybe not, but I bet it won't be long after we get back to the hotel it will be."

"You got me there. Planned on it when we got in the shower." I winked at her. "After that, we'll have to see."

Her laughter lit up my world. Yeah. I was in trouble. And I wasn't even upset about it.

Chapter Eight
El Segador

On the way home, we took a detour. We went to Europe, stopping in Germany, Italy, France, and the UK. We were still ahead of schedule, and there were things on Swan's list I could fulfill.

We marked off taking a hot air balloon ride in Rothenburg, Germany. The balloon was bright orange with a big yellow smiley face. The guide happily let her dictate to him when she demanded they go higher. He just laughed and winked at her. Which got my back up. The guy wasn't as big as me, but he was younger, and women probably thought he was better-looking than me. He didn't have the hard edge to him I did.

He spoke to her in German, telling her how pretty she was. When Swan just smiled at him with a blank look on her face, he gave her a sly grin. I said nothing but suspected he was testing her knowledge of the language. I was proven right when he told her in German he'd love to toss her big motherfucker of a boyfriend over the side and fuck her raw.

I propped my elbow on the side of the basket and replied in the same language. "Her motherfucker of a boyfriend is the right-hand man to the deadliest assassin in the world. Killing you would be no more than an afterthought. Do you really want to take me the fuck on?"

The little prick turned white. Swan frowned at me.

"What did you say to him?"

"Nothing too bad." I grinned at her, pulling her close for a kiss. "Take pictures, baby. It's a beautiful view." It was enough to distract her. Likely because she was a good person and would never suspect the boy would think of doing her harm, or that I'd reciprocate. Or worse.

After our two days in Germany, I took her to see the Colosseum in Rome, the Eiffel Tower in France, and the Tower of London. She protested a little, but wonder had soon won out in every place, and she'd just gone with it. The sex had been every chance I could coax her into a private corner and the most fantastic of my life.

We knocked out taking a cruise, too. Instead of flying back to Palm Beach, we took a seven-day cruise to New York. We didn't take just any old cruise, either. I got us one from Cunard. I'd booked the best suite they had, offering enough money they bumped someone so we got the best suite on the ship. I'd have taken us back to Fort Lauderdale, but it was another seven days and I knew that, though Doc had gotten back from his assignment with ExFil, he'd want some time to study Swan's records. Swan didn't object, because she'd never been to New York. I figured we could take some time there if she wanted.

I got the call from Doc about halfway into our seven-day cruise. He said he wanted to do a biopsy as soon as we got back. Bastard refused to say why he wanted to do it so quickly, but I let it go. Mainly because I didn't want Swan to hear us. The last thing I wanted to do was worry her this close to the end of our vacation. The only thing we hadn't checked off on her bucket list was the Disney World roller-coaster thing, and I intended to do that the second I could.

Other than her little setback at Base Camp, Swan was looking much better than she had when I'd first found her. She wasn't limping, and I had her eating three square meals a day plus snacks. While she hadn't put on much weight yet, her face had filled out slightly, and she didn't look like she'd blow away in a stiff breeze. The cruise was helping tremendously. I got her to sit by the pool or on our balcony most days. When we did go out, I gave her piggyback rides. It got some strange looks, but she just laughed, enjoying the attention.

By the time we got to New York, Swan confessed to being ready to head home. She looked great. Her face had color where she'd been pale before. I took it as a win, even if she was tired. Hell, after being gone so long, I was feeling it, too. And I wanted to ride. I needed my bike, and I suspected she'd love it. It was first on my agenda when we got back to Palm Beach. Then Doc could do whatever Swan was willing to let him do.

We landed around noon. I'd had Swan sleeping as much as I could, distracting her from the fact I wasn't letting her have anything to eat or drink. It had been part of Doc's instructions. Instead of a waiting car, Tank and Iron were there with my bike and a truck. We disembarked, Swan using me for balance so she could put as little pressure on her leg as possible.

"What's this?" she asked, looking up at me. "Are we taking the truck or the motorcycle?"

I stepped forward and took Tank's hand, then Iron's. "We're takin' the bike, darlin'. It goes against everything I believe in, but I'll even let you not wear a helmet if you promise to hang tight to me."

"Oh, boy!" She practically squealed as she bounced in her excitement. "I've never ridden on a motorcycle!"

"It's a bike, baby. My bike."

"Figured El Segador could use all the help he could get. Three weeks with him by yourself? Well, we were takin' bets whether you'd killed him yet."

She laughed. "He was wonderful! We went ballooning in Germany, went to Paris and Rome and England... He took me on a cruise using the Cunard line! It's historic!"

Tank and Iron, the bastards, just looked at me and chuckled. Tank said, "Looks like you got him pussy-whipped, girl. See you keep it that way."

"Don't know about that, but if he's pussy-whipped, I'm dick-whipped. I'd do anything he wanted if he promised me his cock at the end of it." Her smirk said she'd meant it to counter them.

Tank and Iron threw back their heads and laughed. Both of them. Iron pulled her into his arms, hugging her gently. "You decide you don't want him, little sister, I'll take you on. If for no other reason than to listen to that sassy mouth of yours."

"That's enough," I growled. "Give her back."

"Take your time," Tank said. "Fury said Doc'd be at the clinic around one with Mama, Alizay, and Blade."

That brought me up short. "At Fury's clinic?"

"Yeah." Tank shrugged. "He wants this done now. Something about not making Swan suffer needlessly. Had a few things to say about her previous care. I already told him you landed, and that you guys were takin' the bike home."

Fuck.

"What's going on?" Swan looked up at me with big eyes. I could see fear there. Resignation.

"Don't know, babe. Doc's been lookin' into your case. Blade is another doctor at Salvation's Bane. Mama and Alizay are both from Bones. Mama was a surgeon back in the day, and Alizay is a trauma nurse and the wife of one of Bone's patched members. If I had to guess, Doc's assembling his own team to help you."

"Do you need to call him?"

I pulled her into my arms. "I can if you want, babe. Otherwise, we can just ride and enjoy the trip until we get to the compound. Up to you."

She appeared to think about it. "Maybe we could just go. I'll find out soon enough, I guess. I want some time to enjoy the new experience you're getting ready to give me."

"OK, then."

Part of me wanted to purr in satisfaction at her desire to have this with me. Another part wanted to rage at Tank, Iron, and Doc for making her worry without an explanation.

"Did Doc say what he thought the problem was? Why he was assembling everyone?"

Tank shook his head. "I only know he was pissed as all get out."

"About having to look at my case?" Swan looked horrified. "Reaper, I'm so sorry! I never intended to put anyone out --"

"Hush, sweetheart. It's not that. If it were, he'd just tell us all to fuck off."

"I don't want to be a problem, Reaper." She looked up at me, her eyes swimming with unshed tears. Which made me want to punch someone. Probably Tank for saying something in front of her instead of to me directly.

"Honey," Iron said, glancing at Tank and me. "I didn't get the feeling he was upset he was called on to help. I think he was pissed because he didn't think you got the care you should have before you came to us."

"If that's anyone's fault, it's mine. The doctors wanted to do more stuff, but I couldn't afford it and didn't want to drag this out and be miserable the whole time."

"I get you, sweetheart," Tank said. "He does, too. He deals with kids with cancers, so he understands." He looked at Reaper. "Get her home and let Doc do his thing. The sooner you know what her prospects are, the better you can decide on what to do next."

I heard Swan whimper beside me and pulled her into my arms. "It's all gonna be OK, baby. No matter what, I'm here. I'll always be here."

"I'm scared," she whispered. "I'm so scared."

"I know. But remember, you're not alone. I'm here. My club is here. We'll all be with you no matter what."

I wanted to howl in pain. I'd hoped for her first bike ride to be a joyous time. Instead, though she had her arms around me the entire time, I felt the dampness of her tears on my shirt where it clung to my back while she cried. At every stop, I rubbed her hands and her leg, trying to soothe her. By the time we got back to the clubhouse, I'd had all I could take.

I stopped the bike in the front lot and climbed off, taking Swan with me. She clung to me and cried softly.

"I know, baby. But I swear to you, I'll do everything in my power to take care of you. No matter what. You can count on me."

"I know," she whispered, trying to get herself together. "I know."

I'd just scooped her up in my arms when Doc came from inside, his gaze focused entirely on Swan. Holly skipped along beside him, chatting lightly, oblivious to the dynamics with Swan. Mama and Blade tried to distract her, but the girl had a hold of Doc's hand and wasn't letting go.

"What's a matter with Swan? You gonna fix her?"

"If I can, sweetie," Doc said absently, his attention only partially with the girl. "I need you to go back inside now. I need to take Swan to the clinic and see what's goin' on with her."

"I wanna go too," Holly pouted. "She's my best friend."

"Come along, dear," Mama said, trying to pry Holly's hand from Doc's. "You need to go back to your mother for a while. When Doc's finished with Swan, I promise I'll bring you to her. OK?"

"I wanna see Swan first," Holly said stubbornly. "I've missed her!"

Swan sniffed, swiping her hands across her face. "I'm OK. Let me down to see Holly."

"You sure? She'll be all right. You don't have to deal with her just yet."

"No. It's because of her I have you. I owe her more than I can ever repay."

I just grunted, knowing it was true, but I was riding the edge of my control at the moment. If Doc came back with bad news, I wasn't sure I could hold my shit together.

The second I put Swan on her feet, Holly ran into her arms. Swan knelt down and hugged the child.

"Hey there, squirt," she said, trying to sound cheerful when anyone could see she'd been crying.

"Don't worry," Holly said with confidence. "Doc there can fix anything. You'll see." She wrapped her skinny arms around Swan's neck and hugged her fiercely. "When you're done, I'll come see you. And just remember: Needles hurt, but sometimes they can help you get better."

"Thanks, sweetie," Swan said, kissing the child on the cheek. "If I can't see you tonight, I'll see you tomorrow. I promise."

When they were done, I picked Swan back up into my arms, carrying her the distance to Fury's clinic. Doc didn't say a word the whole time. No one did. Alizay and Blade were already there. They talked in hushed voices as they moved around the office collecting items and taking them into what Fury called his procedure room.

"We've got everything ready," Alizay said softly. "Whenever you're ready."

"What's going on?" Swan still clung to me. I sat and she stayed in my lap. I wasn't sure that I didn't hold on to her as tightly as she held to me.

Doc pulled up a stool and sat in front of her. "Two things," he began. "I want to physically examine the knot on your upper thigh. I'll ask you some questions, and you need to answer me as truthfully and accurately as you can."

"OK."

"Second, I want to do a biopsy. I need to see exactly what kind of cells you have in there and in what concentration. That way I know what I've got to work with."

"I don't want you taking out my leg and pelvis and shit." Swan was more sulky than stubborn. It was almost as if she'd resolved herself to doing whatever Doc said, no matter what her wishes were."

"Baby," I said before Doc could say anything. "No one's gonna make you do anything you don't want to. I swear to you on my life, I won't let that happen. I'll kill a motherfucker first."

Doc gave me an exasperated look. "I think I'm more pissed about that than anything else," he muttered. "Look. That kind of surgery shouldn't have even been hinted at before they knew exactly what they were dealing with, and the only way to know that for absolute certainty is to do a biopsy. Besides, what you described was pretty radical. Not something I can do in a clinic, no matter what kind of equipment Fury has. This is strictly a biopsy. I'll get what I need with a small drill and a needle."

She nodded. Then asked softly, "Will it hurt?"

"I'll give you enough medicine you won't care, but I'll numb you up as much as I can. OK?"

"OK," she said, then buried her face back in my neck.

"Good," Doc said, standing. "Let's get the exam finished so we can get all this other shit done. I promise you, you're gonna know one way or the other exactly what we're dealing with and what your options are before you go to bed tonight."

The next few hours were the longest of my life. El Diablo and Jezebel stayed with me the whole time. Once Doc was finished, his samples collected and given to Mama to take wherever she was taking them, Swan slept. I moved her from the exam table to a bed in the back. I sat beside her on a chair, scooting it as close to the bed as I could and holding her hand.

"I can't live without her, Liam," I said softly, knowing my friend would hear me. "She's become my world in so short a time, it's laughable."

"Just let Doc do his work. Don't give up yet."

"I'll never give up on her," I murmured. "Whatever it takes. If it will get her better…"

"I know. Just have a little faith."

"You know, I was El Segador before you were El Diablo. Maybe there's a reason for it."

"You bring monsters to justice, Reaper. Not innocents."

"She commented on the irony of my name when we first met." I sighed, kissing her hand gently. "She loves me. I know she does."

"And you?"

I glanced over at my oldest friend. "You know I love her. More than I ever thought myself capable of loving anyone."

Liam nodded, then put his arm around Jezebel, kissing her temple. "Go let Holly know Swan's going to need to sleep tonight. We'll bring her to breakfast in the morning."

"Sure." Jezebel stood and put a hand on my shoulder. "We're all pulling for her, Reaper."

I smiled. "You're good for Liam," I said. "A remarkable woman. No matter what happens tonight, Swan's going to need friends. I'm a jealous bastard, but I want her to have all the friends she can stand."

"You can count on me. Anything either of you need, I'll be there."

With Jezebel gone, it left me and Liam with Swan. Neither of us spoke for a long time. It was a couple of hours before either of us said anything. Then it was me who broke the silence.

"Until I got the call from Doc, her illness was an abstract thing. It was there, but I could see improvements in her appearance with just rest and food and good care. I'd forget about it sometimes unless her leg hurt." I gave a soft laugh. "I mean, we went to the other side of the fuckin' world, for fuck's sake. She never had the first bit of trouble. Never complained about anything other than the occasional bit of pain when she'd been on her leg too much."

"Doc made it real."

"Yeah." I scrubbed my free hand over my face. "Took me out of my fairy tale."

"We'll make it through this," El Diablo said. "How much did you get done on her bucket list?"

"Everything but the fucking shit at Disney World. And getting her drunk and high. Thought she might like to go to Disney with the girls. The other I wanted to wait until we were back here. Need to know exactly what I give her to get her high. And that I can trust it."

Again, we fell into silence. Holding vigil.

Swan stirred, moaning in her sleep. I stroked her hair softly. "Shh, baby. I'm here."

"Hurt," she said, her eyes still closed.

"I'll go see if Fury can give her something," El Diablo said softly.

"Thanks."

I leaned forward and placed my lips on her forehead. "My precious Swan."

"Reaper?"

"I'm here, baby. I'll always be here."

"You promise?" She sounded sleepy, but also scared and utterly miserable.

"I do, sweetheart. I'll always be with you. No matter what."

Fury entered the room, a small syringe in hand. "I'll give her a small dose. Doc said to keep on the pain but to let her get good and awake."

"Where is he?" I asked, wishing I could talk to the bastard. I needed to know what was going on.

"With the pathologist. He said to give him a few hours, and he'd know exactly what we were dealing with."

"It's already been a few hours," I grumbled.

"Figured you'd be impatient." Swan's words were slurred, but she had a faint smile on her face.

"Always when it concerns you, baby," I said, kissing her hand. "Fury's brought something for pain."

"Ah, good. Hip hurts like a mother."

"I expect it does," Fury said with a smile.

His woman, Noelle, sat beside Swan on the bed. "Hey, honey. Doc bein' mean to you?"

Swan grinned sleepily. "Yeah. Have someone cut off his balls for me, will you?"

"Yeah," Noelle said with a chuckle. "I'll see if I can get Shadow or Millie to get on that for you."

"Nah. Don't really do that. I know he's trying to help."

"If it's my balls you guys are contemplatin' losin', I'd appreciate it if you could at least wait until I've had some offspring." Doc walked in, grinning at Swan.

"We were," Swan said with a smile. She still sounded about half loopy from the drugs he'd given her. "But I think I talked her out of it."

"It was you who suggested it," Noelle said, giggling. "I was just helpin' a bitch out."

Swan chuckled. "I like you, Noelle. You and me and Jezebel are gonna rule the roost around here."

"That you are, my dear," El Diablo said with a smile. "Now, Doc. You have news?"

"Can't we just talk about other things for a while?" Swan looked like she thought she was being led to the gallows. "I don't want to --"

"Relax, Swan." Doc came closer, sitting on the other side of the bed from Noelle. He took her other hand in both of his. "It's not cancer. You're not gonna die. At least, not from this, and not any time soon."

She sucked in a breath that turned into a sob. "What?"

I was afraid to say anything. My grip on Swan's hand tightened fractionally, and I tried to loosen my grip. Last thing I wanted to do was hurt or frighten her.

Doc sighed, frowning. "This is a prime example of why I don't like telling patients a definite diagnosis until I've run all the tests." He took a breath. "You should have been told they were testing for osteosarcoma. And yes, all the imaging pointed to it. Your blood markers were questionable, but the imaging was key in the diagnosis they gave you. The pathology, on the other hand…" He grinned. "You've got what's called myositis ossificans. It can look like cancer in imaging, but it's not. Short of it is, this was caused by your fall in a roundabout way. The resulting injury to your muscle, and probably the bone to a lesser degree, caused an inflammation or swelling around the bone. It's why the chemo didn't work and any kind of surgery or just walking on it will aggravate it because it irritates it. With some rest, anti-inflammatories, and gradually working your way back to full mobility, you're going to be just fine, honey."

Swan's lower lip trembled. "You're serious. You promise you're serious."

"Honey, I would not in any way be that cruel to anyone. You don't have bone cancer. You have an inflammation that will go away on its own given rest and careful physical therapy."

Chapter Nine
Swan

When Doc's news finally settled in, I reached for Reaper and burst into tears. I'm not sure how long I cried, but it seemed like months of worry and fear burst free, and I couldn't stem it. Wasn't sure I wanted to. Other than all the people witnessing my breakdown, there was really no reason to hold it in any longer. In the month or so I'd been with Reaper, I knew for certain he understood my fears and would never make fun of me or allow anyone else to. And these people? Yeah. They were solidly in my corner. I had no idea what would happen next, but right this second it didn't matter. The people in this club and, if I understood it all, two other clubs -- Salvation's Bane and Bones -- had banded together and helped me in my lowest moment. The people from Bones had come all the way from Kentucky! And none of them had asked for anything in return. No one had ever been so caring in my life since my mom died.

"You're OK," Reaper said, his mouth at my ear. "You're good. It's all good." He sounded like he was talking more to himself than me, but I'd take it. He held me tight, trembling nearly as much as I was. That was when I realized the man loved me. At least, in some way he loved me. This changed things. Our relationship was now vastly different.

"Will you help me?" I asked softly. "Help me while I do whatever Doc says I have to do to heal?"

"Of course." He pulled back. "Swan, why would you even ask me that? I'm not leaving."

"But..." I glanced around me. Everyone but El Diablo and Doc had gone. El Diablo had a supportive grip on Reaper's shoulder while Doc watched over both of us. "I'm not dying. You didn't sign up for this."

"I signed up for you, Swan. No matter how long or short a time together. I'm with you."

"Hold on to her, Reaper," El Diablo said before turning to go. He took Doc with him, and the men left us alone.

"You know I'd never hold you to your promise now," I said, even as I gripped his shirt tightly in my fists. Tears streamed down my face at the thought of goodbye from the man who'd come to mean so much to me.

"I know. And you don't have to. I'm not leaving you, Swan. Not when we thought you were sick. Certainly not now that I know you're well. You're my woman. I'm your man."

"I'm gonna live, Reaper." I know it sounded mundane, but I was so relieved. I wanted to shout my thankfulness to the universe but could barely manage to breathe.

"Yeah, baby." Reaper smiled at me. If there was one tear that trickled down his cheek, I didn't mention it. "You're gonna live. If you still want me, I'm all yours. This time, I swear I'll be with you until I die."

"You can have any woman you want, El Segador." He raised an eyebrow at me. Likely because I never called him that. "I've been living in my own little world here, feeling sorry for myself. Eager to experience everything I could before I got too weak to do anything other than wait to die. But I see the way the women here look at you. You're not vice president of the club or whatever. I know that title belongs to Samson. But you're the closest person here to El Diablo, other than Jezebel. That makes you the second most powerful man here."

"Sure. I could have any of them. Hell, I've had

several of them over the years. But the only one I want with my heart and soul, my entire being, Swan, is you." He took a breath and cleared his throat. Looking supremely uncomfortable, he looked away before saying, "I love you, Swan."

God, if I cried any more I was gonna have the headache from hell. But yeah. I started blubbering like an idiot. I wrapped my arms around Reaper's neck as tightly as I could. "I love you, too! I love you, too!" I kissed him hard. Over and over. Then he wrapped his arms around me as tightly as I held him and we just… cried. Both of us. Even my big tough biker.

We stayed like that for a long time. Until my pain medicine started to wear off. I was content to stay like that, but Reaper wasn't having it. He settled me back in bed and called Doc back in.

"Does she need to stay here tonight?"

"Not necessarily," Doc said. "But it would be easier for her. I can give her pain medicine when she needs it. I'd like her to sleep as much as she can and be as pain-free as possible tonight and tomorrow."

"Then that's what we'll do."

"I want you to be with me, Reaper."

"Oh, don't worry, baby. I'm not leaving you. I'll be right by your side, just like I promised." He looked up at Doc. "She's hurting."

"Not to worry." He lifted a small syringe with medicine in it and pushed it into the IV in my arm. "Don't fight it. If you get sleepy, just close your eyes and let your mind drift." He looked back at Reaper. "I'll be in every two hours. It's a small dose, so I'll give it more often to stagger it out. I don't want her pain to get out of control."

"How long she gonna hurt?"

"From the biopsy? A couple of days. Tonight and

tomorrow will be the worst. But it still won't be too bad. Mainly, I want her to rest. If I have to dope her up to get it? I'm good with that." Doc grinned at Reaper, then winked at me.

"Well, I guess I'm about to do something else on my bucket list," I said, my words slurring.

"Getting high?"

"You know it." I giggled. "Though, I'd kind of hoped I'd be getting fucked by you when I got high." Reaper chuckled. I was pretty sure Doc did too, but I couldn't think about that. If I did, I'd be mortified. Instead, I chose to be pleasantly numb.

"That can happen later, baby," Reaper said. "Lots and lots of time for that. And I'll indulge every single, dirty, depraved thing your mind can come up with. But now, you sleep."

With a happy sigh, I obeyed him.

* * *

El Segador

The next several days were some of the happiest of my life. I knew there'd be many more like them. The rest of my life, to be precise. Swan healed and did exactly what Doc told her to do, thanks to me bullying her into letting me do everything for her. And it actually did take me bullying her, though I was pretty sure she and the other women were laughing behind my back at how I jumped every time she opened her mouth.

"How you doin', baby?" I brought her a Captain and Coke to the pool lounger where she sat enjoying the sun. There was a mister set to oscillate so it sprayed her body with a fine mist. It wasn't much. The warm ocean breeze and the hot Florida sun were enough to almost evaporate it between passes. I was doing everything in my power to pamper Swan to within an inch of her life.

"I'm great." I giggled. "Drunk."

"Second to last thing on the bucket list."

"It is. Speaking of that, when we gonna get to go to Disney World? I'm super stoked!"

"Give it a few months. Doc is happy with your progress, but he wants to be sure you're completely healed."

"Fine," she huffed. I grinned.

"You ready to go back home?"

"You mean our house in the compound. Right?" I hated that uncertain look in her eyes, but someday soon, she'd get that I wasn't going anywhere.

"I do. That's our home, unless you decide you want us to move somewhere else. I can move us back into the main house. You know, with all the club girls if you want to keep an eye on them. Make sure they don't trespass on your man."

"Uh, no. I'm good, thanks." She rolled her eyes at me.

"That's what I thought." I bent to scoop her into my arms and carried her to my bike. "You OK to hold on?"

"Yeah. I'm not that drunk." Her laugh was the sweetest music. I hoped I got to hear it for years to come.

I took her the short distance to our home and carried her inside. Stripping her of her little bikini was a pleasure. Washing the suntan oil from her body in the shower was even better. Having her wrap her lithe body around mine when we got into bed? Well. There was never anything sweeter.

I kissed every inch of her, paying special attention to her breasts just because I loved the way she shivered when I swirled my tongue around her nipples. It wasn't long before I made my way to her pussy, where I spread her legs and buried my face between them.

"Fuck!" She arched her back, crying out sharply when I flicked her clit with my tongue. "Love that!"

"Me, too," I said between sucks and licks. "You have the sweetest pussy."

"You have the most talented mouth."

"I got something else, too." I winked at her from between her legs. "You want it?"

"I do." She reached for me as I crawled up her body, pulling me down for a torrid kiss. She seemed to love to taste herself on my lips because she always kissed me eagerly after I'd gone down on her. "Reaper?"

"Yeah?"

"I want you to fuck me without the condom today."

I stilled. "You sure about that? We might oughta wait until you're not under the influence."

She shrugged, but I could tell this meant something to her. "If you say so." She looked away, but I grabbed her chin and turned her face gently back to mine.

"Talk to me, baby. You always talk to me. Remember?"

She closed her eyes then nodded. "Don't you want to fuck me? You know. Like that?"

"More than anything," I said without hesitation, meaning it. "Nothing I want more."

"Then why --"

"Baby, don't tempt me. I'm just bastard enough to take your drunken demands to heart, especially when it's exactly what I want. I get you pregnant, you can't leave me. Not really."

She grinned. "No one said I'd want to leave."

"Fine. But if I knock you up, I'm gonna remind you I gave you an out. Not much of one, but an out just the same."

Not waiting for an answer, I slid inside her. As always, I waited for her to adjust. The very last thing I ever wanted to do was hurt Swan.

When she arched into my shallow thrusts, pulling my hips to her, I took that as my cue to go on. I lay fully on top of her, just like she liked it, wrapping my arms around her. Swan gave a happy sigh and moved with me, urging me to fuck her harder. I did.

She cried out, burying her face in my neck and sucking. I loved that she marked me like that. It had infuriated more than one club girl, but I wore those badges proudly. Because of the ordeal Swan had gone through, none of them had the temerity to say anything to her about our relationship, but I could tell Swan was ready to take them on. And, oh, what a glorious battle it would be. Right now, though, I was just happy she felt like making love.

And it *was* making love. I loved Swan with every fiber of my being. I knew she loved me, too. Sometimes, she'd get insecure, thinking I could do better or some dumb shit. I'd flip her over to her belly and fuck the shit out of her, and she'd come around. I thought about taking her hard and fast now, but this first time bareback, I wanted to look into her eyes and know that we were claiming each other. We belonged to each other.

I surged inside her, flexing my hips as I stroked her hair away from her face. "Can you come for me, Swan? Can you milk my cock and take my cum inside you?"

She gasped, opening her mouth to say something, but nothing came out. She nodded, her nails digging into my ass as she gripped me. "Do it," she finally whispered. "Please, Reaper."

"OK, baby. Hold on."

Picking up my pace, I surged into her, grunting with the effort. Her gaze never left mine as I fucked her. Her breath came in little pants now, little whimpers escaping when my body jarred hers.

It wasn't long before she screamed, arching her back, her pussy milking mine as she came apart in my arms. Her orgasm triggered my own, and I erupted inside her with tremendous force. A hoarse shout ripped from my throat, and I groaned long and loud.

"Fuck, Swan! Fuck!"

"Reaper," she whimpered. Her body shook and erupted in sweat. Her breathing was ragged and broken. Mine too.

I collapsed on top of her, kissing her gently as I tried to recover. I felt like my strength had shot out the end of my dick. The pleasure astounded me. Every time I fucked her, every time I came, it was better than the last. And it was all this woman. Swan. She was everything alive inside me. My heart. My soul.

My woman. "You good, baby?" I managed to ask her between breaths.

"Better than good. That was… Reaper, that was wonderful."

"Yeah. It was absolutely wonderful.

"Thank you. So much."

"For what, baby?"

"For being my hero. You saved me, Reaper. You helped me through the toughest time in my life. Gave me something to look forward to."

"Honey, you've done all the work. I was just here

to support you. I'll always be here. I'll be anything you need me to be."

She cupped my face in both her hands. "Just be mine, Reaper. Always?"

"You know it. I'm yours. You're mine. That's the way it is from now on."

With a happy sigh, Swan wrapped her arms back around my neck and brought me down for a gentle kiss. "Forever."

"Forever, baby. Always and forever."

Marteeka Karland

Erotic romance author by night, emergency room tech/clerk by day, Marteeka Karland works really hard to drive everyone in her life completely and totally nuts. She has been creating stories from her warped imagination since she was in the third grade. Her love of writing blossomed throughout her teenage years until it developed into the totally unorthodox and irreverent style her English teachers tried so hard to rid her of.

Marteeka at Changeling: changelingpress.com/marteeka-karland-a-39

Changeling Press E-Books

More Sci-Fi, Fantasy, Paranormal, and BDSM adventures available in e-book format for immediate download at ChangelingPress.com -- Werewolves, Vampires, Dragons, Shapeshifters and more -- Erotic Tales from the edge of your imagination.

What are E-Books?

E-books, or electronic books, are books designed to be read in digital format -- on your desktop or laptop computer, notebook, tablet, Smart Phone, or any electronic e-book reader.

Where can I get Changeling Press E-Books?

Changeling Press e-books are available at ChangelingPress.com, Amazon, Apple Books, Barnes & Noble, and Kobo/Walmart.

ChangelingPress.com

Printed in Great Britain
by Amazon